CONVICT

A NOVEL BY MICHAEL COLE

SEVERED**PRESS**

CONVICT

CHAPTER 1

It had killed over a thousand organisms on a thousand planets. Its pastime was slaughter, with no regard for age, stature, or species. There was no motive for the murders other than sheer entertainment.

Like all criminals anywhere in the galaxy, it had been on the run. Space was vast, the planets capable of sustaining life relatively sparse, especially in this corner of the galaxy. It was thought by the marshals that traveling here would be a mistake. The ion signatures from its vessel could easily be detected, and furthermore, the desolate planets meant it had limited options for refuge.

The capture was easy. The Convict had put up a little fight, exchanging energy projectiles with the three marshals. The same species as it, he knew the vulnerable areas for a quick kill. Though sometimes, quick was disappointing. It was not only death that brought it pleasure, but also the reactions to projectiles and edged instruments.

The Convict did not pretend to have some tragic backstory that somehow justified its actions. It had been raised well and integrated into society like the rest of its species. Like any civilization, it was presented with options to contribute to the whole. Some members picked construction, some went into medical study and research, some pursued exploration and observation for a grander understanding of the universe. Some chose caretaking, for civility was crucial to a flourishing society. Equally as crucial was security, both in law enforcement, and the military.

It was there that the Convict truly learned the pleasures of killing. There had been signs beforehand. It had spent much time hunting small game on distant planets. The rule was to kill as quickly as possible, and only organisms which could be used for food. The Convict in its earlier days sometimes did not kill slowly, for it held a great fascination for seeing a lifeform react to the anguishes of death. Nor did it limit itself to authorized species. While on its own, searching through the wilderness, it learned that many species tended to their young. It had tracked a herd of Ortonix to a wooded area, the young calves struggling to keep up. To this day, it savored the memory of watching the thigh muscle explode off the back leg, and the sound of wailing as the trunked creature collapsed.

Its mother turned back and tried to get her young back on its feet, the other calves waiting behind her.

One by one, the hunter picked them off, putting their mother into heated turmoil. After putting a plasma bolt through all four of her legs, the Convict decided to approach. The young were still alive, crying to their disabled mother for protection. Slowly, intimately, he killed all four of them with different methods. One was burned. Another was skinned. The third was dismembered. The fourth was baited with an attractant, then dragged to a dirt mound where insects awaited. It watched from afar, listening to the squeals from the calf as it was slowly eaten alive, and the hysterics from its mother.

With the military came conflict, both with rogue terrorist colonies and with neighboring civilizations. It learned how to use advanced weaponry and tactics. More importantly, it learned the thrill of mutilating intelligent beings. It was a thrill far beyond shooting dumb animals to plunge a blade between the ribs of a bipedal organism wearing armor.

Its stint in the defense forces had ended, but its lust for murder was stronger than ever. Hunting on distant planets did not quell that thirst. On its home planet, it grew to despise its civilized neighbors. The veteran quickly became a recluse, its attempt to reenlist in the military declined.

Thus, the Convict had to rely on itself to fulfill its need. It started with the recruitment officer, using tracking skills and stealth to avoid getting caught. The kill was successful, the thrill the most satisfying so far. The next victim was a civilian who the Convict believed was attempting to steal its ship. Very quickly, it realized it did not need a motive to justify these deaths to itself. When the Convict recognized the truth, it was at peace. It loved to kill, and it hated everything around it.

Two deaths became three. Four. Ten. Fifty. One hundred, and so on.

It went from one planet to another, seeking out victims and mutilating them. It traveled from planet to planet, finding new victims of various races in a race to satisfy an unquenchable bloodlust. After a while, it did away with stealth and set out for all-out mass murder. Soon, its identity was discovered, and it was officially on the run.

Soon, it was caught, and given a life sentence at a prison colony. Its punishment was short-lived, for the Convict knew how to stir the pot. It triggered a mass riot, resulting in the breaching of barriers, and access to vehicles. It secured a shuttle and departed, but not before slaughtering some of the guards and fellow prisoners—and raiding the armory.

For years, it traveled across the galaxy, finding new victims along the way. Some of those victims were intergalactic marshals sent to capture it and bring it back for public execution. For many years, they failed, until finally, they tracked their target to the dusty spiral-shaped galaxy. Its nucleus was bright with the energy of stars being sucked into a black hole.

With its ship damaged, the Convict had nowhere to go. So, it found a planet, and wearing a mask for air supply, it made its 'last stand', which ended with its surrender.

It stood in its chamber, eye-to-eye with one of its three captors. Its wrists were bound by metal cuffs, its weapons stripped and taken to the cargo hold. Again and again, it had been searched and scanned, with no signatures of edged or energy weapons found. Its wrist gauntlet was taken, its razor whip, laser traps, and vials of grind worms.

Great for torture, they were. On many occasions, the Convict took joy in pouring those yellow inch-long meat-eaters onto injured prey.

Though their prisoner was disarmed, the marshals were not taking any chances. The commander had ordered a nonstop watch, with orders to kill the Convict at the slightest conviction.

The marshal was patient, having stood in place, unmoving, for seventy-two standard hours. It was armed with a standard wrist blaster, capable of generating a bolt large enough to burn a hole through its target.

Based on the hums and vibrations passing under its feet, the Convict knew the ship was moving at standard speed. They were not out of the galaxy yet, thanks to some mineral from the planet where the capture took place. Unfortunately for them, they were unaware of the gradual acid erosion the sediment had on ion engines, just as they were unaware of the Convict's *reason* for landing there.

Over the seventy-two hours, the engine gears slowly dissolved. The damage was minor at first, only resulting in minor vibrations running through the vessel. Little did the marshals know that the sediment had already dissolved the sensors designed for detecting damage.

Little by little, the ion engine broke down until the starboard shaft finally snapped. The gears failed to turn, and the energy particles were no longer regulated. All of this came to light with an explosive sound that rocked the vessel.

The Convict remained in place, playing the role of the helpless prisoner equally perplexed by the recent development.

His guard was called away, racing to the bridge of the small vessel. Their chatters could be heard from the brig.

The ship was not large. The bridge, quarters, armory, and cell were all one level, the engine rooms down below. The cells were in the aft section, separated by a thick wall, with only a narrow six-foot corridor leading to the rest of the vessel. The cell gate was an energy barrier, capable of dicing any prisoner foolish enough to try and pass through. The restraints binding its wrists were made with steel equivalent to the hulls of warships. Even a specimen as mighty as itself could not break free of them. Even the cell gate energy beams were insufficient for cutting through this metal. It required a small, explosive force, directly in the Z-shaped key slot.

All explosive ordinance developed by its species were too large and powerful. Luckily, the Convict had expanded beyond the known regions, and had made discoveries of its own.

No longer under surveillance, the opportunity was now.

The pointed nail at the end of its finger had been sharpened to a fine point. It ran its fingertip down to its right hip, searching for the scab of a tiny scar. No more than an inch long, the marshals took little notice of it. Just a scratch, a minor inconvenience. Nothing worth tending to.

It clicked its mandibles, hissing quietly in minor discomfort. The pain from reopening the wound was marginal. It was the digging inside its own body that enflamed its nerves. It was a minor inconvenience for freedom, easily made up for by the thrill of bloodshed guaranteed in the near future.

The Convict pulled out a small transparent vial. An inch in length, it was divided into two separate compartments, divided by a thin wall in the center. Both ends had a small lid for access.

On the left side were a few white particles. On the right compartment were a few blood-colored particles. Both were like sand in texture and size, but when combined, created an explosive chemical reaction. It was a tiny amount, easily overlooked, and just enough to provide an adequate blast.

It propped the frame of the righthand cuff upwards. Carefully angling its left hand, it opened one end of the vial and gently inserted the white particles into the slot. Next, it opened the other side, and delicately inserted the maroon-colored particles.

It turned its head away and extended its arms to the max.

A red-hot blast burst from the cuffs, the concussion rocking the gears. The cuffs opened, separating its hands.

Next was the gate.

This was where its military background became useful. Unknown to most members of its species, there was a panel at the front left corner of the cell. Using its sharpened nails and all of its strength, it peeled the panel off the floor. It only managed to widen one end by an inch-and-a-half, but it was enough to expose the energy transfer tubes from the battery. It was here that the rest of the particles came into use. Pulling a small tab on the side of the tube, the Convict removed the divider and shook the vial. The dust particles mixed, their explosive reaction just moments from occurring. The Convict slipped the tube through the panel, then backed away.

This explosion was larger, generating smoke. Already, the Convict could hear the footsteps of suspicious marshals coming toward it.

It exited the cell and waited around the corner of the corridor entrance. Listening to the footsteps, it knew two of its captors were on approach. Uniformed bastards, with their crown-shaped helmets, triangle badges, and sense of superiority—these were the types it enjoyed killing the most.

The first one never had a chance. The Convict turned the corner as soon as it arrived, gouging its eyes with its spear-like fingertips, then redirecting the charged plasma gauntlet toward the second one.

Blue bolts hit their mark, punching football-sized holes in the second marshal. It was dead as soon as it hit the deck.

The Convict proceeded assaulting the blind one, repeatedly bashing its head against the corner before dragging it to the next cell. The energy bars were activated, ready to dice through anything that passed through.

Thus was the fate of the marshal, whose blood burst from its body in a hot green mist as it was diced into a dozen pieces.

The Convict activated the control panel and shut down the energy gate, allowing it to enter unharmed. It knelt by the severed arm of its former guard and removed the gauntlet.

Two down, one to go.

The third was ready and waiting. As soon as the Convict peeked around the corner, the marshal opened fire. It was the leader of the group, its helmet marked with a red lightning bolt. Its projectiles narrowly missed. The Convict returned fire, deliberately aiming past the marshal at the small panel under the control console. Fire erupted from the electrical components, catching the marshal off guard.

The marshal screeched in overwhelming frustration. The Convict was perfectly willing to risk its own demise just to win this shootout. It was between a rock and a hard place. It could not let the control system short circuit, or else life support would be lost and it would be literally dead in space.

The Convict weaponized this knowledge and hit the panel with another shot. The marshal returned fire, driving the Convict back around the corner. Making a split-decision, it knelt by the panel with intent to conduct a fast repair. It immediately regretted taking its eyes off the corridor. The prisoner reappeared and charged toward the bridge.

Frantic, the marshal fired a shot. Its plasma bolts struck flesh and vaporized blood.

The Convict, who had picked up the dead marshal from the hallway deck, tossed the corpse aside and returned fire, hitting the marshal in the shoulder. This time, it screeched in agonizing pain.

Even now, with the ion engines threatening to tear the ship apart, the Convict was not willing to let the thrill of murder get away. It charged the fallen escort, stomping on its right elbow. The bone snapped in multiple places, rendering the marshal incapable of utilizing its gauntlet.

There was no chance to call for backup, no hope of utilizing security protocols designed in the event of a hijacking. The marshal was outmatched, outwitted, and outdone.

In one last ditch effort, it attempted to draw a secondary dagger from its boot. This move was anticipated and countered by a blast to its lower abdomen. Burning pain stunned the marshal. Feeling as though its insides had been exposed to the surface of the sun, it was unable to move. The knife was pried from its left hand and run through its ribcage. It made the mistake of crying out, which again, spurred its killer on.

The knife was plunged into the still-smoking wound, touching literally enflamed nerves.

The fun was cut short by an emergency alarm. The Convict looked at the flashing yellow instruments and accepted that the fun would have to be cut short in favor of stabilizing the vessel.

It raised the dagger and plunged it into the marshal's chest, twisting it twice until the bastard went limp.

A rush of pleasure swept through the fugitive's filthy mind. It had outsmarted these dumb law enforcement agents, just as it had done to so many others. They never learned: the Convict would never see the inside of a prison cell. It was beyond the jurisdiction of its species. Of any species.

Now the new operator of this long-range patrol vessel, the Convict ran a diagnostic.

Starboard engine compromised.

Port engine stable.

Thrusters functional only at half-power.

It would have to land somewhere and conduct repairs. The problem was there were not many planets in this quadrant with suitable atmospheres. It initiated a scan of all stars and planets within five-thousand lightyears.

Only one result came back. It was an ocean planet, with roughly thirty percent of its surface containing land. Its atmosphere contained seventy-eight percent nitrogen and twenty-one percent oxygen. Perfectly breathable without the use of regulators. Its landscapes provided a great range of temperatures and terrain. There were valleys, forests, canyons, mountains, deserts, and so much more.

There was a special bonus which alone made landing here a solid choice: The scans revealed satellite technology and abundant life.

A second diagnostic revealed that the cloaking systems were functional. The Convict would be able to pass through the systems undetected, set down in an area with cover, and be free to explore.

And kill.

CHAPTER 2

The planet was an impressive sight from space. It was spherical in shape, not perfectly round. Its greatest radius was at its center. There were multiple bodies of water separated by stretches of land. The poles were flat and white, the landscapes showing a variety of green, tan, and grey. As its scans had suggested, this planet had cities, deserts, and forests.

The machines hovering above its atmosphere failed to detect it. The cloaking mechanism was functioning perfectly. There was still the possibility that the dominant species on this planet could detect the ion trail leaking from its damaged engine. With the engine breaking down, there would be no fast getaway should it get detected. Though the cloaking tech would remain active, the Convict preferred to land in an area with plenty of cover.

It had to choose carefully. This planet, and all life existing on it, had never been cataloged. The technology proved that intelligent life existed—the most fun victim of all. There was a thrill to slaughtering animals, but intelligent species felt a whole new level of fear and pain.

Just the thought made the criminal click his mandibles. It could not wait to discover what was on this new world.

It settled for an area in the western hemisphere. It was a green area, indicating thick forest. Detailed scans revealed a scattered population. It was sparse, though not desolate. It was enough for the Convict to explore and still manage to get a taste of the offerings this world provided. Soon enough, its multi-purpose drone would be able to fly around and scope out the rest of this region.

With a press of touchpad buttons, the ship plunged through the atmosphere. This region was on the verge of nightfall, providing even more cover. The shields activated, protecting the ship from the burn of atmospheric entry.

The wooded landscape came into view. It was an area consisting of several large hills, a few habitat structures, and a five-mile-long lake on the eastern side of the woods.

Scans revealed heat signatures throughout the area. Some were in groups, others isolated. There were a few habitats on the south side of the lake, and one on the northern part. The Convict located an area on the north side, not too far from the lone structure. It detected three heat signatures within a quarter mile, two to the northwest, and one near the habitat.

It was a perfect distance. The Convict was eager to explore and take part in its favorite pastime.

***

Chrissie Young spat and groaned. She had been told starting a campfire would be easy. All she had to do was stack the wood together and light a flame. Clearly, there was more to it than that. Every single time she touched a match to the wood, it fizzled out.

She looked to her right at Martin, who was almost done setting up their little tent.

"Will you do this? I'm getting so pissed, I can't even think."

"Just light the match and toss it in," he said.

"I did like five times! It's not lighting!"

"Ugh. Hold on." He finished setting up their yellow tent, then padded the inside with their sleeping gear. It had been a long day of hiking and he was looking forward to some beer, food, and hopefully a good time with Chrissie.

She sat on a log and plucked a splinter from her thumb. "Ow."

"What's the matter now?"

"I'm tired and starving," she said. "Plus, I'm about to kill for some beer."

"It's in the truck," he said. "Go help yourself. There's whiskey in there too."

"Good to know!" She got up, then stopped to remember which direction the truck was. They had arrived that morning, then spent the rest of the day hiking around the lake. Her feet were sore and her patience was thin.

"Oh, no wonder it won't burn," Martin said. "You didn't put any tinder in."

Chrissie did an about face, pointing at the yet-to-be campfire with both hands. "The hell are you talking about, Martin? There's tinder right there. You're looking at it."

"No, this is firewood."

Chrissie dropped her hands. "Is that not the same thing?"

"No!" Martin burst into laughter. "Tinder wood is little shavings you put under the firewood. Thin twigs, dry grass, thin strips you can slice off a log. That's why I gave you the knife."

"Oh..." Chrissie shrugged and continued for the truck. She *really* needed a drink right now.

She reached into the backseat, pulled out the little cooler, and a small bag with canned groceries… and the bottle of whiskey.

"Oh, yeah. I'm gonna put this to good use." She unscrewed the cap and downed a slug. The whiskey hit her empty stomach and went straight for her head. When she returned to the campsite, Martin was slicing a dead branch into shavings. After placing the tinder under the firewood, he grabbed the matches, shaking them in front of his girlfriend's face.

"Watch and learn, sweetness."

"Right, right," she said. "I'm waiting for my lesson, oh-Martin, the god of fire."

"I thought it was thunder."

She shook her head. "Sorry. You're no Thor. *Definitely* no Chris Hemsworth."

"Thanks a lot," he said. He leaned close to the logs, then struck a match.

Growling thunder rolled in the east, followed by a warm gust of wind.

Chrissie stood up. "What the hell was that?"

"Isn't it obvious?" Martin said, smiling. "I am the god of fire *and* thunder. I control both with a flick of my wrist. I bet Chris Hemsworth can't do that."

Chrissie rolled her eyes and waved him off. "Believe me, I'd happily let him generate all kinds of warmth and sounds."

Martin thought about that statement, then perked up. "Hey!"

"Shh!" She held a finger up, then listened to the distance. Something was moving through the woods a few hundred yards out. Whatever it was, it was large enough to snap large branches. "You hear that?"

Now, Martin was serious. "Yeah." There was a faint rumble, then silence, except for the sound of woodland critters being scared from their burrows. A minute followed, and there was nothing. Martin shook his head. "Weird."

"Let's check it out," Chrissie said.

"You spent the evening hike complaining about having sore feet."

"Because we've literally been hiking since eight this morning," she said. "I enjoy it, but holy shit, it gets tedious after over twelve hours. But this is different. That almost sounded like something was coming down in the woods, like a helicopter or something."

"If a helicopter is setting down in the woods, I don't think we should be anywhere near it."

"Fine. I'll just go myself," she said. She kicked off her flip flops and put her hiking boots back on. Just for fun, she took a couple more swigs of the whiskey. "Oh, man. That's the good stuff." The buzz added to the fun. Already, her imagination was conjuring up ideas of what that sound could be.

She tied her laces, then darted toward the east, waving bye to her boyfriend. "See ya!"

"Oh, for godsake! Hold on!" He grabbed his flashlight and took off after her.

***

The ramp yawned open, revealing a world warmed by summer heat, now cooled by the night. The trees were similar to those on several other planets. There were a few mild differences, but overall, they were the same. This appeared to be a standard forest with no poisonous flora. An extensive study was needed to be sure, but the Convict was confident in its hypothesis. Even the animals bore some resemblance to those on planets neighboring its home world. Some were small and furry, others feathered and capable of flight.

Boring. The Convict had no use for such inferior lifeforms aside from sustenance.

It returned to the ship's interior, stepping over the body of the marshal in the bridge.

A bubbly sound of gasping breath caught its attention. It turned around and looked at the fallen foe. The marshal twitched, its right hand clenching into a fist. The brief seizure came to an end, and the marshal remained motionless.

The Convict watched the blood pooling around its most recent victim. The memory of stabbing it was fresh and satisfying.

Satisfied that there was no life left in the corpse, the Convict entered a small corridor leading to the armory. There, it found the small arms carried by the patrol team. It was mostly wrist gauntlets, standard issue. The Convict had no interest in them, for it already had seized one from one of the dead marshals. It was the weapons stored in a compartment on the left which contained the items it sought.

The compartment unveiled like a metal flower, revealing its prized possessions. The weapons were displayed on their own individual racks. Its favorite of which was the razor whip. A good lash, when properly handled, could either lacerate the target, or, as the Convict enjoyed doing, wrap the end around the victim. With the target snagged, a good yank would reduce it to bloody fragments.

Beside it were two other storage compartments. One contained several vials of razor worms, the other holding vials of explosive dust. Further down the wall were displays of laser cutter traps, an acid pistol with a whole cannister full of projectiles, marble-shaped explosive booby traps, and more gauntlets. The Convict clipped on a weapons harness and armed itself with its toys. It packed its acid pistol, vials of worms and powder, some marble explosives, then double checked the blades on its gauntlet. They extended nearly two feet from the end of the device, both sharp enough to slice bone with little effort. It decided to leave the whip for another day. By the looks of it, the fugitive was gonna be enjoying its stay for quite a while.

It tapped a key on its gauntlet, waking up the ship's multipurpose drone unit. Insectoid-shaped, it was designed for repair, medical treatment, reconnaissance, sabotage, and—with a little tinkering—assassinations.

The ship's computer beeped, alerting it to approaching heat signatures. The screen zoomed in on the bipedal figures. They were five hundred feet out and gradually closing in.

It was the same two lifeforms the scanners detected northwest of its position. They had likely heard the landing and wandered over out of curiosity. The Convict was a good flyer, but the woods were thick, the trees tightly packed, and it did not have the time for a seamless landing.

With the press of a button on its gauntlet, the Convict opened the exit ramp again, then stepped out into the woods. It kept low, easily blending into the trees. Its species was adept for night hunting, the chemistry of its eyes altering once the starlight's UV levels dropped below two.

Its night vision was active, allowing it to see through the woods as clearly as if it were daylight.

It spotted the indigenous lifeforms. Immediately, it deduced a few characteristics. The taller one with broader shoulders and facial hair was a male. The smaller companion had longer, brighter hair, smoother skin, and an extension to her chest area that indicated milk-feeders, similar to the females of its own species. They wore clothing and communicated with each other through language and gestures. There was no doubt that these were members of the dominant species on this planet.

They were smaller than itself. Though the male was stronger than the female, the Convict was certain his strength was inferior to its own.

Neither appeared to be alarmed. They approached at a steady pace, looking around for the source of the noise. There was no operation of technology, no attempt to alert the planetary authorities. Just a mated couple, walking at night, straight for its camp.

Only one question remained: how fun were they to kill?

It clicked its mandibles in excitement and extended its wrist blade. Slowly, it circled around them with intent to take out the male first.

***

"Holy shit, Chrissie."

Chrissie took another swig of the whiskey, then laughed. "Sorry. I'm pounding it down on an empty stomach and it's making me feel really whoopsie!"

"You mean tipsy…" Martin smacked himself on the forehead. "Why am I correcting a drunk person?"

"Hey!" She turned around and pointed a finger. "I'm not drunk. I'm… half? Drunk? Maybe sixty percent, uh, drunk." She took another drink, then laughed when she saw Martin's face. "Sorry. I'm just on a roll. I've worked up a hell of an appetite, I've got no food in me, this stuff is working at lightspeed, and shit! I love it. I've never been drunk in the woods before…" She pointed again. "*Half* drunk!"

"Well, I'm not looking forward to whatever mess that might come from this. You hurl in the tent, you're cleaning it up." He waved his hand at the trees. "And I thought we were looking for, I don't know, whatever caused that noise."

"We will! We will! I promise, we will find the helicopter, or bulldozer, or the spaceship…"

"Spaceship? You really *are* drunk."

"*Half* drunk."

"More like a hundred-and-ten percent."

Chrissie stepped forward to protest. "I take issue with…" Her foot hit a branch, sending her falling against Martin. He grabbed her by the shoulders and kept her upright.

Chrissie threw her head back and started laughing. Its contagious effect finally got the better of Martin.

"You really are having a good time, aren't you?" he said, grinning ear to ear.

"Maybe too much fun… I might puke some time tonight," Chrissie said. She laughed again. "I'll try to make it out of the tent."

"I appreciate that."

"Did I really say spaceship?"

Martin nodded. "You sure did."

"Oh, GOD! I must really be drunk if I believe aliens have touched down." She squeezed her eyes shut and threw her head back in another fit of drunken laughter.

Her eyes opened, and her laughter turned into a scream. Martin, shocked by the sudden change in her demeanor, was blissfully unaware of the six-foot-eight humanoid thing standing behind him—until its blades punched through his back. He convulsed, spitting blood, twitching in a mix of pain and confusion.

The thing lifted him with one arm, keeping him skewered on a dual-bladed protrusion that came from its wrist. Martin's arms and legs shook, his eyes focused on the knife tips protruding from his chest. He looked over his shoulder and saw the alien's insectoid face.

He let out a scream, which came out as a gasp due to deflated lungs. The thing held on to him with its other hand, then ripped its blades out through his shoulders. Martin's torso split in two, the right shoulder and head peeling one way, the left shoulder going the other.

Chrissie screamed, unsure if this was reality or an alcohol-induced nightmare. The splashing of warm blood on her face confirmed the former.

The creature advanced with intention, tossing her dead boyfriend aside.

Chrissie threw her arms out. "No! No!"

A slash of its blades literally disarmed her. She stared at her elbow stubs as they jetted blood, eventually redirecting her eyes at her killer.

The humanoid thing looked at the blood-stained dual blades, then at her eyes, noticing the perfect spacing of both.

Thrust.

Splat!

Her body twitched, held upright by the blades that had plunged through her eye sockets.

The Convict watched the twitching in utter fascination. The blood was red and warm, the flesh no match for its strength and weaponry. Better yet, they displayed immense fear.

These kills were among the most thrilling yet. The Convict needed more. It dropped the female and marched in the direction of that third heat signature. Like a child in a brand-new playground, it was having too much fun.

CHAPTER 3

Patrick Gawdy lifted his eyes from his flyrod and turned to look into the woods. He wasn't sure if he heard a scream or if it was just his imagination. Often, younger people enjoyed fooling around in the woods, and they tended to get a little 'vocal'. There was nothing but silence now. Perhaps their little game had reached its conclusion.

Then again, that almost sounded like a panicked scream, but it was from deep in the woods, at least a thousand feet out. Too far away for him to be able to do anything about it.

What can I do anyway? Wander the woods and look around? Maybe call the cops and say 'hey, there's someone screaming somewhere in the woods... Where exactly? I don't know. Hard to pinpoint from where I'm at?... No, I'm not sure there's even an emergency or just people horseplaying, which happens often.'

After playing that imaginary conversation in his head, he shrugged it off and returned to his leisurely activity.

Since retiring from his roofing company, Patrick spent most of his summers at his private cabin. All of his life, he had worked around noisy people and tools, and relished the peace and quiet of his getaway time. Whenever he was home, it seemed there was always something going on. One of his adult kids needed something fixed, or a grandchild needed babysitting, or some of his old work buddies wanted to drop by and chat. His siblings were not any better. The minute he retired and actually had time on his hands to work on his own home projects and leisure, they all had requests for him. Help with the roof, building a new deck, installing a pool, electrical work. One, living in a rural area, phoned him up to request he help build an extension to her barn. Patrick had nothing against any of them, aside from the fact they were blatantly taking advantage of his generosity to save money on labor.

Still, it quickly began to feel like retirement life was just as busy as his working days. The fact was, Patrick enjoyed a certain amount of solitude, and it seemed like every day he had to interrupt his own plans in favor of someone else's needs. Only when he came to his cabin was he truly able to get away. His phone barely got any signal in these woods, so any texts or calls never made it through.

Lit only by the glow of the porchlight on his lakeshore cabin, he stepped into the water, stopping a few yards out. Knee-deep in water, he began flicking his wrist back and forth, whipping the line into a loop. He swung the line forward, planting the fly in the water, then pulled it back.

***

The Convict arrived at the location of the third heat signature. This one was a male, and judging by his features, appeared to be much older than the others. Just as it predicted, he was blissfully unaware of his presence.

It stood in the tree line, watching the indigenous swing the long line into the water. After a moment, the Convict realized what this activity was. There was animal life in the water, and the male was trying to catch it for sport. This theory was confirmed when the indigenous being laughed while pulling on a taut line. After a few tugs, he lifted the aquatic creature from the water. It was pan-shaped, clearly not intelligent in the slightest. It struggled to get away from its captor by thrashing in his hand.

However, no struggle was necessary. After the resident dislodged a barbed hook from its mouth, he tossed the animal back into the lake. Perhaps it was a sport which did not require death of the animal. Either that, or it was too small for consumption. Whichever the case, the elderly male was not done. He cast his line again, whipping it back and forth before planting the lure in the water. A few moments later, he was pulling in another catch.

The Convict's fascination subsided. It had no real interest in studying lifeforms in their natural habitat, even if it was the first of its kind to discover them. Generally, it only observed to benefit its own twisted goals.

Now, it was time to decide which method it wanted to use. The Convict drew the acid pistol. It had been a while since it had put this tool to use, and now was as good a time as any. It pulled an acid pellet from a pouch in its belt and loaded it into the chamber. Though only as large as a pebble, it was more than enough to burn an adult member of its own species down to the bone.

The male took no notice of the intruder, his attention on his catch. He held it by the jaw and pried the hook free.

The Convict stepped through the open yard, then took aim.

***

Patrick held the largemouth by its lower jaw, finally getting the hook free from the corner of its mouth. It was a good-sized catch, weighing a few pounds at least. Originally, he was only doing catch and release, but he was tempted to hang on to this one. He guessed it was nineteen inches.

An official measurement was in order. Patrick turned around to walk to his front porch, stopping suddenly at the sight of a large individual standing in his side yard.

"Holy—who the hell are you? This is private prop—" He squinted, noticing the intruder's physical oddities. He was so taken by its goblin-shaped head and insect-like mouth, he did not realize it was pointing a pistol at him until it fired.

Two feet in front of him, the pellet exploded into a huge yellow mist that completely encompassed him.

Patrick dropped his fish and grabbed his throat. Everything, inside and out, felt as though it was on fire. He tried to yell, but spat blood instead. He extended his hand like a blind man, seeing his own skin dripping off the bone. Then it went dark, his eyeballs dissolving in their sockets.

***

Now this was something the Convict could watch endlessly. The senior seemed determined to cling to life, even after parts of his charred skeleton was revealed to the world. Cheeks and muscle tissue fell from the jawline, which then extended twice beyond its normal capacity. The tongue flopped between his teeth like a Lovecraftian tentacle, gradually dissolving along with the rest of him. The eyes were completely gone, leaving dark, rounded sockets. The forearms were made up of two bones, the upper arms only of one.

The midsection opened up, spilling smoking contents into the water. It was then that the male finally collapsed.

The Convict stepped over the corpse. After a few additional moments, everything above the knees was eaten away. His lower legs, having been protected by the water, were still intact. That wasn't to say the acid had no effect on the water. Throughout the cove, a few pan-shaped bodies floated to the surface, their bodies discolored from exposure where the mist touched the lake.

It wasn't often the intergalactic criminal got a buzz. It had only killed three of these lifeforms so far, and already it had concluded they were among the most fun. Most creatures displayed some level of emotion, but these ones surpassed them all. It could not wait to kill more.

First it needed to get to work on repairing its ship. The Convict wasn't too concerned. Judging by the readings on its scanner, it had plenty of opportunities to kill.

CHAPTER 4

"Tensions between protestors and the Denver Police Department are still high following last week's verdict. Two nights ago, hundreds of people marched to the District One police station, demanding justice for the death of Willie Stader, who was shot and killed by former Detective Diego Tritton. It is unclear if Tritton, who was acquitted of all charges on Wednesday morning, will be reinstated with the department. We've spoken to some of the protesters this morning, and here's what they had to say..."

*"This is bull-sh****BLEEP***! If we lived in a just society, that **BLEEP** would be under the jail right now!"*

*"I don't know, man, this seems pretty fu****BLEEP****ed-up. From what I can see, the Denver Police just legalized gunning down unarmed civilians, even if they have no serious record."*

"THIS IS AN OUTRAGE! PEOPLE SHOULD BE MAKING NOISE ACROSS THE COUNTRY!!!"

"Watch your back, Officer Tritton!"

"I mean, didn't Willie Stader like assault the cops while they were trying to arrest a rapist?"

"This department needs a new chief! It's time for things to change!"

"... While our reporters were on the steps of the District One station, they captured this footage of the crowd chanting in honor of Willie Stader..."

"JUSTICE FOR WILLIE STADER! JUSTICE FOR WILLIE STADER!"

No matter where he went, he could not avoid the news. Even in a little gas station in the middle of nowhere, Diego Tritton was bombarded with the news. Everybody had their narrative about what happened and why it happened. The mainstream outlets were a united front, covering the incident in the same general manner. They showed the same footage from the same camera angle, leaving out the segment leading up to it.

Diego, against his better judgment, looked at the screen above the checkout counter. There, he saw himself in black Kevlar, pressing a gun against the driver's side window of a twelve-year-old Toyota Camry. His memory matched the audio airing on the screen.

"Stop! Put your foot on the brake. Don't... don't reach into that glove compartment..."

The footage stopped right there, but it didn't stop the memory from going on. He saw the twenty-one-year-old reach into that glove box with intention, defying his orders to give up. He yelled a second time for Willie to withdraw his hand. When he did not comply, Diego fired.

Of course, the news agencies neglected to show the footage of him being dragged down the road for a hundred feet. Nor did most of them report the fact that he fired his taser first but missed his shot.

Plenty of onlookers recorded the event on their smartphones, most of them starting at the moment he put his weapon to the window. Only a handful caught the incident from the starting point, and they were several yards away.

"The medical report concluded that Mr. Stader suffered multiple gunshot wounds to his chest and neck," the news anchor said. *"He was pronounced dead twenty minutes after the shooting."*

Diego groaned. His eyes went to the counter. On the other side, the gas station owner quickly broke eye contact. Diego saw the way he was fidgeting with his pencil. The guy was just waiting for him to leave.

So much for not getting recognized.

Diego set his items on the counter. He had planned on purchasing more things, but now had a feeling he wasn't welcome. He would have to settle for milk, a case of beer, and the pack of hot dogs he had already selected.

The owner slowly stood up, keeping an eye on Diego while he scanned the items.

"Holy shit," a customer said from behind Diego. "You're the guy. You're that piece of shit from Denver. How's it feel getting away with murder, you motherfucker?"

Exhaling slowly, Diego turned his head just enough to see the busybody in his peripheral vision. As he suspected, he was in his early twenties, obviously influenced heavily by so-called intellectual college professors. The prick was as stupid as he was skinny, thinking himself brave for confronting the former detective.

The store owner finished his excruciatingly slow scanning of the four items. "That'll be seventeen-forty."

Diego paid in cash, much to his regret. The owner, maybe unnerved by his presence, fumbled with the change, miscounting it twice, even though all he required were a pair of ones, two quarters, and a dime.

Fed up, both with the owner's ineptitude and the white knight customer's eyes on his back, Diego scooped up his items.

"Just keep it."

He went for the exit, ignoring the young right-fighter who watched him up to the moment the door shut behind him.

As Diego went to his truck, he happily gazed at the world of trees that made up Poncho County. It was an area of rolling hills, thick woods, several lakes, and best of all, few people. Relatively few people. It was summer, and many were in the town of Rainwater for camping, fishing, and hiking.

Diego tossed his items in the backseat of his truck, then removed the pump. As he returned it to its slot, his eyes turned to the Poncho County Sheriff's Department SUV parked across the street.

Though he couldn't see his face, Diego was tempted to flip Sheriff Eddie Wingard the bird. The Sheriff knew who he was, knew he had a cabin over by the lake, and knew he would likely be getting away from the drama taking place in Denver. Clearly, he was keeping an eye out for him. Eddie knew what Diego drove, and also knew he stopped at this gas station for fuel and groceries when in town.

Yeah, fine. Keep an eye on me if that makes you feel better.

He heard the gas station door open and rapidly approaching footsteps.

"So?! How's it feel?"

"Aw, fuck," Diego muttered. He turned around, seeing the young busybody step toward him. "What?"

"You didn't answer my question. How does it feel to get away with murder?" The guy put his arms out, as though daring Diego to take him on. His baggy shirt, at least two sizes too large for his skinny physique, waved in the breeze.

"Kid, two words of advice," Diego said. "Mind your own business, and for heaven's sake, eat a sandwich. I swear, you're about to blow away." He walked to the driver's seat, determined not to waste any more time with this moron.

The moron ran in front of his truck, waving to a couple of vehicles that pulled into the lot. Their occupants turned their attention toward him, believing he may have been in distress.

"This is the murderer from Denver! Everyone has a right to know this man is in town. He got away with killing Willie Stader. He's protected by the law. Demand justice for this man's crimes!"

The people in the nearest vehicle rolled their eyes and waved him off.

"Oh, geez. Freaking nut," the husband said. "Kid, get a life."

"Better yet, get a damn job," the wife said. They both went inside.

The next vehicle simply ignored him and pulled up to a pump to fill up.

Diego stood at his open truck door, keeping his temper in check. "Kid, you mind moving?"

The guy turned toward an RV which coasted around the building from a pump on the other side, then parallel parked into a row of parking spaces. Unfortunately, its occupants paid the moron some much-desired attention.

"This is the murderer from Denver, the one who got away with shooting Willie Stader to death!"

The passenger got out. Diego groaned as soon as he saw the heavyset figure with piercings in the nose and eyebrows march toward him. Her boyfriend, a slightly-less fat individual with a neckbeard, followed her over.

"Are you serious?" the woman asked.

"That's him," the skinny guy said.

By the way they spoke to each other, it was obvious they knew each other. Eager to leave, Diego tried to measure the distance between the edge of the lot and the skinny guy. If he could back away, he could just swing around him and take off...

Right as he had that thought, a big camper came up behind him, its engine creeping within inches of his truck. The moron inside peeked out the window, trying to line his fuel cap perfectly with his pump.

"Hey! Watch it!" Diego said. "Gosh, did all the dumbest idiots in Colorado decide to follow me here?"

"Have something to say, racist?" the fat woman with piercings said.

Diego gestured at the exit. "Just let me leave in peace, will ya?"

"You don't deserve to have peace! Not after what you did!"

He gritted his teeth. "Okay, so you think I'm a murderer. Use some measure of logic, if you can: you see someone you think is a murderer, and the first thing you think to do is walk up and antagonize them? Does that sound like a smart thing to do?"

The woman's mouth dropped. "He just threatened me!" She turned to the walking twinkie that was her boyfriend. "You hear that? He threatened me! Are you filming?!"

He held his iPhone out. "I sure am. Smile, asshole."

The skinny fella was still standing in front of his truck.

Diego inhaled deeply. This was a no-win situation. Being nice and civil was doing nothing but prolonging this encounter. Yet, losing his temper would only bring more misery. He exhaled slowly, sensing his patience on the verge of running out.

"Young fella, I'm gonna ask nice once more: move your ass, or I'll move it for ya. I'm not gonna say it ag—"

The camper behind him inched forward again. *Thump.* Diego watched it back away from his tailgate, and the small scratch it left behind.

The driver poked his head out. "Whoops."

It was all downhill from here.

Diego marched to the driver's side window, hands out, eyes blazing.

"Are you serious?! You dumb motherfucker! Was it so important to line up precisely with the damn thing?! You forget there's a hose that allows you eight feet of extra space?"

"Get away from my camper, man!" the driver said.

The three activist-types moved closer, each with an iPhone aimed at the former cop.

"This is the kind of aggression that led up to Willie Stader's death!" the skinny one said.

Finally, the Sheriff switched on his lights and sped across the street. He entered the lot and parked near the exit. He stepped out and walked over, accompanied by a tall, fairly skinny deputy whose nametag read Ford.

Eddie Wingard put his hands on his belt, like a dad ready to scold his teenage kids.

"Sheriff! You gonna do something about this guy?" the fat guy said.

Eddie shook his head. "Listen, people. It's Friday. The weather is beautiful. Supposed to be like this all through next week. Don't waste time getting involved with petty drama."

"It's not petty. You know what he did, right?" the skinny guy said.

"All I see are three kids harassing someone who just got rear-ended in a parking lot. Do me a favor and go on about your business. Are we clear?"

The three of them stepped back, their iPhones still recording.

"You see this? The cops don't care," the woman said.

They took their sweet time, but they eventually backed off and regrouped near their RV.

Eddie shook his head and approached Diego. "This generation, I swear. Instagram, TikTok, and Twitter have turned them into a bunch of narcissists." He stepped behind Diego's truck and looked at the tailgate. "Luckily, there's no damage."

"Except for the scratches."

"Eh, they're barely noticeable."

Diego eyed the fifty-year-old officer with greying hair. He was able to read between the lines. In Eddie's eyes, Diego was a magnet for drama, which in turn meant more business for the Sheriff's Office.

"How lucky is it you happened to be over there," he said.

Eddie chuckled. "I had a feeling you'd come over."

"And?" Diego tilted his head, waiting for the rest of that statement.

"*And...* I wish you picked a different spot."

"Telling me I can't go to my cabin?"

Eddie shook his head. "Not at all. But after everything that happened, people aren't comfortable around you. What you did... in today's political and social climate, it's a bad look."

"I think you've spent a little too much time checking fishing permits while guys like me performed actual police work," Diego said. "You mean to tell me you didn't look at the rest of the video? That you're happily going along with the media spin?"

"It doesn't matter," Eddie said. "The court of public opinion has deemed you as, let's just say, a controversial figure. Mr. Tritton, I am sorry you went through all of that. Killing someone cannot be easy. Especially someone that young—"

"If you don't mind, I'd like to get going," Diego said.

"Well..." Eddie shrugged. "In any case, I am sorry to hear the department fired you. Maybe they did it to save face, maybe it was justified... we'll never know. All I ask is for you to avoid disputes with the people camping around here. You know the media frenzy that would ensue should you throw hands with someone."

Diego considered a hundred replies before silently getting in his truck.

"Good to see you again, Sheriff." He shut the door and started the engine. As he pulled out, he noticed Eddie and the deputy named Ford grinning at each other. Both were wise enough to know what Diego *truly* meant with that statement. 'Kiss my ass, Sheriff.'

He nudged his truck out through the exit, then hit the brakes, barely avoiding collision with a speeding van.

"Christ alive! So much for peace and quiet." He cautiously checked his left side, then finally made a right turn. Soon, his truck disappeared in the thick of the woods.

Finally, he was isolated from human life.

Almost isolated. That van was still up ahead, going in the same direction as him. Aside from a few campgrounds, the only destination this road led to was Lake Fairview.

Diego sighed, and prayed they'd hang a left at some point.

Considering how unlucky I've been so far...

CHAPTER 5

Fingernails dug into the cushion, gripping for dear life. Not that it would do any good. If the hormone-driven Ted Leevie veered into a tree or an oncoming vehicle, Kelly Dawson would be plastered against the back windshield. The little make-out session in front nearly caused one accident already. It was only the fact that the guy pulling out of the gas station was paying attention that prevented an accident.

"Mmm, I love you baby," Ted said.

Pam giggled, leaning over the center console, her mouth digging into his. "I love you too."

Kelly watched the road, seeing the vehicle drift into the opposite lane. "Hey guys? You mind?!"

Ted broke away and turned his eyes to the road.

"Whoops!" He put the van back into the right lane, grinning ear-to-ear while squeezing Pam's thigh. Looking into the rear-view mirror, he noticed his nervous passenger pressed against the back of her seat. "Sorry!"

Kelly filtered a hundred different responses, settling on silence. She was still embarrassed from their near-accident a couple of miles back. She looked back to see if that vehicle was still behind them.

Sure enough, it was still there, the same blue pickup truck from the gas station. Fortunately, there did not appear to be any sign of road rage. The driver was simply going in the same direction.

"Oh, baby. Not here. Not with Kelly in the back," Ted said.

Kelly turned her eyes forward, seeing Pam's hand slipping under Ted's khaki shorts. "Yeah, for once I agree with Ted. You guys are like fifteen-year-olds. Can't you wait another fifteen minutes till we get to the cabin?"

Pam put her knees on the seat and turned to face her, her movements unrestricted due to not bothering to buckle in.

"What's the matter, Kelly? Still heartbroken over Gordon?"

"No. I'd just prefer to make it to the cabin in one piece," she said. She looked away, watching the trees scrolling by the window. "And believe me, I'm way over Gordon."

"Ha. I'm sure."

"Norman's single," Ted said. "And according to trusted sources, very confident in raising profits in the southern regions."

Kelly shook her head. "You always were a pig, Ted. You and Pam deserve each other."

"Whaaaat?!" Pam said, feigning shock and offense. "What's that supposed to imply? You saying I'm a whore or something?"

"Damn right I am."

Ted's smile widened. He reached over, cupped his hand under Pam's chin, then pulled her over for another make-out session.

"Damn right you are."

"Yours." She giggled and kissed him more.

Kelly swallowed in an attempt to keep from throwing up in her mouth. This wasn't a new occasion. Three times each summer, the three of them would meet Ross, Jamie, and Norman at Ross' cabin. Every single time, Ted and Pam couldn't keep their lips off each other. It had practically become a running joke that someone would wander into the woods and find the two of them getting down and dirty.

She would never admit the smidge of jealousy she felt towards them. She had no interest in Ted whatsoever, but the crazy passion that would drive two people to such high levels of stupidity. Only in her last relationship did she feel anything close to that. Gordon was quite the looker, and very much the charmer. Too much, in fact, as she learned when she found him in his apartment with an eighteen-year-old girl. Woman? Girl? Technically the former, though the latter in appearance. Small breasted, somewhat baby-faced. It was disgusting to see a thirty-two-year-old with her. Not only that, but he was cheating on Kelly, a twenty-nine-year-old master's graduate, with her.

Yeah, perhaps there was a little jealousy seeing Ted and Pam acting crazy together, even if it had nearly got her killed twice so far on this drive.

The two of them behaved themselves for the rest of the drive, aside from a few thigh squeezes. Being in the woods of Poncho County sparked a sense of freedom and carelessness. It didn't matter that they had visited Ross' cabin several dozen times beforehand. The thrill of vacation never grew old.

Kelly, despite her stone-faced expression and lackluster energy, was excited too. In fact, she needed this trip more than ever. With her boring personal life, uninspiring career, and relationship failures, these trips were all she truly had to look forward to. Hell, they even beat Thanksgiving and Christmas, though those weren't high marks to beat. Kelly dreaded the holidays and the consumerism that came with it.

Here in Poncho County, however, it was just her and nature...

She looked at Ted and Pam.

...and these guys.

Kelly shut her eyes and tried to relax. All she needed right now was to survive long enough to get on a paddleboat. Lake Fairview was calling her name.

****

She breathed a sigh of relief when they pulled into the driveway in one piece. As soon as the van came to a stop, she was out the door. Finally, a genuine smile took form as she admired the cabin, a two-story structure constructed out of royal oak trees. Kelly could see the kitchen and living room area through the side window.

"About damn time," she said. The sound of car tires behind her made her squirm. That blue truck had followed them all the way up here. She looked back, anticipating the guy to pull in behind them and go on a fit about how they nearly t-boned him.

Instead, the vehicle kept going, the driver not even giving them a glance. It was at that moment she remembered there was another cabin a couple of hundred feet up the shoreline. She knew the cabin was there, but never saw anyone in it. It was easy to assume that the time of their visits never overlapped. Until now, of course.

Ted got out of the van. "Hey, Norman. What's up?!"

Kelly turned her attention to the back of the cabin, where Norman was chopping wood. He was shirtless, his tan muscular form glistening in the hot sun. He had an ax in his hand and a pile of wood at his feet. He tossed it aside and slapped hands with Ted.

"About time you showed up."

Ted tried to keep from being pulled in for a hug but was overpowered by Norman's immense strength. He grimaced, freshly greased by the Army veteran's sweat.

"Oh, God! Get off me, man! You're sweatier than a whore in a Vietnamese brothel."

"Well, I wouldn't know about that," Norman said. "The Korean ones, however…" He clicked his tongue and winked, then finally released his buddy.

Ted winced at the mental image. "Don't wanna know about that. Where's Jamie and Ross?"

A window opened. "Over here!"

The four friends looked at the kitchen window, seeing it still shut. When Jamie finally repeated himself, they realized he was yelling from the rear window.

Kelly got there first. She stared at the droopy-eyed, shaggy-haired math whiz, who was practically hanging off the windowsill. He looked at her, a beer in his hand and an obnoxious grin on his face.

"Hey, Kel. How's you and Gordon?"

She didn't answer, instead turning her attention to Norman. He was gritting his teeth, looking embarrassed for their pathetic mutual friend.

"Yeah… he's only been here two hours."

"And he's already shit-faced," Kelly said.

"Shit-faced?! No, I'm not!" he said. "I'm on vacation. It doesn't count. It's like Vegas! Whatever happens here stays here."

Pam joined Kelly by the window, watching the pitiful alcoholic half-dangling out of the window.

"Where's Ross?" she asked.

"Out in front," Norman said. "Doing something on his computer."

"Probably writing another article," Kelly said.

Jamie's upper body swung as he tried pulling himself back into the cabin. "Hey! How'd this happen? Someone mind lending a hand?"

Kelly stepped forward. "Sure!"

"Oh, you're the best!" Jamie reached for her.

"I sure am." Kelly took him by the wrist and gave him a good yank. A squealing Jamie tumbled from the window and landed flat on his back. Staring straight up, he admired the sky and the trees, then Kelly's face. "You're pretty. When you're done with Gordon, give me a call."

Kelly scoffed, then walked away. *Pathetic.*

"Hi, Norman," she said, the greeting an afterthought.

After turning the corner to the front of the cabin, she found Ross seated at the picnic table, fingers tapping the keyboard.

"Hey, Ross."

Ross didn't hear her, thanks to the tunes in his earphones. He stared into the computer screen, in a trance-like state, clicking those keys with precision.

She picked up a pebble and tossed it at his shoulder. "Hey!" The skinny journalist shook, nearly swiping his computer off the table.

Kelly laughed at his clumsiness.

"Why, hello to you too." Ross removed his headphones and stood up.

At five-foot-six, he and Jamie were tied for the shortest men in the group. It was a running joke that he, Jamie, Kelly, and Pam could stand against a piece of wallpaper, and someone could easily draw a straight line over their heads. Their heights matched perfectly, making Ted and Norman feel superior and masculine.

Ross straightened his computer and untangled his headphone cords.

"How was the drive?"

"Well, we survived," Kelly said. She looked at the computer screen. "Working while on vacation?"

"Caught wind of a story before I left home. This homophobic hardware shop owner in Aurora who fired one of his LGBT employees. It's just another example of the bigotry that's running rampant in these places."

Kelly regretted asking. She was more than happy to conclude the topic right there.

Unfortunately, Norman overheard and approached.

"Dude?" he said with a condescending laugh. "A hardware shop guy nobody's heard of until now? How is that even newsworthy?"

"I wouldn't expect *you* to understand," Ross said.

"That right?" Norman twirled the ax, catching it by the handle. At six-three and built like an ox, he towered over everyone else. The former Army infantryman gladly relished his role as the alpha male of the group. Even while on vacation, he radiated testosterone. He had a large knife strapped to his belt at all times. Not that he needed it. Like a Viking, he always carried that ax, as though ready to raid an enemy village. The rest of the group didn't complain. They loved keeping the firepit burning, and splitting wood was just one way for Norman to maintain that impressive figure.

Ross was probably the only one who was not impressed. Either that, or he was secretly envious.

He watched Norman play with the ax, shaking his head with contempt. The two often debated about social issues. Whenever something hit the news, they often took opposite sides. To Kelly's relief, they surprisingly managed to keep their debates snarky and humorous. There were insults hurled at each other, but it was all part of their banter. It rarely got truly heated.

"Well, I wouldn't expect a caveman to understand anything but, 'Oh, look! Mammoth! Must kill! Oh, look! Woman. Must fuck!'"

"Hey, at least one of us has experienced that second one," Norman said.

"With *women*?" Kelly said. Everyone in the group erupted with laughter.

"Alright, you closeted homophobes," Ross said. "Go fight over which rooms you want. I gotta finish this up."

Norman raised an eyebrow, sensing a new opportunity to antagonize Ross.

"Not sure if you can be a closeted homophobe. Closeted homosexual, sure. But closeted homophobe?"

"Oh, ha-ha," Ross said. Before he returned his attention to his computer, he noticed someone was missing. He looked around, then stood back up. "Where's Jamie?"

"He was back there," Kelly said.

The five of them walked to the rear of the cabin, then erupted with laughter after finding Jamie snoring away where they left him. Even in slumber, he remembered to prop his beer bottle at his lips, bottom up.

"How cute," Pam said. "He has his pacifier."

"Come on guys," Kelly said. "Let's get to the cooler ourselves before he wakes up and hogs the rest of the beer."

***

"Just great. The one time I'm counting on nobody being around…" Diego muttered to himself. He pulled his duffle bag out of the bed of his truck and carried it to his cabin. The obnoxious laughter from the neighboring cabin carried over, souring his already grouchy mood. All he wanted was peace, quiet, and most importantly, isolation. Instead, he would have to share this portion of the lake with a bunch of twenty-somethings, who likely would spend the week boozed out of their minds. Luckily, there were plenty of trees in-between their cabin and his. At least he wouldn't have to look at them.

He opened the door and stepped into the sunroom, admiring the wooden table and folding chair facing the screen window. Two fishing poles were racked on the wall next to a couple of shovels and other maintenance items. Something about being in this little space helped lift his spirits. Often, he enjoyed staying up at night, admiring the lake while seated at the table. Diego was a man of simple tastes. Though he usually packed novels for his pastime, he generally found pleasure in simply watching the lake and the trees. Working in the city, tracking down the worst people society had to offer, made him appreciate the lush tranquility.

Since the department canned him, he now had all the time in the world to appreciate it.

He unlocked the next door and let himself into the main part of the cabin. The living room area was as clean and neat as when he left it. There was wood in the fireplace, stacks of newspaper in the corner, and a soft couch across the room. Further back was the kitchen, cleaned and organized to perfection. All of the coffee cup handles faced the same direction, the pots and pans were arranged by size, and the cleaning materials lined up at the windowsill.

To the right was a small hallway. On the right was the master bedroom. On the other end was a guest bedroom, which was never used, and in the middle was the restroom, as sparkly clean as the rest of the cabin interior. Diego was no germaphobe—he made fun of those types— but working in police work, he had endured more than his fair share of ratty kitchens and bathrooms.

Diego tossed his bag on the end of his bed, then plopped down next to it. Welcoming the soft fabric underneath him, he shut his eyes.

Finally! Back to my place of Zen. Away from the rest of the world.

A distant splash interrupted his meditation. Obnoxious laughter followed, then chatter.

"Hey, Ted! You'll scare the fish jumping in there like that!" one of the females shouted.

"Nah, that only happens when Jamie jumps in."

"Yeah… scares away the fish *and* everything else."

"Alright, alright. That's enough. Don't need to be reminded of his skinny-dipping habits."

More laughter.

Diego sneeringly stared through the ceiling, picturing the heavens above.

"Why, God? Three-hundred-sixty-five days in a year, and these assholes had to show up *today*."

He inhaled deeply and tried to ignore them. Gradually, his mood started to shift back in the right direction. After all, it wasn't as though he owned the lake, and it wasn't like these people were setting out to irritate him. They were a bunch of young people having fun.

"Oh… Hey! You assholes let me doze off there!" someone yelled.

"Uh-oh! Jamie's awake."

"You were gonna let me sleep in the grass like that? You guys are real assh—oh."

"Oh, God," one of the guys shouted. "Jamie, get away from the A/C unit…"

"BLECH!"

There was a mix of laughter and disgusted groans. The fella named Jamie coughed, getting his cookies back in order.

"Whoops. Sorry man."

"I'm gonna kill you!"

Diego was back to questioning God. "Why am I stuck with these people?"

CHAPTER 6

The night had fallen and the crickets were singing their nightly melody. The frogs splashed in the lake, chasing after mosquitoes and flies. The loons called to each other in their eerie, yet beautiful voices. Critters moved about in the woods, either burrowing somewhere to settle in for the night, or setting out to take advantage of the dark in their forage for food.

For most campers, these sounds were part of the thrill of sleeping in the woods. For Kathleen Hargle, they were just an annoying hindrance. One of many, in fact.

She stepped out of the RV, dressed in a nightgown that was a size too small for her hefty mass.

"Ah-hem!" She waited for her slightly less fat boyfriend to look her way. He was scratching his neckbeard, nervously anticipating a verbal chastisement in front of their three friends.

"Want a marshmallow?" he said, grinning innocently. He raised a sharpened stick with a charred cylindrical mass made of sugar, corn syrup, and gelatin.

Kathleen kicked the cooler, which had been set near the RV door. "I see you remembered five cases of beer."

"Well…" he gestured to Charlie, Drew, and Lindsay. "I'm very considerate."

"So considerate, that you failed to pack paper towels and disinfectant." She yelped, slapping her neck. She proceeded to swat at the air in a pitiful attempt to shoo the mosquitoes away. "God! I hate that you dragged me out here. I'm never gonna let you talk me into this again."

Aden put his marshmallow stick down and snatched up a beer bottle.

"You said you wanted a vacation."

"At the spa. Not in *Deliverance*-Ville."

"Yeah, a two-thousand dollar stay at a spa," Aden said. "Forget the fact that our credit cards are maxed out. Thanks to my uncle lending us his RV, we can have a vacation without spending any serious money." He pointed his elbow at Drew and Lindsay. "They seem to be happy we're here."

Kathleen looked at the half-drunken couple, mouths connected as though welded together.

"Christ. How can they breathe?" She slapped her neck again, then her thigh, then thrashed at the air to get at the offending bugs. At her wit's end, she marched into the RV, then returned with a can of spray. She unleashed its contents, creating a chemical cloud in their little camp area.

Drew and Lindsay, two sweethearts that were considerably more attractive than their overweight counterparts, broke from their makeout session.

"Whoa, there," Drew said. "You trying to fog the place? You'll only drive them away for a few minutes at best."

"Better to stay by the fire," Lindsay said. "The heat seems to keep the bugs away. At least, I haven't noticed any."

"How the hell would you notice anything while you're busy digging your faces into each other?" Kathleen said.

Aden shrugged. "At least somebody's having a good time."

Lindsay sat straight... at least she attempted to. The three beers and the fifth of Scotch had done wonders for her mood and drive. She straightened her tank top straps, then brushed her pink hair back in an attempt to make herself more presentable. After five seconds, she realized she didn't care. It wasn't as if anyone else did either. Certainly not the big blob standing in an outfit *nobody* wanted to see her in.

The only one with no opinion on the matter was Charlie. Skinny as a twig, he was buried in his phone. Repeatedly, the group had to endure the audio from his encounter with the cops back at the gas station.

"This is the murderer from Denver, the one who got away with beating Willie Stader to death!"

"Are you serious?"

"That's him."

"Hey! Watch it! Gosh, did all the idiots in Colorado decide to follow me here?"

"Have something to say, racist?"

"Just let me leave, will ya?"

"You don't deserve to have peace! Not after what you did!"

"Geez, Charlie," Drew said. "You're quite proud of yourself, aren't ya? You gonna play that video another hundred times? Perhaps it's not engrained in our memories quite enough yet..."

Charlie shook his head. "I'm trying to upload it, but I can't get a freaking signal."

"Just as well," Drew said. "No need to broadcast that level of stupidity to the world."

"You know who that guy was, right?" Aden said.

"Yes," Drew said. "As I've said, I've had the displeasure of listening to the recording ten-thousand times."

"Then you know he killed that innocent man in Denver," Kathleen said.

"And?"

"And you're okay with that?"

"I didn't say that," Drew said. "I'm pointing out the retardation that was you three attempting to mess with him. Yeah, go up and harass an ex-cop, who probably has a gun, and probably a bad temper. Yeah, smart."

His criticism was lost on Charlie, who was raising his phone high over his head.

"Come on, you piece of shit."

Lindsay finished her beer, then stretched her arms while deliberately leaning against her boyfriend. Those arms closed around him, and her mouth was reconnected with his.

"Good grief," Kathleen said. "Don't you guys have a tent? Use it, will ya?"

Lindsay broke away and smiled naughtily. "That's not a bad idea." She got up and strutted into the woods, heading in the direction of their truck and tent.

Drew slapped his thighs, then stood up, noticeably pleased.

"Y'all have a good night." He turned on his heel and marched after his girlfriend.

Aden smirked, amused and slightly jealous.

"Aden?"

The tone of her voice was even harsher than before. Aden swallowed, then looked at Kathleen.

"Yes?"

"You expect me to clean up your mess in the kitchen?" she said, pointing at the RV.

"I'll get it tomorrow."

"No, you'll get it now. Don't feel like waking up to a bunch of bugs helping themselves to the buffet you left them."

Aden groaned, then stood up. He rarely said no to Kathleen, despite the resentment he often felt toward her. He stepped into the RV and switched on the light.

Charlie got up and started wandering into the woods, phone still raised high.

"Where are you going?" Kathleen said.

"Seeing if I can upload this damn video to Facebook," he said. Barely watching where he was going, he stumbled into the woods, panning the phone back and forth.

Kathleen slapped her neck again, then looked at her hand. The fact that she missed was more irritating than the constant buzzing. It was as though these mosquitoes were trying to get her to beat herself up.

"Fuck! I hate it here."

***

It had enjoyed a period of rest after a long session of repairs. The power cell had been recharged and the cloak was still holding, rendering the ship invisible to the naked eye. From the outside, it looked like just another section of forest.

The Convict stepped outside, giving one final inspection of the ship's camouflage. Aside from the occasional ripple, there was no way anyone would know it was there. The fluctuation in the cloak did not occur often. For someone to notice it, they would have to be standing in the right place at the right time. It was nothing the Convict was too worried about.

It had done enough work. Now, it was ready to enjoy some recreation. Its scanner picked up signals to the northwest. There was a settlement, not too far from the lake. According to the scanner, this group had split in two. Two of the members had departed for a separate, smaller settlement, while the other three were each busy doing their own individual tasks.

The activity between the pair sparked intrigue. Slowly, it advanced, its night vision spotting a small shelter made of a draped fabric. The inside was lit, the silhouettes of the occupants standing out against the yellow tarp. One was on top of the other, shifting vigorously while making intense panting noises.

Just as the Convict suspected—a mating session. Simultaneously amused and curious, it moved closer, settling by a tree nearest to the habitat. The pair were going at it hard. Judging by their shapes, it appeared that the female was on top. Then, in a seemingly violent shift, the male took charge, rolling his mate onto her back and began thrusting with intensity. Now, the female's gasping had grown more passionate.

Just like its own species, these creatures mated for pleasure. Though they were different creatures, it appeared their method of copulation was very much the same.

Vile fascination took over. Before it would quench its need for slaughter, it needed to satisfy its curiosity. Cautiously, it approached.

The shelter entrance was partially open, the top peeled outward allowing for the Convict's viewing pleasure.

It took each step carefully, making sure not to alert its victims. Then again, their coupling was so intense, they probably would not have heard it even if it approached with loud childish stomps.

Now outside the entrance, it peeked. There they were, both stripped of their garments, engaged in a physical union. The male was still on top, pleasuring the female with each shift in his body. Though enjoying his actions, the female seemed to be the domineering type. She grabbed him by the shoulder and rolled him over, taking charge of the situation by mounting. She sat upright, head leaned back, now slowly grinding against him.

The curiosity had subsided. The Convict eyed its gauntlet blade, feeling a murderous itch more extreme than any sexual urge.

***

"Oh yeah, baby," Drew said. He watched Lindsay rise and fall, her pink hair all over her shoulders. He admired the form of her body, his hands making sure to grab the goods.

Lindsay looked up, eyes closed, her jaw parted. Gasps became moans, and moans became yells. The pleasure reached its peak.

The tent ripped. She opened her eyes, catching a glimmer from the long silver blades slicing at her neck.

Her yell became a scream.

Her scream became silence.

That silence was overtaken by Drew's screaming. He flailed, seeing his headless girlfriend, still mounted on him, spurting blood from the stump.

Her killer brushed her body away, then stomped a heavy foot on his torso, impaling his lungs with broken ribs.

The humanoid thing looked down with its insect-like face, watching the naked male squirm under its foot. It reached into a pouch, pulling out a vial. Little worms squirmed inside the little glass tube. It opened the lid and dropped a few on Drew's busted abdomen.

A world of pain that he never knew was possible engulfed him. These worms, with jaws like razors, dug into his flesh. Attempts to scream resulted in blood spitting from his mouth.

The thing stood and watched as the little creatures ate at his flesh. Then it stepped out, alerted to the sound of rustling bushes nearby.

***

"Damn!"

Charlie lowered his phone, hearing the intense howls coming from Drew and Lindsay's little hideout. The two of them must be having a hell of a time to be making that much noise.

A smirk came over his face. He could not help himself. His judgement partially impaired by alcohol, he succumbed to the urge to head over and spy on them. Besides, it would grant an opportunity to get a look at Lindsay's breasts. Knowing those two, they had probably left their tent partially open. They were always so eager to get down to business that they half-assed any attempt to be tactful.

He pushed through some thick undergrowth, stumbling over an exposed tree root.

"Damn it." He stood quietly, listening for any further activity. It had gone silent, aside from some rustling. Perhaps he had missed the show. He kept going, figuring it was worth a perverted peek.

Charlie's fellow activists would likely criticize him if they were here. "You're a creep," some would probably say. Alas, they were not here. What they didn't know would not hurt them, nor would it impact the movements they stood for.

He could see the tent and the two figures inside. One of them seemed to be shuddering nonstop, while the other was still.

Damn. Something tells me I missed a hell of a performance.

Charlie grinned.

His amusement turned to terror when he saw the broad-shouldered monstrosity step from behind a tree on his right. He stumbled back, his eyes so focused on the pincer mouth and the big black eyes that they didn't notice the twin blades extending from its wrist.

It grabbed him by the throat with its other hand, lifting him effortlessly. Charlie kicked and gagged, unable to yell out, despite his best attempts.

The thing studied his form, intrigued by his thinness. It retracted its wrist blades and lowered its right arm.

Charlie clung to its wrist, his feet kicking above the ground. He was uncertain if the thing was showing mercy, or if it had other plans.

All of a sudden, he was raised high over its head. The thing held him by the shoulder and crotch, its victim's kicking doing little to impede its horrific act. Slowly, it bent his body backward.

Charlie squealed, then squeaked pathetically as his spine snapped at the center. His fingers clenched, his nerves firing all kinds of conflicting signals throughout his paralyzed body.

There were no final thoughts. No feelings of remorse or regret. Cognitive thought was hardly possible when experiencing such overwhelming pain and terror. He couldn't even comprehend who or what this killer was. All he could comprehend was the motion of its rising foot, the stomp that followed, and the brief sensation of his skull imploding.

Blood, bone, and brains splattered onto the dirt.

His killer raised its foot, then watched the bent, headless corpse twitch. It turned and moved in on the campfire, its bloodlust now directed at the fattest members of the group.

***

"Aden?"

"What?"

"Can you come out here?"

"I thought you wanted me to clean!"

"Just come out here, will you?"

"Fine!" Aden stepped out of the RV, wiping his hands with a towel. Kathleen was standing by the fire, fretfully watching the woods. "What's the matter?"

"I thought I heard something," she said.

"Probably just an owl."

"No… it sounded like someone was starting to yell."

"But then they didn't?" Aden chuckled. "Probably nothing, Kathleen."

She cupped her hands around her mouth. "Charlie? Where'd you go?" Her voice carried through the woods, with no reply. "Charlie?!"

"Oh… shit," Aden said, looking down.

"What?"

"I think I know where he's at."

"Where?"

"Well, uh… you know what Lindsay and Drew are doing…"

Kathleen's jaw dropped. "You think he went over there to *spy*?"

"Maybe."

"He wouldn't. You know the kind of stuff he stands for," Kathleen said. "He would never disrespect women like that. Sneaking on them, watching while they're exposed."

Aden scoffed. "Yeah. Okay. Sure."

Kathleen shuddered. After giving the subject a moment of consideration, she recognized the likely truth.

"Yeah, alright, fine. Go get him. Make sure that's not what he's doing."

Aden slapped his arms against his sides and groaned. "Fine."

He delved into the woods, yelping as he grazed a thorn bush at the grove of trees right outside their campsite.

"Ow!" He plucked a few thorns from his wrist, then looked at Kathleen. Her glare spurred him back into action. With a sigh, he continued his quest. He passed the bush and ventured into the woods. "Charlie? You out here?"

Kathleen stayed behind, keeping close to the fire. Another bug landed on her neck, driving her to madness. She slapped herself, then grabbed the bug spray. For the second time, she showered herself with its contents.

"I hate this place." She settled down, her skin moistened by the repellent. She looked past the fire at the woods where Aden had gone. His silhouette was somewhat visible in the far reaches of its glow. Even at night, his large figure stood out fairly easily.

"Hurry up," she said.

"I'm looking!" he called back. He pressed deeper, almost vanishing completely.

"You see him?" she shouted.

"You know, it's easier to do this when you're not…Whoa!"

Thud!

Kathleen shivered. "Aden?"

There was no response. All she could hear was mild rustling. She kept close to the RV, unsure whether to be frustrated or concerned.

"Aden, speak up, will ya? You couldn't have fallen *that* hard." She crossed her arms and waited for a reply. Now, she was frustrated. "Come on, dipshit. Where'd you go?"

The thorn bush swished, a mass behind it bobbing up and down. Finally, she could see his hair peeking over the top.

Kathleen shook her head. "Alright, dude. What kind of game are you playing?"

Aden's head rose higher, his raised eyebrows near his hairline. It was impossible to tell what kind of comical expression he was trying to make, but Kathleen was not amused.

Her patience lost, she marched over to the thorn bush.

"Alright, you dumbass. Enough is enough. Time for you to…"

Aden's severed head came into full view, propped on the blades of some—*thing*.

It bobbed the head like a puppet, then with a flick of its wrist, it flung it to the side. Kathleen screamed and stumbled backward. Her foot came down on one of the beer bottles, which rolled from under her foot. Her scream became a high-pitched squeal as she tumbled backward.

Right into the blazing fire.

Her nightgown lit up instantly. The fire spread to her repellent-covered skin, lighting up her entire bloated body.

The Convict stood by, watching the fat, clumsy local squirming on the ground. Its work was cut out for it in this case. She was so wide, that she could not manage to stand up or even roll out of place. Eventually, she stopped trying, instead succumbing to the mindlessness of overwhelming agony. She reached to the heavens, fingers coiling as she was slowly cooked alive. Her skin blistered, then turned crisp. Her hair lit up, encasing her entire skull with flame.

Meanwhile, the Convict further entertained itself by exploring the campsite. By the looks of it, the locals were roasting some small white things on sticks. Judging by the way the pointed ends were charred, these foods were prepped by being roasted over a flame. Easy enough. There was no harm in trying the foods here. Luckily for the Convict, there was already a nice flame currently ablaze.

It stuck one on the end of a stick and extended it over the fire. Cooking the item, it reached for one of the brown bottles that the locals drank from. Why not try that too? It twisted the seal off and tilted the bottle into its mouth. Whatever this drink was, the Convict liked it.

It drained the bottle, then helped itself to another, drinking away while roasting the little white comestible over the flame.

CHAPTER 7

Diego opened his eyes to a world of sunlight and singing birds. If there was anything about unemployment that he found positive, it was the extra hours of sleep. For the first time in twenty years, he did not wake up to an alarm clock. His time was devoted to the Denver Police Department ever since his graduation from the academy. Constant sixteen-hour days prevented him from having much of a life. He never married or had children. How could he? He was married to his work. His mistress was this vacation home, where he spent a couple weeks out of the year if he was lucky. Luckily, not having much of a personal life allowed him to save a significant amount of money. A stocked savings account granted him the ability to take some time to himself before initiating the inevitable job hunt.

He spent the morning hours enjoying a couple cups of coffee in his sunroom. The water was gentle and welcoming, making him consider a swim. The tranquility was quickly interrupted by the sound of splashing and laughing from next door. The group in the other cabin was already out and about this morning.

Relax, dickhead. It's not like you own the lake. They're just out having fun.

Yeah? Well, ask me if I give a shit?

Diego believed people had two sides of their brain. The rational side and the irrational side. They were usually at war with each other.

The rational side was usually more empathetic and understanding. It was usually the side that dominated his personality when on the job. Then there was the irrational side, which essentially said "To hell with everyone else. My way or the highway." In this case, he cared little for the fact that other people were trying to get away from the world and relax. For once in his life, Diego wanted complete and total isolation. Go figure, those dickheads in the next cabin had to pick this exact weekend to show up.

Diego watched the grove of trees that separated his property from the neighbors'. At least they couldn't see him for the most part. The last thing he needed was for another nosey person to recognize him.

Done with his reading for the morning, he stood up and went to his bedroom. Not since college had he remained in his sweats at ten a.m. It was enjoyable, but the time had come to feel somewhat presentable to the world, even if he planned to remain isolated. It was not a matter of impressing anyone. It was a simple matter of discipline.

He stripped down, folded his laundry, then placed it in a basket near his closet. Before heading into the shower, he reached for the top shelf and found his Glock 17. It was his personal weapon, passed down from his father who retired from the Denver department nine years ago.

It was routine for Diego to perform safety checks on the weapon. Even if he kept it loaded, he would still check the muzzles for blockages, and make sure the slide was sufficiently lubricated. Too often, he responded to homicide scenes which were the result of improper gun handling. Murders, accidents, they were all homicides and fell under his jurisdiction. Then there was the occasional screw-up from cadets or even veteran officers, usually at the firing range. He had witnessed the results of improper weapons handling too many times in his life. When it came to his personal firearms, he treated it as though his academy instructor was always looking over his shoulder.

The gun was clean, oiled, and ready to go.

Diego placed it back on the top shelf, then took his shower. Having short hair, it was a quick five-minute process.

He stepped out and went to the kitchen pantry, wearing only a towel. Something about taking showers triggered his appetite. Diego often skipped breakfast. For whatever reason, he didn't have much of an appetite in the morning except for coffee. It was between ten and eleven when his body would finally demand real sustenance.

He was low on food, which he was aware of when he arrived. His attempt to rectify this situation at the gas station was foiled, thanks to those nosey jerks. The thought of them made his blood pressure rise.

It was time to look over his options. He could make a run into town and grab a few things or make do with what he had.

Diego looked at his fishing rod and tackle box, which were placed in the sunroom corner.

To hell with the gas station. Let's catch some lunch.

He grabbed his shovel from the sunroom and a tin can off the shelf, then marched into the woods. He found an area with loose soil where he usually dug for bait. The dead leaves and decaying wood in this little patch of forest served him well. Nightcrawlers were abundant, just waiting to be placed on a hook. He filled the can, sealed it, then went back inside.

After scarfing a multigrain bar to settle his stomach, he filled a travel mug with hot coffee, then grabbed his gear.

Time to forget about the world. His boat was right there at the dock, waiting for him.

***

"Alright, you jokers," Ross said. He stepped out of the cabin with two large plates in his hands. "Brunch is served. Got eggs, pancakes, French toast, sausage patties… and yes, Norman, bacon."

Norman was kneeling on the dock, power drill in hand. "Better not be any of that gay tofu garbage."

"No, you animal," Ross said. He placed the plates down on the picnic table. "Just the same barbaric, cholesterol-raising normal stuff."

"Is it the pre-cooked stuff, or the *real* bacon that you buy frozen? Because that's the good stuff!" Norman continued. Ross raised a middle finger, sparking laughter from the veteran.

Ross sat at the picnic table with his cup of coffee, then began helping himself to the assortment of food.

"Ungrateful ogre. I ought to start charging you for your stay, instead of giving you a free ride all the time."

"Ungrateful soy boy," Norman retorted. "I ought to charge *you* for fixing this dock for the umpteenth time, not to mention the picnic table last year, and for doing the roofing and repairing the water damage. Oh, and *who* clogged the drain three years ago?"

Ross snorted and raised his coffee to hide a smile. "Well, uh… Jamie, of course."

"Hey!" Jamie shouted, splashing water. He pulled himself onto the swimming platform, then turned to face Ted and Pam, who were busy frolicking in the water. "CANNONBALL!"

SPLASH!

"Jesus, Jamie!" Ted shouted, splashing at the goofball.

Jamie surfaced, spitting water as he laughed. "I'm sorry! Did I interrupt something?"

Pam brushed the water from her eyes and backstroked away from him.

"You're right, Ross. It is easy to blame everything on Jamie," she said.

"That's fabulous! Love you guys too."

Norman drilled the last screw into place, then marched to the picnic table with purpose.

"No need for the *too*, Jamie. That would imply your reciprocating feelings."

"Oh, be nice," Kelly said. She was standing up from a lounge chair with a book in hand, ready to join the buffet that Ross prepared. "Let's give Jamie a little bit of credit where it's due."

"Yeah?" Norman said. "What would that be? Actually managing to put the milk in the fridge instead of the pantry?"

"There's that," she said. "And he is buying the beer tonight."

"You're assuming he won't consume half of it before he even returns," Ross said.

Kelly sat down and shrugged. "Yeah, you got a point there."

"You guys are mean, you know that?" Jamie shouted from the water. "I'm unworthy of such abuse. I'm an angel in an earth suit, in case you didn't know." He stuck his tongue out at them and blew raspberries like a six-year-old.

Kelly rolled her eyes, then grabbed a paper plate. First, she grabbed some pancakes, then some bacon.

"Tongs, please," Ross said.

"Sorry. Guess I'm used to being too casual," Kelly said.

"Aw, don't worry," Norman said. He happily reached onto the platter and grabbed some bacon, sausage, and pancakes. "He's just a germaphobe. Why he enjoys the outdoors, I'll never know."

"I'm not a germaphobe," Ross said. "I'm just sanitary when it comes to preparing food. You know, the stuff we put in our bodies?" He looked at the pile of bacon on Norman's plate. "Guess I shouldn't kid myself. Like you would care about what goes down your gullet."

"You're just jealous." Norman pulled his open shirt apart and tapped his abs. He bit down on a strip of bacon. "Aw! Ross, this *is* the pre-cooked stuff!"

"You'll live, you damn lion."

Norman cracked a smile. "You say that like it's an insult. That actually sounds awesome! Norman, the Lion of Rainwater."

"Enjoy being awesome in your own mind," Ross said.

"Jeez oh Pete's," Kelly said. "You guys would make a great married couple, you know that?" She noted the disgusted look on both men's faces. Chuckling, she reached for the tongs. "Don't worry, Ross. I'll keep my grubby fingers off of the platter."

"It's not that," he said. "You work at a chemical plant. God knows what stuff is on your fingers."

Kelly leaned back, perplexed by that notion. "I work at a water treatment plant, for one."

"Oh…" Ross thought for a second. "But you're a chemist."

"Yeah. How do you think we clean the water?" she said.

Ross chuckled, feeling a little embarrassed. "I guess you have a point. Sorry, I knew you worked at a plant, but I didn't realize what kind of plant. You never really talk much about your job."

"Not much to tell," Kelly said. She played with her food while staring at her plate. "We just test water samples from various communities and businesses that were ordered to by local authorities. I'm not part of the staff that manages the cleaning of the city water."

"They probably put stuff in it to dumb down the population. Makes them easier for the government to control," Norman said.

"Oh, here we go. More conspiracy theories about governments," Ross muttered.

"Right," Norman said. "Because world history has totally proven that governments are totally trustworthy. They would never drum up ways to control their populace."

"You probably believe in that lizard people crap too," Ross said.

"No, but I believe there's an effort to move us to globalization."

"Is that necessarily a bad thing?"

"Considering the people who'd be running it, *yeah*!"

"Better than the one percent," Ross said.

"People in government *are* the one percent, dipshit!" Norman said. "That, and they gladly take money from the rest of the one percent."

"Oh, for heaven's sake." Kelly scarfed her food down and stood up. The last thing she needed was to witness another political debate between Norman and Ross.

She tossed her paper plate in the trash and returned to the lounge chair. The twenty feet of distance was not enough.

"Why do you think the media pits us all against each other?" Norman said.

"Which media? Fox?"

Kelly had known those two long enough to know this useless debate would go on for at least another half hour. With that in the background, she would not be able to focus on her book. Their back-and-forth was like nails on a chalkboard for everybody, even Jamie.

The three swimmers were looking at the picnic table.

"Oh, here we go again," Pam said.

"Nothing ever changes," Ted said. He leaned in toward his girlfriend. "Except my desire to grab your ass." Pam let out a high-pitched laugh as he helped himself to her right cheek.

Kelly smirked as she walked to the dock. She took a seat on the paddleboat and unmoored it.

"Going on a voyage?" Pam said.

"Might as well," she said. "Beats listening to that." She pointed her thumb at Ross and Norman. Jamie leveled himself with the water, then swam like an eel in her direction. "The hell are you doing, Jamie?"

"I'm escorting you on your journey."

"By being weird?"

"No need to use that word. Just say he's being himself," Pam said.

"Touché." Kelly waved goodbye, then backpedaled into the lake. The goofball Jamie traveled parallel to the boat's right side. He kicked his feet to increase speed. Now, Kelly had to carefully watch how she turned the boat in order to avoid hitting him. "Damn it, Jamie! The hell are you doing, ya freak?!"

"I'm a sea monster, hungry for pretty ladies in the middle of the ocean!"

"Good God." She pointed the boat south and paddled in that direction. Go figure, the dummy kept swimming after her.

"I'm gonna getcha!"

"You'll run out of breath before you'll even get close." She increased her speed. "Ha-ha! See ya, sucker!"

"Not so fast!"

Kelly looked back. Jamie had grabbed onto the mooring and was now dragging behind her. She wasn't sure what his endgame was, or if he even had one. Jamie was the type of guy who just felt like he needed to be funny all the time, even if the jokes did not make sense. As long as they made sense in his mind, he was content.

"You're a nut, you know that?" she said. The guy was refusing to let go of the line. The water tugged at his body, inching his trunks down his hips, exposing his butt crack. "Dude, you better let go or you're gonna be so embarrassed."

Jamie raised his head. "You forget who you're talking to?"

Kelly giggled. At least he was self-aware.

"Alright, have it your way." She continued paddling, keeping her eyes behind the boat to make sure he was alright—and to see if the trunks would hold. Kelly usually considered herself a modest individual, but that didn't mean she didn't enjoy a good laugh once in a while.

Jamie maintained his grip, his trunks slowly slipping.

"Excuse me?!"

Kelly perked up. "What'd you say, Jamie?"

He raised his head from the water. "Blech! What?!"

"Did you say something?"

He shook his head. "No."

"Excuse me!!!"

Kelly's eyes widened. That wasn't Jamie, but somebody *in front* of her. She faced forward just in time to witness her collision with the twelve-foot aluminum boat.

The man aboard, an athletically-built fella in his mid-to-late-thirties with dark hair, shouted as the boat leaned to the side.

Splash!

Down he went, along with his fishing rods. The boat teetered on its side for a short moment before leveling out.

The guy emerged, as frustrated as she expected him to be.

"Goddamnit! You dumb broad! You not look where you're going? You have the entire goddamn lake, and you *had* to smack into me."

Kelly felt the blood rushing to her face.

"I'm sorry, I… I wasn't paying attention."

"Oh, really?! I wouldn't have guessed."

Jamie swam alongside her boat. "Listen man, have a sense of humor, will ya? It was clearly an accident. Maybe we can…"

"Who the hell's talking to you, pencil neck?"

Kelly extended her hand. "I'm so sorry, mister. Here, let me help you out."

"No, I got it," he said in a low, growly tone. He grabbed the side of his boat and lifted himself up and over. He stood up in the same position he happened to be in when the impact occurred. Right away, he was looking into the water again. "Great. Lost both rods. And to top it off, I had a big one on the line. Thanks a lot, lady."

"How much do they cost?" Kelly said. "I'll pay you for them."

The guy ignored her attempts to rectify the situation. Instead, he pulled up his anchor and began rowing to shore.

Kelly started paddling after him. "Sir, just tell me how I can make this right."

"By shutting the fuck up and leaving me alone."

"Hey! What's going on?!" Ross shouted.

The man groaned, seeing the other four friends running onto his property.

"You alright, Kelly?" Norman called out.

"It's alright. Had a little run-in, was all."

"You don't say!" the man snapped.

Kelly facepalmed, regretting the poor choice of words.

"Dude, chill out, alright," Norman said. "Whatever happened, I'm sure it was an accident."

"Fuck off, beef," the man said.

Ross stepped ahead of the group, studying the man's features. "You look familiar. Do I know you?"

"I've been in this cabin for years," the man said. "Mind heading back to yours?"

Ross narrowed his gaze. "I swear I recognize you."

"Come on, dude," Ted said. "Let's head back."

Ross wasn't satisfied. He knew this guy from somewhere, and he *needed* to solve the mystery.

Then it hit him.

"Holy shit! It's the cop from Denver!" He scoffed in a combination of astonishment and disgust. "I can't believe it. We're cabin neighbors with the killer of Willie Stader. I see the little scar near your eyebrow. I know it's you. Diego Tritton! That's the name, isn't it?"

The man named Diego moored his boat then started walking to his cabin. "That's the name. Seems everyone knows it now."

"That's what happens when you shoot an unarmed kid," Ross said. "How much did you pay the investigators to let you off scot-free?"

Diego stopped, then stood in place for what seemed like an eternity. His hunched shoulders indicated tension—the kind one felt when on the verge of snapping.

Norman grabbed Ross by the shoulder. "Come on, dude. Let's head back."

For once, Ross leaned toward Norman's way of thinking. Perhaps being the activist type wasn't always the best idea… especially when you were out in the middle of the woods, miles from civilization. For all he knew, this guy was armed and willing to unload on the lot of them.

Kelly watched as the four of them turned around, then breathed a sigh of relief as Diego resumed walking to his cabin. Further incidents had been avoided.

"You alright?" Jamie said in a rare moment of sincerity.

"Yeah. My nerves are a little shot, is all," she said. Her hands quivered, her heart acting as though it was trying to make an escape. "Hey, Jamie? How deep is it here?"

"Maybe six, seven feet," he said.

"You a good diver?"

Jamie realized what she was getting at. "Oh, you want me to go down there?!"

"It's the least we can do."

"No, it's the least *I* can do. You're the one who ran into him."

"All because of your silly antics."

"Hmm." He thought about that for a moment. "Yeah, fine. I guess you have a point."

He took a breath and disappeared under the water.

Kelly waited on the paddleboat, dreading her inner desire to do the right thing. She had heard the reports of Diego Tritton and the controversy surrounding him. His name had been dragged through the mud by the mainstream press. It seemed anyone who paid attention to the actual reports, given directly from the investigators on live television, knew any of the real facts. Everyone else was out to make a headline from the ordeal.

Jamie popped back up and raised a fishing rod over his head like a gladiator with his sword.

"Found it!"

Kelly took it and placed it in the left seat. "Both of them?"

"He had two?"

"Yeah."

"Ugh." Jamie took a breath and vanished for the second time.

Slowly but truly, Kelly's nerves began to settle down. She rested in her seat, watching the bugs dancing on the water. Over at the center of the lake, a bird swooped down, its talons scraping the water. When it ascended, it was clear it had grabbed a fish.

When it reached a hundred feet, it suddenly dropped its catch, which splashed down in the middle of the lake.

"Whoa!" Kelly looked up. The bird continued flying off, showing no further interest in its meal. She could see the fish floating on the water, obviously dead. "Hmm. That's odd. I wonder if it's common for birds to abandon easy meals like that."

Jamie reemerged and raised the second fishing pole. "What? Common birds? Did I miss something?"

"Huh? Oh… nothing. Just thinking out loud." She took the pole from him. "Thanks."

"No problem. I'm beat. You mind giving me a lift?"

"Actually, I'm gonna head over to the neighbor's cabin and return his stuff," Kelly said.

Jamie grumbled. "You're gonna make me swim all the way back there?"

"No." She pointed at the shore. "You can swim over there and walk back to Ross' cabin."

Jamie gave Diego's cabin a look as though it were haunted.

"Nah, I could use the exercise anyway. See ya!" He doggy paddled back home, stopping every few yards to fix his trunks.

"There's a drawstring, you know!" she said. The moment of levity had passed, and now she was dreading her do-good attitude. Now, she was watching the cabin as though it contained a masked killer. That Diego guy certainly had an attitude. Then again, so would she if someone rammed into her boat because they weren't paying any attention.

She took a deep breath.

"Alright, let's get this over with."

She pedaled her boat to his dock, moored, then went up to the cabin. Nervousness made her throat tighten. She felt as though she was walking up to a haunted house.

Kelly arrived at the sunroom. It was a nice little front area facing the lake. She imagined it would be especially relaxing during a thunderstorm. Already, she found herself wishing Ross' cabin had such a room. She would awaken at dawn and watch the morning fog part over the lake.

The door was on the right side. Kelly went over and rested the fishing rods against the screen, then held her fist to knock on the door.

Nervousness gripped her again. She knocked on the door, quickly stopping after she saw how wobbly it was. The thing needed new hinges. Worried she might damage it further, she decided to peek through the front screen to see if Diego was inside.

***

Diego stepped inside his cabin, tracking water with each step. He pulled his shirt off and threw it on the sunroom table. After stripping himself of his boots, socks, and pants, he went to the bathroom. He grabbed a towel, wrapped it around his waist, then immediately dropped it after seeing a white fuzzy patch. Standing naked in the hallway, he used his foot to lay the towel out.

Sure enough, there was mold growing on the damn thing.

"You've got to be kidding me."

The presence of mold meant that moisture had somehow gotten on the towel. Diego was not lazy with his laundry. He always made sure everything was washed and dried thoroughly.

He checked the bathroom closet, silently praying that the mold spot was just an anomaly. As it turned out, luck was not on Diego's side. All of the towels in the cabinet had mold growth on them. The ceiling above them was cracked and discolored.

Diego clenched his jaw, barely holding off a mental breakdown. Water damage meant a leak. The state of the damage indicated the leak had been happening for a while. The ruined towels were the least of his problems. His cabin had roof damage.

"Just what I need." He stepped into the kitchen, still naked and dripping wet. It was time to put one of those beers to use. Who cares if it was only eleven in the morning?

He opened the fridge, pulled a cold one out, and guzzled it down.

A knock on the door made him jump. He looked to the sunroom, its door out of view.

"Hello?"

He recognized the voice of the woman on the paddleboat. Kelly was what her friends called her.

"Sir? You inside?"

Before he could duck for cover, Kelly moved around to the front of the sunroom and peered through the screen window, where she could see through the open doorway into the kitchen.

"OH!" She turned around, cupping a hand over her eyes. "I'm so sorry! I was coming back to—"

"You are on a roll today, lady!" Diego said.

"I'm sorry! I'm so sorry! I'm going now." She retreated to the dock and hopped aboard her paddleboat. Incredibly frantic, she tried backing out before unmooring it. After paddling in place, she finally noticed her mistake and corrected it. She raced from the dock as though fleeing from the scene of a murder.

Diego took a breath, then shut his eyes. Seeing the girl's panicked reaction shifted his anger into guilt. Obviously, she did not mean to see him in this state.

Nice one, Detective. Good work. No wonder everybody hates your guts.

It only took a minute for his frustration to take hold again. There was work to be done in the bathroom.

Diego put on some dry clothes, then went out the backdoor to his shed. He unlocked the padlock and let himself in.

His charcoal grill was on the left, with half a bag of charcoal and a bottle of lighter fluid beside it. For a moment, he considered cooking on it later. The problem was he had nothing to cook! Perhaps he could have grilled a few bullheads, but that would require a fishing rod.

More issues. More misery.

Diego grabbed his tools and turned around.

A buzzing sound made him stop and listen. He prayed he was listening to the wings of a horsefly. That hope was squandered when he saw the black hornet whizzing around the doorway.

A second one appeared, followed by a third.

"Oh, no. Oh *please* no."

He exited the shed and went around the corner. There it was, the big walnut-shaped hornet's nest tucked under the awning. This damn colony had been here for some time, for the nest was nearly as big as a damn football.

Several drones crawled from the entrance and took to the sky.

"Oh, shit!" Diego turned around, tucking his head down as he retreated from an angry swarm. "SHIT! DAMN! FUCK! SON OF A BITCH!!!"

***

Kelly ventured farther into the lake, repeatedly glancing over her shoulder at Diego's cabin. Hearing his crazed ranting, she half-expected to see him running to the shore to yell at her more. The guy must have been *really* pissed.

She couldn't blame him too much. First, she dumped him into the water, then walked in on him while he was in his birthday suit and already in a bad mood, understandably so.

So far, it appeared he was staying in the cabin.

After a few moments, the shouting came to an end. Certain the chaos would not escalate, Kelly faced forward. Her desire to explore the lake was gone now. The only thing that sounded good was a drink. Unfortunately, it was still morning, and she was disciplined enough to hold off, even when stressed. A cup of coffee would have to do.

That thought went to the back of her mind after she looked at the lake. That dead fish was still floating. A dead fish in a lake was nothing new, but the residue clouding the water around it certainly was.

"What the hell?"

She paddled closer to the thing, then plugged her nose as she came alongside it. The thing was way past dead. Its side was wide open, exposing its bones and a blob of flesh that appeared to be an accumulation of its innards. Several scales on its back were burnt off.

Burnt off, not rotted. Kelly knew what burns looked like, particularly acid burns. This was not the result of natural decay.

There was something in its mouth. Whatever it was, it was blue and yellow. Kelly leaned down and splashed the water to get the fish to turn. Its mouth faced her, revealing the fishing lure embedded in its lower jaw. There was at least eighteen inches of fishing line attached to it.

It was a lure from a flyfishing rod, resembling an orange dragonfly. Normally, Kelly wouldn't have thought much of it. However, there was only one person on this lake who used those lures. They were handmade by Patrick Gawdy, who had a cabin on the north end of the lake.

"Wonder if he's there now?" she said to herself. Curiosity was getting the better of her. Chemical burns did not happen out of the blue in a place like this. Whatever caused this was likely man-made.

She turned around and paddled back to Ross' cabin. When she arrived, the group was gathered by the picnic table, listening to Ross talk about something in a lecturing tone.

"That's really him?" Jamie asked. "The guy who shot what's-his-name through his car window in Denver?"

"Without a doubt," Ross said. "And the name was Willie Stader."

"I'm trying to remember," Jamie said. "Weren't the cops executing an arrest warrant for his brother, and ended up shooting Willie?"

"Yep," Ross said. "I can't believe we've got a cabin right next to that dipshit."

"That sounds a little judgmental," Norman said. "Wasn't he cleared by the department?"

"Same department that fired his ass."

"Sounds like they did it to save face," Norman said. "They were probably willing to get rid of him to lessen the media backlash but didn't have the evidence to actually convict him of anything."

"Sure, there are people who believe that," Ross said. "Then there's those of us who saw the video."

Kelly moored the paddleboat and marched up the dock.

"The *whole* video, or just the snippet they played on the news over and over again?"

All eyes turned to her.

Ross rolled his eyes and sighed. "Kelly? Did you really go over there?"

"Yeah?"

"Why?"

"I was returning his belongings. I did knock him off his boat, after all."

"Probably wasn't a good idea."

"No," she admitted. "Not really. I should've left his things at his dock instead of going up to his door."

"See, I knew it!" Ross said. "We need to be careful around that guy. Kelly especially."

Kelly stood quiet for a moment, absorbing that statement. "Why me, exactly?"

"Well, because you're…" Ross pointed in her direction. It was evident he was addressing her skin tone.

"He wasn't pissed at me because I'm black," she said. "I walked in on him while he was changing. Anyone would be pissed."

Ross searched for something more to say, which irritated Kelly. The problem with those with moral virtue was that they were unable to part from a debate without getting the last word in. That issue paled to the actual validity of their statements. Ross was a nice guy with a decent heart at his core, but he embodied the stereotype of the white guy who believed he knew what was best for other groups.

Kelly, and everyone else was ready to change the subject. Interestingly, it was Jamie who managed to divert them from the topic.

Ironically, the means in which he did so made the group even *more* uncomfortable.

"You know what, guys! I'm feeling wild!" He slipped off his trunks and ran into the lake. "Skinny dip time!"

Like looking at a car wreck, the group couldn't help but watch his pasty white ass as he raced to the dock and dived into the water.

Ross pushed his plate away, his appetite long gone. "You know? I already forgot what we were talking about."

Jamie popped back up. "Anyone gonna join me?! Kel? Pam?"

Norman chuckled. "I don't think anyone's going near that lake ever again."

CHAPTER 8

There were two things Jim Reeves cherished over everything else: Solitude and exercise. Whenever he wasn't at the office, he was in the gym or at the track. Often, he would go to the gym at night or early in the morning while it wasn't too busy. He was a friendly man, but he loved himself more than anyone else. Though he enjoyed female companionship, he was not the type to settle down. Too often, Jim had to listen to friends and family complain about their married lives. It seemed after two years, things gradually got duller, especially if kids were involved.

If Jim had a third and fourth love, it was sex, then the woods—sometimes both at the same time. Today, it was just the latter. It was no great loss, for his first love was solitude. While his friends and family enjoyed vacationing in Disneyland or similar theme parks, Jim preferred being somewhere fairly isolated. The woods around Lake Fairview satisfied that need. He had his truck, his tent, some fishing supplies, and no interruptions.

The best part about this vacation was the variety of workouts it provided him. He started the day with a two-hour swim in the lake. After finishing up, he ate a small meal and moved on to his next workout.

Even people at the gym hated running. Jim, on the other hand, loved it. It was the best way to test oneself, especially when electronics weren't involved.

Seated on a log, Jim tied his running shoes. In love with his own physique, he wore a t-shirt that was a size too small. After all, while the population around here was sparse, it still provided space for campers. One never knew: perhaps he would come across a gorgeous blond or brunette who would take notice of his abs and biceps. His muscles had served him well in the past.

One memory, in particular, brought a smile to his face. It was in the grocery store of all places. It was a Saturday morning, and Jim had completed a four-hour workout. His pump, combined with the smell of his shampoo, managed to attract a few gazes. Being the confident type, Jim played it cool and pretended not to notice. It was at the checkout when one of his admirers made sure to end up in line behind him. Some mild flirting took place right there, which led to 'coffee at her place'.

Coffee had never tasted so good.

Though he was already loose from his swimming exercise, Jim made sure to start his stretches. He had pulled a hamstring at the age of twenty-one, and to this day, never forgot the pain.

As he stretched, he took a glance at his camp. His truck was locked, his wallet secured in the glove compartment. His keys were in his shorts pocket, not that he was worried about anyone breaking in. He knew this area fairly well, and usually camped in the same spot.

His favorite location was a third of a mile from the north end of the lake. He was a hundred feet from the shore, in a nice clearing on level ground. This campsite was surrounded by thick woods, which guaranteed nobody else would be camping nearby. Solitude came before anything else.

Jim jogged in place for a moment, then began his run. He sprinted through the woods until he found one of the hiking trails, which he followed to the north.

***

The Convict needed very little sleep. A couple hours would supply it with over twenty-four hours of energy.

Following the end of its slumber, it resumed repairs on the ship's ion engines, while the ship continued scans of the surrounding area. Throughout the night, nobody ventured nearby, which benefited its efforts to remain undetected while conducting repairs. This planet undoubtedly supplied it the most enjoyable prey to slaughter, one that it wasn't sure it would ever tire of. Though it was still too early to judge, the Convict even considered settling here. These things—humans, as it had learned from the rectangular databases they carried in their pockets—were so pathetic and diverse, slaughtering them was glorious.

It had spent much of the night trying to get the ship's computer to analyze the little rectangular devices the humans were so oddly obsessed with. They were used for communication, data storage, social collaboration on strange wireless platforms, gathering of materialistic goods, among other things. The computer took some time to decipher the language, but once it did, the Convict was given a whole new understanding of these creatures.

Humans.

As it determined from their physical features, the larger, broad-shouldered ones were male and the ones with rounded breasts were female. Though in its research, it learned that certain sects of this species were up in arms about sexual identity. Whatever that meant. Apparently, these creatures had way too much time on their hands.

It didn't matter. As far as the Convict was concerned, the dumber the species, the more fun they were to kill.

Enough time had been spent analyzing the data. The Convict stepped away from the cockpit and returned to the armory.

In its hand was the severed arm from one of the marshals. The arm itself was useless. The bio-chip inside the wrist, however, was necessary to access some equipment stored in a compartment.

It scanned the reader, opening a portion of the armory wall. Inside were three combat masks. Molded to complement the skull of its genus, the masks were essential to guerilla warfare. They could scan the area for other lifeforms, be programmed to track down specific species, and could link with a small drone to map the nearby area.

As much as the Convict enjoyed hunting, it preferred knowing where the targets were. While outside, it could not reference the ship's computer, which forced it to rely on old-fashioned tracking. The technology made this a lot easier.

It slipped the mask on then took a breath of the filtrated air. It now resembled the ancient warriors of a million eons past, who fought giant beasts with their claws and basic edged weapons. It was a time of worshipping ancient gods and dominating a single planet, before the age of space technology.

The Convict did not hold any appreciation for its past. It just liked the helmet. Its mandibles were given just enough space to move freely and not be cramped.

Now, it was time to resume its pastime.

As soon as it was out the door, it launched its drone. No larger than a dragonfly, the device zipped through the woods, conducting detailed scans and transmitting them to the helmet.

Immediately, it picked up movement.

In the mask, the Convict watched the greenish-blue figure running through the woods. It was a human, moving considerably fast, though not with any serious intent. Nothing was chasing it, nor did it appear to be pursuing anything. Probably just endurance building.

With the press of a button on its gauntlet, the Convict mapped the jogger's likely path. It was then that it realized it was following a trail.

Immediately, it knew exactly how it would eliminate this target.

The Convict highlighted an intercept point, then charged through the woods. The target was still a mile away at least, giving it enough time to place the trap.

After passing through several hundred yards of woods, it arrived at the destination.

From its vest, it removed one of its laser traps. The pyramid-shaped device was able to change color to blend with its surroundings. When placed on the dirt trail, it resembled a dirt mound or a rock. Nothing that its victim would take notice of.

The scanner in its helmet warned of the human's approach. The Convict backed into the woods, finding a thick patch of vegetation to conceal its bulky mass while it watched its handiwork play out.

***

Sweat drizzled down his body as Jim approached the two-mile mark. Just a half-mile more, then he would run back to camp. Five miles, followed by another swim in the lake, this time to cool off, would conclude his exercise routine for today. After that, the rest of his day would consist of reading and fishing.

Jim followed the trail, peeking every so often at his Fitbit. One-quarter mile to go.

This was Heaven for him. He crossed over two miles and had hardly seen anyone else. From the looks of it, he truly did have this entire area to himself. Occasionally, there had been instances in which he came out here to get away from the rest of the world, only for the world to follow him. One time, he was in camp, enjoying his campfire, when a dad and his two young kids arrived nearby. Over the course of the night, the kids hollered and fought, their old man losing his patience. Jim couldn't believe it. They had the entire lakeside, and yet, they decided to pitch a tent less than fifty feet from him.

Luckily, it appeared he would not suffer that particular misfortune today. Unless there was someone hiding nearby in the woods, Jim Reeves was truly alone. Everything was perfect. Even the trail was smooth, mostly void of obstacles, save for one little rock up ahead.

Jim didn't even notice it—until he passed over it. He saw a red flash, then three thin lines extending from the ground. Lasers. There was brief heat and pain as he passed through the lasers. Then nothing.

***

Five slabs of human collapsed onto the dirt trail. The Convict emerged from hiding and approached. It was interesting to observe the inner body spilling out from the five vertical slices. The laser had cut through him like a hot knife through butter. His head was split right down the middle. Even the nose was perfectly divided in two. The arms were intact, though the legs were diced vertically down the middle.

The Convict used these traps quite often, but rarely did a target manage to get so perfectly divided into equally sized parts. Usually, the Convict did not get this level of thrill from using traps. Primarily, it used them to prevent enemies and prey from escaping. In this case, it was curious to see how effective the device would be. The results were not disappointing in the slightest.

Next, the Convict removed a small vial containing a green dissolving liquid from its vest. Normally, in this kind of environment, it was content with the woods obscuring any bodies it left behind. However, with these remains in a fairly open area, the Convict determined it was best to dissolve them into oblivion.

It drizzled a small stream onto the mound of flesh and bone, then watched it collapse on a molecular level. After a few moments, there was nothing except a wet stain in the dirt.

After securing the laser trap and the vial of dissolvent in its vest, the Convict did another scan of the nearby area. There were larger populations to the west, away from this large lake. Its drone picked up larger vehicles, similar to the one it saw last night near the camp.

Those settlements were a few miles away. Perhaps it would venture in that direction soon, but first, it wanted to remain fairly close to its ship. It was still a stranger on a new planet, and it would be wise to finish repairs before venturing into more populated areas.

It directed its drone to the south side of the lake. Two results flashed before its eyes.

On the lakeside were two structures, one of which contained nearly a half dozen humans. There were males and females in this group, with only one life detection in the second habitat. Seven overall. The drone buzzed around it, detecting no other life signs in the nearby vicinity. It was perfect.

Bloodlust caused its heart to race. Like an addict seeking a narcotic, it traveled south to get its fix.

CHAPTER 9

"So much for peace, quiet, and relaxation."

Diego dusted his hands, looking at the two trash bags' worth of ruined toiletries and mold-infested plywood. The cabin now smelled of bleach, disinfectant, and sawdust. With the luck Diego was having, he was certain he would find termites as he cut away at the infected cabinet. The fact that he did not find any brought little comfort. At this point, it was a certainty that something would come along and taint his vacation further.

"Let's see," he thought out loud, "I've got those jackasses over there, making a ruckus. I have a pair of clothes and boots now soaked. Now my roof is leaking, my cabinet is screwed up beyond belief, and to top it off, I don't even get to go fishing thanks to Dummy-Dumb-Dumb over there."

Diego stared at his tools and the sawdust from the cabinet's surgery. He would have to make a run into town to get lumber for reconstructing the shelves and back wall. He would also need a tarp for the roof. If it was leaking this bad, he was more than likely looking at a complete roof replacement. A couple grand at least.

The thought ignited a desire for fresh air.

He turned around and stepped out of the bathroom. Right away, he nearly faceplanted on the floor. Diego hopped on one leg, freeing the other from the cord to his buzzsaw that nearly tripped him. He raised his foot, brought it over the cord, then stepped down… onto the hammer, which then skidded on the floor. For the second time, he stumbled off balance, this time falling against the bathroom mirror.

Crack!

Diego looked at the tiny shards in his elbow, then at the spider-web of cracked glass.

Diego kicked the hammer, as though it had deliberately set him up.

"Son of a bitch! Piece of shit!"

Every little misfortune added to a mountain of misery. Misery required medication. For some, it was painkillers. Others, antidepressants. For Diego, it was beer. He downed his second can of the day, crushed it with his fist, then stepped into his sunroom.

He sat in his chair and focused on the outdoors. The sun was out, the leaves and grass were green as ever, the lake smooth and reflecting the canopy around it.

It eased his temper for a moment. Looking at his boat, his blood pressure started to rise again. He wanted to be out on that lake, tossing a few casts, forgetting about all of his problems. Instead, it felt like coming here was only adding to his misery.

He heard one of the friends jump into the lake with a flamboyant "Woohoo!"

"Stupid bastards," he muttered.

He needed to walk. Staying in here was causing him to dwell on his issues. Perhaps getting a little exercise would help.

As he stood up, he checked the frame above the screen windows.

"Maybe I should consider getting shades, so no more dumb morons come peeking like that dumb…" He looked to the window by the door and saw the two rods leaning against it. He stared confused for a moment, then stepped outside.

Leaning on his screen window were his two fishing poles. The reels were still dripping wet, but it was nothing serious. All he would have to do was dismantle it and dry off the line.

His hot temper subsided. Suddenly, it was clear why what's-her-name came to his door. She had fished the poles from the bottom of the lake and was trying to return them. If only he had shut the main door—or better yet, not walked around bare—he would not have had a misunderstanding.

"Well, shit."

For several minutes, he contemplated what to do. Part of him felt he should say nothing and leave well enough alone. Those kids probably wouldn't want to talk to him anyway.

In other words, do the easier thing.

Then there was the more thoughtful part of him, which demanded he go apologize and thank Kelly for retrieving his items.

KELLY! That's what her friends called her.

Diego leaned on his desire for solitude as an excuse to do nothing. After all, it wasn't like Kelly wasn't the one to knock his stuff into the lake. Also, her friends, especially the one named Ross, did not seem so fond of him. From what it seemed, they believed the media spin regarding the Willie Stader incident.

Truly, he could not escape that.

Damn you, kid. You had your whole life ahead of you. Why did you have to reach into that glove box?

If only things played out differently. If only Willie surrendered, or better yet, stood aside and did not interfere with the arrest. Then he would be alive, and the world would not hate Diego Tritton.

Nor would he hate himself.

While Diego leaned toward doing nothing, he couldn't take his eyes off those poles. It was more than the simple fact they were fished out and returned. Kelly did it in spite of all the stuff her friend told her about him.

There was something to be said about a small act of kindness.

Oh, hell...

Diego took a breath, braced for the storm, then started walking to the neighboring cabin.

***

"Ross?"

He ignored Norman's drill instructor-style voice, instead keeping his attention on the document on his screen.

"Ross? Roooooosssss."

Finally, he looked over at his muscled friend. "Aren't there more fun things for you to spend your time on instead of annoying the hell out of me?"

Norman bit his lip then thought for a moment.

"No, actually! Nothing tops annoying the hell out of you."

"Why am I not surprised?" Ross put his nose back to the screen. Norman approached, badminton racquet in hand. Ross had heard him spending the last half hour setting up the net and posts.

"You know, dude, there's better things to do on vacation than fornicate on your computer," Norman said.

"What? I'm not doing any such thing! I'm working."

"Oh, did I say fornicating? I mean fuck around," Norman said. He batted the racquet against his palm. "Up for a game?"

Ross looked at him. "Your grand plan to get me to play with you is to insult my work?"

"To be fair, it's so easy. Besides, why the hell are you working while up here on vacay?"

"My work is my joy," Ross said.

Norman shrugged. "If you call taking the piss out of people for a living your joy, then okay, I guess."

Oh, here we go again.

"Maybe my next article will be about you," Ross said.

"It'll be about how you got your ass stomped in badminton." Norman mimicked whacking a birdie over an imaginary net.

Ross shook his head. "Ask Ted and Pam."

"They're busy making out on the lounge chairs," Norman said.

Ross, so fixated on his computer work, did not even notice until he looked in their direction. He winced and adjusted in his seat to block the view with his laptop.

"Jesus. No decency."

"You're just jealous," Pam shouted. She and Ted resumed making out with exaggerated loud kisses.

"See what I mean?" Norman said.

Ross groaned. "Ask Jamie."

"Yeah, I'd rather have my right nut jammed in a box fan," Norman said.

"Kelly?"

"No idea where she's at."

"Ugh." Ross shut his eyes. "Fine. I'll whoop your ass in a minute. Just let me finish this article first, you dumb gorilla."

"Ha!" Norman leaned back and laughed. "First off, gorillas are really smart. That's… species-ist… for you to make that comment. Second, thanks for the laugh. The thought of you besting me in anything is worthy to be the subject of an article."

"Yeah, yeah. I'll keep that in mind. Especially after I win. Now, leave me alone for a couple minutes."

Norman did not, in fact, leave Ross alone. As the journalist finished writing his three-thousand-word article, the Army vet antagonized him with taunts.

"Hey, Ross?" Norman said.

Ross shut his eyes, suppressing an outburst.

"Dude, I'm starting to think you have the hots for me."

"Only in your dreams," Norman said. "No, we have a visitor."

Ross turned to his right, then stood up after seeing Diego Tritton walking into his yard. Immediately, he started searching his pockets for his phone. The only feasible solution he could think of to defend himself against this violent cop was… to call the police.

"What are you doing here, man? Don't do anything stupid. I'll call the Sheriff!"

Diego raised his hands. "Relax. I come in peace."

Ross clumsily backed away. "Yeah right!"

"Dude, chill please!" Diego said. He turned his attention to Norman, who, while guarded, was less on edge. "Listen, we got off on the wrong foot. I'm Diego, I'm obviously the guy in the cabin next door. I'm sorry

I ruined your guys' morning. If it's not too much trouble, I was hoping to speak with that young lady. I believe her name is Kelly."

Ross watched him with a narrow gaze, as though Diego was a hyena that would spring into action at any given moment.

"Why do you want to talk to her?"

"To apologize for earlier."

"Well, I don't know where she is," Ross said. "Might be best for you to head back, Mister."

Diego rolled his eyes, obviously fed up with the effort to keep his neighbors at ease. He looked again to Norman.

"Can I appeal to your sensibilities?"

Norman chuckled. "Yeah, you're alright, man."

Diego lowered his hands, much to Ross' resentment. If anything positive came from Diego's visit, it was that it broke up Ted and Pam's extensive makeout session.

The front door opened. Out stepped Jamie, beer in hand, a smile only a man oblivious to the world around him could have.

"Hey guys! What's going on?" He looked at his friends, then turned in the direction they were staring. The beer flung from his hand as he jumped at the sight of the killer detective. "Holy shit! Sweet Mary and Baby Jesus!" He spun in place, then hopped on his feet, unsure whether to remain outside or retreat into the cabin. "Don't do anything foolish, Mister! I've got a…" He dug in his pocket for anything he could pretend was a weapon. "I've got a gun!"

Diego squinted. "That's a bottle opener."

"No, it's not!"

"Unless I'm a beer tab, I think I'm safe," Diego said, pointing at Jamie's pocket.

The cabin door opened again. Out came Kelly, equally as confused as everyone else.

"What's going on?" The answer became obvious when she saw Diego. Her next emotion was a mixture of anxiety and relief, the latter of which prevailed when she saw the former detective grin. He was clearly at ease, nothing like the angry leviathan she awoke earlier. Better yet, he had clothes on. Then again, 'better' was a matter of perspective. Minus the temper, the image of him in the kitchen wasn't necessarily a bad one in her mind.

"Kelly, right?"

She relaxed and walked toward him. "Yeah, that's me." She pointed at him. "Diego, right?"

"Yeah… we've met."

"I remember." A nervous chuckle followed the statement.

Diego struggled to maintain his own smile. With all the other pairs of eyes on him, he felt like his every movement was being monitored. At this point, it was surprising no smartphones were recording him.

"Mind if we talk?" he asked.

"Not at all," she said.

Ross gritted his teeth. "Kelly…"

"Ross, I'll be fine," she said. "Jamie, get back to your day-drinking. Ted, Pam… get a room. And Norman… you playing with yourself?" She tilted her head at his racquet.

Norman winced. It wasn't often he got burned that good.

"Damn!"

Ross stood there and watched bitterly as Kelly walked into the woods with Diego.

"You alright, man?" Norman said.

"Can you believe this?" Ross said, pointing at the detective.

"Dude, I don't think he's an ax murderer," Norman said.

"Right." Ross took his seat at the picnic table and tried to resume work on his article. Not a single key was tapped, for his attention was locked on the interaction taking place in the woods.

"Son of a bitch!" Norman said, pointing at him.

Ross shut his eyes as though in pain. "What?"

"You're worried about her *because* you've got a *crush*!"

"What?!"

"It's obvious!" Norman said.

"Hmm." Jamie put his fingers to his chin, appearing deep in thought. "Yeah, that makes sense."

"Stop being ridiculous," Ross said.

"Alright, let me ask you this," Norman said. "If it was me having the private meeting with Mr. Detective in the woods, would you be equally as concerned?"

Ross didn't answer.

Norman snapped his fingers. "Case and point."

Ross slapped the table and stood up. "Where's that other racquet? I'm gonna beat your barbarian ass."

"WHOA!" Jamie ran inside, then reemerged with beers, margaritas mini bottles, and a bottle of bourbon. "Ted, Pam? You gonna join this spectacle?"

They broke apart from their embrace and joined him by the picnic table.

"I guess I could use a little sporting entertainment," Ted said. "We placing bets?"

"I won't make bets. *But...*" Jamie raised a shot glass and a bottle of bourbon. "I'll take a shot every time Norman scores against Ross."

"My money's on Ross," Pam said.

"Alright then," Ted said. "My money's on Norman. What are we betting, anyway?"

Pam smiled and leaned toward his ear. "Position." She nipped his earlobe before turning her attention to the game.

Ted licked his lips. "Norman! Kick his ass!"

Norman twirled his racquet. "With pleasure."

"Bring it. I'll even let you have first serve," Ross said. He leaned forward, ready to take on his muscular opponent. His eyes shifted, magnetized to the two figures in the woods. He could hear Kelly and Diego laughing. What could they be laughing about?

More laughter filled the air, this time from Norman and the other three friends. Ross looked down, seeing the birdie at his feet.

On the other side of the net, Norman was doing a lude pose.

"One, nothing."

***

Diego wiped the tears from his eyes as he and Kelly reminisced over his indignity that morning.

"Well, I suppose there are worse ways you could've walked in on me," he said.

Kelly laughed at the mental image. "Yeah, I could've caught you fondling yourself." They both bent over laughing. "Oh, God. Now we're getting into really outrageous territory."

"After the day we've had?" Diego said. He took a deep breath and regained control. The awkward feeling had lifted, leaving both of them feeling enriched with positive emotions. Diego felt good turning the morning's awkwardness into a funny memory. "Listen, I'm sorry I behaved the way I did. Especially at the cabin. Needless to say, I was already on edge. Next thing I know, I see you there, and my brain jumped to the dumbest conclusions."

"Oh, there's nothing to apologize for," Kelly said. "I would've knocked, but that door didn't look like it was in good shape."

"Ugh. That damn door. The bane of my existence. In fact, that whole cabin is practically falling apart. I guess that's the price for not visiting as often as I should."

"Something wrong?" Kelly asked.

Diego tucked his hands into his pockets and looked at his vacation home. "Something. Everything. Nothing I can't fix." He chuckled and looked at her. "I'm impressed you were able to find the fishing poles."

"Oh." She laughed again. "Technically, we have Jamie to thank for that. Then again, he was the reason I wasn't paying attention and ended up ramming your boat in the first place."

"He seems the, let's just say, outlandish type," Diego said. A few moments of silence passed between them. Diego had made his apology. Now, he wasn't sure what else to say. "Well, uh, I guess I better let you get back to your vacation. Thanks for being patient with me."

"Gosh, Mr. Tritton…"

"Just call me Diego," he said. "Mr. Tritton makes me feel like I'm investigating a juvenile delinquent."

"Okay, Diego. It's I who thanks you for being patient with me. Don't forget, I'm the one who sent you for a swim."

"Eh." He waved his hand. "I needed a bath anyway. Besides, we've established it was your friend Jamie's fault. Right?"

Kelly smiled. "That's right."

"Right. Well, take it easy." With one last smile, Diego started walking for his cabin.

Kelly took a step after him. "Hey, Diego?" He stopped and looked at her again. "If you need some work done at your cabin, we have a guy that can help. Norman's really handy, and he's always looking for something to do."

"Oh, that's really generous of you to offer," Diego said. "But I don't want to impose on you. Besides, I doubt any of your friends would be comfortable hanging out with me, considering my reputation these days."

"Listen, since we're on that subject…" Kelly walked up to him, while trying to figure out how to articulate her feelings without sounding too naïve or cliché. "I don't know how to phrase this, so I'll do the best I can. I saw the footage—the *unedited* footage that was floating around on the internet. I know you didn't shoot that guy maliciously. He dragged you for God knows how far. Then he started reaching for a gun…"

"There was no gun," Diego said.

"Oh!" Kelly said, genuinely surprised. "But he opened the glove compartment. What was he reaching for, then?"

"He was wearing glasses, which fell onto the floor on the passenger side," Diego said. "The forensics found that the latch to the glove compartment was broken. It was already open."

Kelly bit her lip. She immediately regretted pursuing the topic, even though she had the best of intentions.

"I… gosh! I'm sorry to hear that. I didn't know."

"It's not like there was a big, televised trial," Diego said. "Just a bunch of news footage, questionable reporting, and poor judgment all around. Including on my part." He sighed and watched the lake. More silence came in between the two of them. "What can I say? I thought he was reaching for a weapon. I told him not to go for it. He probably didn't register what I was saying due to adrenaline. He reached down, I shot him, the rest is history."

"Diego, I get how you feel, but don't treat yourself as though you're some kind of hideous monster," Kelly said. "If anyone should be blamed, shouldn't it be Willie Stader's brother? You were serving an arrest warrant. Wasn't he a rape suspect who had three restraining orders? That was the reason you were at their apartment, yes?"

Diego nodded.

"Then Willie should've stood by and not intervened," Kelly continued. "I'm not saying he deserved to get killed, but it's not the same thing as cops who exercise actual excessive use of force."

Diego chose not to reply. Instead, he glanced at his cabin, then at the big muscular guy named Norman who appeared to be whooping Ross' ass in badminton.

"You know what? If Norman's willing, maybe I wouldn't mind having him take a look at my place. I might need an extra set of eyes to help me determine how much lumber I need to buy."

Kelly read between the lines. She was certain he was grateful for her kind words, but it would take more than that for Diego to forgive himself for the burden he carried. Only he could accomplish that.

"I can make that happen," she said. "How long you gonna be here?"

"For a week at least. Maybe longer," Diego said. "Not like I have anywhere else to be."

"Good. Then I'll see you around," Kelly replied. "Maybe we can go fishing sometime."

Diego's heart fluttered. "Absolutely."

He watched her walk away. Right away, his mind began pondering all the possibilities that were implied with that statement.

Hmm…. For chrissake, Diego, she's almost a decade younger than you. Get those thoughts out of your head… She is gorgeous, though… Alright, that's enough. Stop staring.

He spun on his heel and returned to his own cabin. Though he didn't want to admit it, being the loner that he was, there was a weight lifted off of his shoulders from conversing with Kelly. It felt good to laugh for once in his life. That thought made him look forward all the more to a possible fishing trip with her.

***

"Son of a bitch." Ross swung the racquet so hard, he thought for a moment that his arm was about to fly out of its socket. The irony was that he shouldn't have swung at all. Had he let the birdie go, it would have landed out of bounds and he would have scored the point. Instead, he took the swing and grazed the birdie, sending it twirling under the net.

He looked at Norman and the others. "Yeah, yeah. Laugh at my expense. Douchebags."

Jamie leaned side-to-side, holding a bottle of bourbon in one hand and a shot glass in the other. He filled it and threw it back, wincing from the twentieth burn in a row.

"Whew! Yeah, believe me I am. And more!"

The nauseated look on Kelly's face took form without any conscious effort. *No shit.* She had nothing against drinking, especially on vacation, but Jamie had a tendency of going a little overboard. Or a lot overboard.

Pam chugged her beer, withholding her laugh. She clung to Ted, putting her head on his shoulder.

"I'm starting to regret my bet."

"I'm not," he replied with a wide smile. He grabbed her ass to hint at his intentions.

"It's not over yet," she said.

"That's right," Ross said. "It's not."

"It's twenty-to-five," Norman said. "Trust me, 'over' is just one serving away."

"Alright, ya freak," Ross said.

"That's what the ladies call me in the sheets," Norman said.

"Good lord," Ross muttered. He picked up the birdie, noticing Kelly standing to his left, watching. "Hey. Did your talk go okay?"

"It went just fine," she replied. "He seems very nice and genuine. Maybe we should have him over for a barbeque."

Ross scoffed. "Sure."

"Hey, lover boy," Norman said, waving his racquet. "You gonna toss that thing over this year, or…"

Ross tossed the birdie over. "Your serve. Show me whatcha got."

"Lover boy?" Kelly said with a smirk. "What does that mean?"

"Nothing," Ross said.

"It means he's hoping to land a shot in your goal net," Jamie said.

"Jesus, dude!!!" Ross said.

"Twenty-to-five!" With his opponent's attention on the drunkard, Norman made the serve. By the time Ross looked back, the birdie had cleared the net and landed at his feet. Norman tossed the racquet on the ground and threw his hands up victoriously. "OH! Who's the man! I know… *I'm* the man!" He turned to the spectators. "Let's hear it."

They didn't give him the 'you're the man' response he was hoping for, but he settled for the round of applause for his win, and the laughter at Ross' expense.

"Oh, come on!" Ross said. "That was horse shit."

"You loooost," Norman said.

"That's right. You did," a very happy Ted said.

Ross shot him a glare, studying the more-than-usual happy look on his face. It wasn't just happiness, but mischief in that expression.

"Why are you so glad?"

"No reason," Ted said. His not-so-subtle grabbing of Pam's ass said it all. "Nothing at all."

She gave a sarcastic groan. "Thanks a lot, Ross."

"You're welcome," he replied in an equally sarcastic tone.

Norman continued his victorious poses as though he was an NFL player who made a winning touchdown. He picked up his racquet and pointed it at Kelly.

"Who's next? How 'bout you, Kel? Wanna take on the world champion?"

"Maybe another time," she said. "I have a suggestion for ya to show off your manliness, though."

Norman clicked his tongue and winked, taking great joy in Ross' souring expression. "Whatcha got in mind?"

"Diego, over next door, is having some maintenance issues with his cabin. I told him you're pretty handy and could help him out."

"Oh." It wasn't the response he had in mind, but after a moment, he set aside the obnoxious persona and started walking to his truck. "Sure. Let me grab my toolbox and I'll head over there."

"Thanks." Stretching her arms, Kelly walked into the cabin. "Sorry for your wipeout, Ross."

"It wasn't a wipeout!" he said.

"Twenty-one to five? Hmm…" Kelly tried to keep from chuckling, but failed. "That's cutting pretty close to a wipeout."

"Fabulous," Ross said. He shrugged, then collected the racquets and birdie. "Oh well. I suppose there are worse things that could happen this vacation than losing to Norman."

"Ross, if you need to take your mind off your defeat, there's something you can do," Kelly said.

"Like what? Chew on glass?" he muttered.

"There's that, or you could drive me up to Patrick Gawdy's cabin," she said.

"Patrick Gawdy's cabin?" Ross said. "Why do you want to go up there? Remember the last time we met him? He's not the friendliest guy."

"He's friendly enough," Kelly said. "Our sour interaction might've had something to do with you not being able to keep your opinion to yourself."

"The guy was tossing his beer bottles in the woods," Ross said. "He was littering. It takes that shit thousands of years to decompose, if ever."

"Alright, you kinda have a point," Kelly said. "But still, would you be willing to give me a ride over there? I found something weird in the lake and I think he might know something about it."

"Something weird in the lake? Like what?"

"A dead fish."

"A dead fish?" Ross scoffed. "Listen, I love animals, Kel. But even I can tell you that the lake is full of fish. Alive and dead. What's so different about this one?"

"Well, I..." Kelly looked away, concerned that her answer would make her sound foolish or paranoid. "At first, I thought it was rotted away. Then I took a closer look, then I realized the wound in its side was not decay, but resembled chemical burns of some kind."

Now, Ross was interested. "Chemical burns?"

"Yeah."

"And what's this have to do with Gawdy?"

"One of his lures was in the fish's mouth."

Ross nodded with interest. "Let me grab my wallet and keys." As he turned to walk into the cabin, he couldn't help but notice Ted feeling up his smirking girlfriend with increased enthusiasm. "Something tells me that I won't want to be here anyway, otherwise I'd have to endure listening to a certain event."

CHAPTER 10

The trek through the woods was easy work for the Convict. It considered itself among the strongest of a species that was already adept for physical endurance. Sitting still was not its forte, even when it wasn't killing. Maintenance work on the ship, while necessary, was beyond boring. It was a creature that needed to move about.

Its fellow citizens on its home world had taken notice of this strange quirk. Perhaps, it was a symptom of whatever drove it to pursue its favorite hobby. The Convict did not concern itself with these so-called concerns. It enjoyed its life. Here, on the planet referred to as Earth according to the rectangular databank, it was happier than ever.

It had originally come to this planet out of necessity. Now, it was strongly considering a prolonged stay. Maybe even for years. It did not see itself tiring of this life anytime soon.

It was getting close to the habitats. The scans sent by its drone relayed images to its helmet. The humans were moving all over the place, each doing their own thing. One of them had a bottle containing a substance similar to the ones it found at the camp last night. Whatever that substance was, the Convict enjoyed it.

One human with a fairly broad frame was walking south to the second facility. The thermal scans showed the single resident stepping out to meet him. They shook hands, communicated to each other, then went inside the building.

Two other humans went inside the building, their behavior similar, appearing to be the prelude to an intense mating session. Then there was the last pair, also male and female, walking toward one of the vehicles. They got inside the cab, started the engine, then backed out of the driveway.

The Convict was not disappointed. It wanted to savor each kill, which meant slaughtering each human one at a time. The more they spread out, the easier gutting them would be. Those that left were probably going to return later on.

All the Convict needed was patience, something that didn't come easy, but always paid off. And there was no doubt its patience would be handsomely rewarded.

***

Kelly watched the woods streaming past her window as Ross drove the truck north. As soon as they exited the driveway, she could feel his angst lift from his shoulders. He hummed with whatever song that was coming through the broken radio signal.

"I didn't realize going to see Patrick Gawdy made you that happy," she said.

"Hmm? Oh, no it doesn't. I guess I needed something to do," he replied.

"Something to do? Badminton didn't fulfill that urge?"

He grinned. "Maybe if it was anyone except Norman." A small chuckle followed the statement. For a moment, Ross had the look of a comic book villain envisioning his evil scheme. "Who knows? Maybe he'll get on that cop's bad side while he's over there."

"Ross, that's horrible!" Kelly said.

His grin vanished. Now, he could feel the blood rushing to his face. Pride and embarrassment began to clash within him. He didn't like being told off by Kelly, but at the same time, he was firm in his opinion of Diego Tritton.

"Alright, I'm sorry. It was a bad joke. I wouldn't want that to happen to Norman." Kelly punched him in the shoulder. "Ow!"

"I'm serious, Ross. You're a good guy, but you really need to get the stick out of your ass," she said.

Ross sighed, then looked at her. "You seem to like that guy."

"I've only dealt with him the one time."

"Twice. Don't forget the time he was about to kill you."

"Seriously, dude. He wasn't…" Kelly shook her head. "I think if you and he sat down and had a serious chat, you guys would probably appreciate each other. He's put away some serious hardcore criminals, you know? Who knows? Being a journalist, maybe you can get an official interview. Ask fair questions, get honest answers… just say'n."

Ross shook his head. "Nah. I don't interview murderers."

"Murderers don't get interviews?" Kelly said. "Isn't that an important way of learning about the criminal mindset?"

"No, I…" Ross thought for a moment, realizing she had a fair point. "I don't know. We'll see."

"Why are you so concerned with me talking to the guy, but not Norman?"

Ross snorted. "I'm trying not to answer sarcastically."

"Doesn't have anything to do with that lover boy comment he made, does it?"

Ross bit his lip unconsciously, then stopped the moment he realized he was making the answer too obvious.

Kelly didn't press him. The guy had a crush. It was cute. The fact that he was jealous of someone he was vehemently opposed to on a personal and social level made it funnier in a way. She wasn't interested. Ross was a nice guy, and with that realization came guilt. She didn't like friend-zoning people. However, there was no interest beyond a normal friendship.

Then there was the fact she was now constantly thinking about Diego. They had only one meaningful interaction. Perhaps it was the shift in the dynamic. Their first interaction being hostile, the second being extremely pleasant. In addition, he was a good-looking guy. A little older than her, but she didn't mind. She definitely felt a degree of sympathy for what he had gone through, which probably added to her feelings. Then there was another side; a part she didn't want to admit consciously. There was a sense of taboo in the idea of seeing a guy like Diego. She personally didn't see him as bad, but society had deemed him controversial. In a way, that made the thought of a relationship more exciting.

Okay, stop. You've literally just met the guy. You're letting your imagination get out of control.

"Yeah, stop."

Ross looked over. "What?"

Kelly realized she had thought out loud. "Oh! Uh… nothing. Sorry." *Fuck, I HATE IT when I do that!*

"What were you thinking about?"

"Nothing."

"Oh, God! Listen, don't take that lover boy thing too seriously!" Ross shut his eyes.

"Oh, no, Ross. Don't worry…"

"Damn that stupid Norman. I hope he does piss off that ex-cop."

"No, it's not that… ROSS, LOOK OUT!"

He opened his eyes just in time to see the root on the side of the road. *Thump-thump!*

Immediately, the truck became sluggish and the tire light came on.

"SHIT!" Ross found a decent clearing on the side of the road and parked. After a moment of dread, he and Kelly stepped out. As luck would have it, both the front and back tires were flat.

He slapped his hands against his legs, defeated. "Well, this about sums up my whole day."

"Got a spare?" Kelly asked.

"I did," Ross said, pointing to the rear tire. "That was it."

"Great." Kelly looked at the rough road, then at the truck. "How far are we from the cabins?"

"Closer to the north end of the lake," Ross said.

"Don't suppose we can drive back on this thing?"

"HA! We'd be grinding metal before we got halfway."

Kelly slipped her hands into her pockets and thought over their options.

"Okay, there's no way around it. Either we call Norman to come help tow us out, or…"

"Norman's not gonna tow us back with Ted's van. He rode up here with me and Jamie. He needs a pickup. Like… Oh, fuck."

Kelly realized it too. Diego's truck had at least one spare tire that was compatible with Ross'.

"This has got to be some kind of sick joke," Ross said.

"Well, it's that or ask Patrick Gawdy for help," Kelly said.

Ross hung his head down, obviously conflicted as to which was worse. At least he was used to Norman's ridiculousness and Kelly could be a buffer between him and Diego.

"Alright. Try giving Norman a call."

Kelly dug out her smartphone and began the tedious trek to find a decent signal.

***

Norman set his stepladder up against Diego's cabin and ascended to the top. As soon as he arrived up top, he was gritting his teeth.

"Ooooo! Yeah, hate to be the breaker of bad news…"

"Oh, don't worry," Diego said. "I doubt you can top the moment I found the mold in my bathroom."

Norman peeled off a rotted shingle and tossed it down. "Glad to hear that, because you're looking at a new roof. This whole section looks worse than a batch of vegan crumb cake."

Diego wasn't sure which was more flustering, the extent of his repairs, or the analogy used by Norman.

"Vegan crumb cake? They make such a thing?" He immediately felt stupid for asking. "Who am I kidding? Of course, they do. I guess I shouldn't be surprised."

Norman climbed down the ladder.

"You didn't know that? I thought you were a detective."

"Not the tofu detective."

Norman snickered at that. His phone began to buzz in his back pocket. When he looked at the screen, a full laugh burst out.

"Speaking of tofu."

"Ross calling you?"

"No, Kelly is, but she's *with* Ross. Overheard them saying something about driving to a place on the north end of the lake." Norman answered the phone. "Hey, Kel. Ross driving you so insane that you need Norman to come to the rescue?"

"Quite literally," Kelly said.

"Uh-oh. What happened."

"We… and flat-… managed to…"

"Kel? Hang on a sec. I'm losing ya."

"Damn… Hang…"

The line went dead. Norman waited a minute, after which Kelly called again.

"Second time's the charm."

"Stupid signal," she said. *"Anyway, Ross hit a dead branch and flattened two of our tires. We managed to pull off to the side, but I'm not sure if we can drive it back with two flats. Maybe one, if we go really slow."*

"That guy drives as well as he plays badminton!"

Ross' voice quickly entered the background. *"I heard that!"*

Norman took great pleasure in that statement. "What do you need, Kel? You want me to pick you guys up? We'll have to drive an hour to get new tires for that truck."

"Ross really doesn't want to leave it out here. We were wondering if Diego would be willing to lend us his spare. We'd be able to limp it back to the cabin."

Norman looked at Diego, who could hear Kelly on the phone.

"I have a better idea," Diego said. "I'll head over there with ya, and we can drive into town. The auto shop and the hardware store are right next to each other. We can grab Ross some tires, then get some lumber for me to start getting ready for my roof replacement. At the very least, I'm gonna need a tarp."

"Hmm." Norman nodded and grinned. "Kel, did you hear that?"

"I did. I think that's a great idea."

"I don't know if that's necessary," Ross said.

"Gonna have to run into town at some point, dufus," Norman said. "And there's no freaking way we're stuffing the tires into the back of Ted's van. Just hang tight and we'll come pick you up."

"Sounds great," Kelly said.

"See ya soon." Norman hung up and looked at Diego with an ear-to-ear grin. "This'll be fun."

Diego forced a grin, only partially amused. "That Ross fella really has it in for me, doesn't he?"

"Ah, despite the shit I give him, he's not a bad guy. Just a little overzealous. He has brought to light a few genuine cases of injustice. It's just that it's gotten to his head, and now he sees racism and sexism everywhere, especially where it doesn't exist. I take great joy in antagonizing him, but all in all, he's a good friend."

"You'd get along great with the guys back at my station," Diego said. "Give me a sec. I'll grab my keys."

"Just a heads-up," Norman said, looking to the sky in the south, "I'd probably plan on buying a tarp from the hardware store. Looks like we might have some rain rolling in."

Diego gave the sky a glance. "Great. Seems like the weather waits for us to come out here before delivering the rain."

"Typical," Norman said with a chuckle. "Let me say something to the rest of my crew. Meet ya at the truck."

***

Kelly hung up and turned to Ross. "Good news. They're coming."

He turned around, hands tucked in his pockets. "Yay. Great. I get to spend two hours in a truck with Norman and..." He held back from the name-calling, knowing it would aggravate Kelly, "... and Mr. Tritton."

"Well, you *did* survive a longer road trip with Norman," Kelly said. "I'm sure two hours won't make it much worse."

"If you say so." Ross strolled past a few more trees. "That's not to say I want to spend any more time trapped with him than I have—" His voice trailed off. As though in a trance, Ross stared into the woods, stiff as a board.

At first, Kelly thought he was goofing around, about to make some derogatory reference about Norman.

"What?" When she stepped beside him, her grin vanished. Watching in the direction Ross was staring, she could see the RV through the maze of trees. There was nothing unusual about an RV in the middle of the woods. It was the smell that was radiating from that direction that they found most odd. It was a strange combination of cooked meat and decay. Definitely not a typical campfire cookout. Whatever it was, it was vile.

"Maybe we should check," Ross said. His voice made his nervousness plain as day.

Kelly felt the same way. They were caught between their own selfish concern and the moral ethics of checking on someone possibly in trouble.

"Yeah." They stuck close to each other, slowly moving toward the camp. "Hello? Anyone there?" *Please answer. Please answer.* There was no answer. "Shit. I don't like this."

Ross nodded. There was a strange 'sixth sense' warning them that they were approaching something horrible. That same feeling acted as an internal voice in their minds, screaming at them to turn around and leave. If not for inherent human decency, they would have.

They stepped into the campsite. Right away, they both cupped their hands over their mouths.

Right there, on a burnt-out campfire, was a charred, deflated corpse. Blackened flesh still clung to the hands and feet, while everything in-between was skeletal. The jaw was wide open, the eye sockets dark and empty, aside from the juicy brain matter behind them.

"Oh God..." Kelly backed away. It was so horrid, so fantastical, so horrifyingly bizarre, that it took several seconds for her mind to register what she was looking at. When it did, pure terror took hold. "OH MY GOD!   ROSS?!"

He was already stumbling into the woods, making it only a few yards away before he leaned forward and vomited. Hunched over, he stumbled back into the clearing, frantically pointing behind him.

"Th—th—there..." It was all his stammering jaws could get out.

Against her better judgement, Kelly walked over, then immediately turned away after seeing the shredded corpse lying on the ground. Centipedes, mosquitoes, flies, and even frogs hopped over the corpse.

There was no head. Not on the body, anyway. When Kelly went to turn, she saw it lying in the grass near the tree line, eyes wide, eyebrows raised, mouth agape with the tongue sticking out.

It was her turn to vomit.

CHAPTER 11

"Well, well, well," Ted said, shutting the bedroom door behind him. His girlfriend, still in her bikini, was leaning on the edge of the bed, smirking as she endured his obnoxious grandstanding. "As I recall, I am victorious in our bet. I seem to recall you stating the terms."

Pam maintained her smirk, blinking slowly as she played the role of the defeated, reluctant woman. Of course, there was nothing reluctant at all in what was about to transpire, except the power of being the dominant player in this instance. She liked being the 'master' and having Ted as her 'slave'. In a rare twist of fate, today was going to be the other way around.

"You're enjoying yourself, aren't you?"

"You're damn right I am!" he said. He brushed her hair behind her ears, then softly planted a kiss on her lips. It was the only gentle action that would occur. He shoved her on her back and put himself on top of her, pinning her wrists above her head. Pam pretended to try and outmuscle him, obviously failing.

She tilted her chin up, enjoying his wet mouth moving down her neck to her right shoulder and cleavage.

"Pretty basic for you," she whispered between intense breaths. "Considering what was promised."

"I'm just getting warmed up," he said. He began pulling at her bikini top with his teeth. "I'd say relax, but with what I have in mind—"

"BLECH!!!"

Both of them jumped out of bed and turned to the door. For a moment, their drive was lost. Near the stairs, they could hear someone stumbling around. Since Norman had informed them that he was heading out, and knowing that Ross and Kelly were gone, the only person who could be stumbling around was Jamie. The dummy, despite being an alcoholic, could not hold his bourbon.

Pam groaned. "That's it. We might need to set up an intervention when we get back. Not speaking figuratively there. A *literal* intervention."

"I agree," Ted muttered. He marched to the door and found Jamie seated on the top step with a near-empty bottle in hand. "Dude, please tell me you made it to the bathroom."

"Of course I did," Jamie said. He gave a wobbly thumbs up. "I'm just waiting for my ducks to get back in a row."

"We've been waiting for that for years," Ted replied.

"Oh, yeah? Well I…" Jamie swallowed, then belched.

Ted tensed, thinking he was about to witness the worst. To his relief, nothing came out. Still, it was common sense to know it was only a matter of time. No way was he going to let this idiot ruin his reign of power in the bedroom.

"Dude, do me a huge favor. Go outside and puke out there. Better yet, don't come back inside at all. At least not for a couple hours. Take your booze with you. And some water."

Jamie pouted his lower lip. "Aww! You don't want me around?"

"NO! Absolutely, I *don't*!"

Jamie finally grinned. He knew what was about to happen.

"Alright then." He stood up and went down the steps. "Even though this place will be mostly empty, I suspect it's going to get plenty noisy in here."

Ted said nothing and waited for Jamie to vacate, not only for his own self-interests, but to ensure the guy made it out the door without falling on his face. Once the front door swung shut, he was back in the bedroom.

Pam was seated up, frustrated, but also relieved. At least the hindrance was outside doing his own thing.

"'Take your booze with you'? So much for that intervention."

"Just wanted him distracted," Ted said. "I've got more important things to attend to."

"Yeah?" Pam leaned back, licking her lips. "Like what?"

Ted took charge. He grabbed her off the bed and kissed her hard. In doing so, the bikini top came off, followed by the bottoms. Next were his trunks.

Mouth agape and breathing heavily, Pam was spun toward the bed. She smiled and gasped as her man pushed her legs apart and bent her over.

Ted began to enjoy his winnings.

Pam reared her head back and moaned loudly with each mighty thrust.

***

Jamie looked back at the cabin, hearing the faint echoes of what almost sounded like screaming.

"Geez. Freaks."

There was mild jealousy. It had been a while since Jamie had been with a woman. Few showed interest in him, and those that did usually were just looking for free drinks before letting him down easy. Though it never felt easy. Maybe to them it did.

Chugging his bottle of bourbon, Jamie stumbled toward the beach. Midway there, his bladder began giving him signals.

"Oh! Little Jamie says something needs to happen." He gave brief thought to just letting it go right there on the sand. There was just barely enough self-control and human decency intact for him to reconsider. He likely wouldn't be caught, even though he couldn't shake this weird feeling that he was being watched. There was no justification for that feeling. Ted and Pam were getting their freak on, and everyone else was gone. There was nobody in the woods or on the lake.

Jamie looked at the booze. *Hmm. Maybe I should start cutting back on this shit.*

"Eh, who am I kidding?!" He swallowed the rest, then tossed the bottle aside.

The bladder signals increased, as though the booze had fallen straight through him.

Into the woods he marched. After a few yards, he found a tree and unzipped his fly.

Next came the repugnant self-aggrandizing humor that the rest of the world was fortunate to not witness. Jamie admired his equipment, greeting it with a drunken smile.

"Hey, big boy. If Ms. Pam saw you, she'd dump Ted in a heartbeat." He stopped and listened to the faint moans. Though distant, they were getting increasingly intense. *Damn. Maybe it's the booze, but that's kinda hot to listen to. Makes me wanna... well, first let's take care of the pressing issue, shall we?*

He took aim at a tree and opened fire. A long, steady stream splattered against the trunk.

Being Jamie, he couldn't just take a leak and call it a day. He had to make a game out of it. First came some 'phew, phew, phew!' sound effects as though he was in some science fiction movie. Next, he began whipping it around, trying to make shapes in midair with his pee.

"Woohoo!"

He pivoted to his left, splattering another huge tree trunk... A tree trunk that was not there before... a tree with hands and feet, wearing some kind of metallic clothing. It stood seven feet high, its midsection dripping with Jamie's filth.

It stared at him through a metallic helmet that reminded him of the sculptures of ancient Roman and Japanese warriors. Except there was something… *alien* about this one.

With hands clenched at its sides, the figure looked down at the droplets running down its front. Before long, that metallic face slowly tilted in Jamie's direction.

The drunkard teetered on his feet, fright and drunkenness putting his brain on a merry-go-round.

"Oh…"

Two long blades extended from a gauntlet on its wrist. With a single swipe, 'Little Jamie' was made even smaller.

Jamie looked down at his severed anatomy.

Mouth agape, he moaned. His head started to spin. He staggered backward, watching the blood pump from the fleshy stub.

"Uh… uh…." He couldn't form words. Drunkenness and blood loss took their toll, though not enough to spare him from the next wave of terror.

The visitor raised its arm, then swung down vertically, the two blades splitting his head into three slabs.

The Convict withdrew its blades, then watched the stupid human fall backward. The three slabs of bone and meat that used to be his skull swayed on the neck. The feet and arms twitched.

Picking the dummy by the ankle, it dragged him farther into the woods. It needed to go far enough away to create confusion. It wasn't sure if it wanted to go after the other two.

As it decided, it conducted a fresh scan of the building. Two figures were on the top floor, the male dominating the female in a vigorous manner. The creature let curiosity get the better of it. Utilizing the control system, it ordered the drone to slowly move to the window.

The machine moved in, its motors at minimal power to eliminate the noise. Its presence went unnoticed as it settled outside the window and switched from thermal imaging to plain video, delivering a sensational event to its master's helmet. The Convict clicked its mandibles excitedly, watching as the two humans copulated. The female was gripping the fabric hard as though in pain. But the Convict knew otherwise. She liked what was going on.

It took time to admire her form, ignoring that of the male. Despite being a different species, it couldn't help but feel somewhat aroused by her figure. It was taboo on its home planet to copulate with any other species. But the Convict did not subscribe to the laws of its home world.

It enjoyed slaughter, and the other forbidden pleasures the general populace found detestable.

Right now, it enjoyed this.

As the coupling began to reach its peak, the Convict noticed the male's head begin to turn to the window. With a swipe of the control module, it directed the drone away.

The fun was over for now. It needed to prep for its next endeavors. Those other humans would certainly return in their vehicles before long. Those vehicles ran on four wheels comprised of a thick, yet vulnerable substance.

It held one of its marble-shaped pressure bursters to its eye. A new plan took form. The Convict exited the woods and made its way to the parking zone. The mated pair would be too busy to notice the surprise it would lay for the returning vehicles.

***

Pam clawed at the sheets, relishing in the pleasure Ted was delivering. She noticed his actions ease up briefly. Glancing over her shoulder, she noticed he was looking at the window.

"Babe? What's wrong?"

He shrugged. "Oh, nothing. I think some big ass bird was looking through the window."

She smiled. "It wants to watch. Goes to show you're doing something right. Keep going, big guy. Don't stop, don't stop… yes… *yes!*"

With a few more heavy motions, they simultaneously reached their climax.

CHAPTER 12

It had been in and out of consciousness since its prisoner had broken out of confinement. Its body, resilient and stubborn as its mind, refused to die, even as blood continued to ooze from its wound. The knife had missed its heart by a couple of centimeters, though it still severed plenty of veins. Its lower injuries were mostly cauterized due to the plasma scoring, but still ached horridly.

It lacked the strength to get the stim packs, which were in a medical cabinet in storage. The prisoner had taken the ones the marshal and its comrades carried on hand. By this point, they probably would do no good anyway. The marshal needed a medical droid, which did not respond to the distress signal on its gauntlet. The Convict had probably taken the machine and reprogrammed it for its own sick use.

Inch by inch, it crawled from the cell room where its seemingly dead corpse lay with what remained of its two comrades. They, regrettably, were truly dead. Moving down the corridor took time. Not only was the marshal void of strength, but it was operating with one good arm. The other, having been broken in its struggle with the Convict, was now swollen and ached terribly.

There was no comprehension of how much time had passed. It took what felt like three lifetimes just for the marshal to get around the corner, and many times that for it to crawl to the bridge.

As it had speculated, the Convict was not there. In all likelihood, it was out on another murdering spree. There was no way of knowing when it would be back, but the bastard would return eventually. And it would kill again and again unless it was stopped. Reinforcements was its only hope.

Now in the bridge, the marshal reached at the control console, but could not reach from the floor. It had no choice, it had to summon all of its strength to get up on its knees. Growling in immense pain, it lifted itself. The first attempt resulted in it falling forward. The second time, it managed to keep ahold of the control console and stay upright. Leaning against the edge, it reached for the transmitter and swiped the appropriate key.

Nothing.

Again and again, it swiped its clawed fingertips over the key. The truth became obvious. The Convict had disabled it, for any transmissions, either sent out or received, could be tracked by the galactic authority. The emergency beacon was also disabled. There was no way the marshal could get word out for help.

Its weak heart increased its rhythm. The marshal could not die knowing it had failed. It needed to do something. *Anything*. Its species, aside from rare outliers like the Convict, was gifted with a conscience. There was no joy taken in having one of their own savagely mutilate innocent members of other species, especially those that posed no threat. This was not hunting for sport in which the slain victim was used for nourishment. Only one word described the Convict and its actions.

Evil.

Its frantic mind skimmed through various courses of action, only to settle on one basic truth. Only *it* could stop the Convict. Nobody knew where it was. The galactic authority did not even know this planet existed. For a murderous fiend like the Convict, this situation was a dream come true.

The marshal looked to the second passageway. Down there was the armory, sealed shut.

A moment of realization took place.

The Convict clearly thought all three captors were dead, putting the element of surprise in the marshal's favor. It just needed to stay alive long enough to catch its target off guard and put an energy bolt through its chest. The marshal's scanner, which would have provided access to the weapons, had been taken by the Convict, probably for the bastard's own use. However, the marshal knew of another method in which it could gain access.

It crawled to the end of the console, finding a small emergency panel, roughly the size of a pocketbook. When the little door opened, the secret emergency control system activated. Designed in the event of a hijacking, it allowed the pilots access to the internal compartments within the ship. Sweeping its finger over the control, it dialed its secret code.

There was a droning sound of the security system being deactivated. Locked doors unlatched with a metallic popping sound. There was a humming sound as the backup computer started up. The override had shut down the camouflage, which in turn, caused the backup unit to activate and keep the ship hidden. Warping noises from the power cell indicated that the computer was struggling to maintain the cloak.

With a sharp hiss, the armory door opened.

The marshal, straining with each movement, made its way inside, leaving a trail of green blood in the process. Arriving at the end of the corridor, it rested on its good elbow, staring in dismay. The drone had been taken, likely reprogrammed for recon purposes. Insectoid in its shape, it was a machine capable of multiple different functions, one of which was administering medical treatment. With its two comrades dead, the marshal had no choice but to tend to its own wounds.

The infirmary and armory shared one large room. Unfortunately, the stim packs were in a sealed wall-mounted container which required a scanner to open. No special code would work in this instance. This would not be a problem if the droid was present, for it would be able to open the doors and access the stim packs. But it wasn't, thus the marshal was on its own.

Without a key, there was only one other solution: blast the container.

Fortunately, the gauntlets were intact. The cases were open, likely due to the Convict rummaging through the supplies. It grabbed one from the rack, then sat against the wall as it tried to figure out how to put it on. With its right arm busted, it had to wear the gauntlet on its left.

A task easier said than done.

The marshal placed the gauntlet on its lap, intending to use its legs to hold it in place while it slid its arm through. At this moment, it began to waver back and forth. Its vision grew foggy, its balance off kilter. Even leaning against the wall, it struggled to remain upright. Gravity seemed to demand that its body hit the floor. The marshal fought hard, remembering its sworn duty. It could not let the Convict win.

The battle was lost.

Consciousness slipped away once again. The marshal fell to its left, the gauntlet rolling several feet from its outstretched hand.

CHAPTER 13

"…So, then I went into the barracks, and I find the dumb doughboy on his bunk, pants off, drunk out of his mind. I walk on over and yell, "Private Dweeb! On your feet!"

Diego chuckled as he listened to Norman's Army story. "Yeah, with a last name like Weeb, that nickname is inevitable."

"Yeah, we all took full advantage of that," Norman said. "The idiot falls off his bunk. There he was, face-down, ass up—staring me in the face. Almost literally."

Diego smirked, unsure what to make of that statement. "His *ass* was staring at you?"

"Practically. Someone took a sharpie and drew an eye on each cheek. Added eyelashes and everything!"

Diego laughed loudly. "Oh, geez."

"Man, sometimes I wish I stayed in," Norman said. "Did all that training thinking I was gonna go kick some ass, ended up policing a base instead. A lot of standing around, staring into the distance, pretending you're rock hard and unfazed by boredom."

"Been there," Diego said. "Not in the service, but back in my patrol days. Had to stand guard at a warehouse for all eight hours of my shift. That was before everyone had a smartphone in their hand. At least there was coffee."

"Lucky bastard," Norman said. He looked up ahead. "Oh, I think I see them."

Diego saw them too. They were behind the truck, hunched over. Kelly was holding her stomach and Ross had both hands clasped behind his head. Alarm bells went off in his mind. He wasn't sure what was going on, but he knew what distress looked like.

"Something's wrong."

Norman noticed it too. "Yeah…"

Diego parked the truck behind Ross' and stepped out. "Hey guys. What's the matter?"

"We… they…" Ross stammered, then pointed a shaky finger into the woods. "Out there. We tried to call, but… no signal."

Diego and Norman looked into the woods.

"Slow down," Diego said. "What happened?"

"Massacre," Kelly said. "There's a camp over there. Something hap—they're all dead."

Diego's stomach tightened and his heart pressure spiked. There was a feeling of danger and vulnerability. He hadn't bothered bringing his pistol on this drive, a decision he now regretted immensely. He had a pocketknife clipped to his belt, his only defense against whatever threat which may be lurking in these woods.

His eyes skimmed his surroundings. There was no movement that he could see, nor were there any unusual sounds. That wasn't a comfort. If there was a killer around here, they would likely try and keep hidden. For all he knew, he was being watched at this very moment.

"Are you serious?" Norman muttered. He kept his voice low. Like Diego, he was concerned as to who may be lurking nearby.

"You think we would joke about this?!" Ross hissed.

"Everybody keep calm," Diego said. "I'm gonna go take a look. The rest of you might wanna stay here."

"I'll go with you," Norman said.

"I'm going wherever Diego goes," Kelly added.

"The fuck?" Ross muttered. He swung his hands out to the side in protest. It didn't make a difference. The other three were back in the woods, leaving him alone by the truck. Clearly, Kelly did not see him as an efficient protector against a possible mass murderer.

The feeling of safety in numbers hit him hard. Cursing under his breath, Ross caught up with the others, straggling behind as soon as they neared the camp.

Diego winced, recognizing the smell of burnt and decaying flesh. Right away, he recognized the RV. It was the same group that he had an altercation with at the gas station.

Right there in the firepit was the deflated, skeletal corpse of the heavy woman who seemingly was the matriarch of the group. The only reason he was able to identify her was by the pink flipflops near her feet. Flies were picking at her toes.

Empty beer bottles and smore makings were scattered across the camp. All of the marshmallow bags had been torn open.

To his right was the source of the decayed smell. The severed head was on the ground at the edge of camp. Gripping his knife, Diego approached the trees nearby, finding the body the head belonged to.

"Jesus."

"We should call the Sheriff," Norman said.

"Absolutely."

"We already tried," Ross said. "The damn signal. Can't even get a call to 9-1-1."

"Everybody stay calm," Diego said.

"Stay calm?" Ross said. "You do realize…"

Kelly elbowed him in the ribs and shushed hard. He pursed his lips, bitterly, then took a deep breath. It was meant to calm himself, but instead, all it did was give him a big whiff of the putrid smells. Groaning, he walked in the direction they came and dry heaved.

Diego knelt by the severed head, pressing a handkerchief over his face to mask the smell. It was the neckbeard fella from the gas station. He could see the vertebrae, which was almost as smoothly cut as the muscle tissue. Whoever did this used an extremely sharp instrument.

Even more odd were the puncture wounds going straight up into the stub. There were two of them driven deep into the meat, probably into the brain. The detective mindset went to work. Looking at this, Diego couldn't help but feel as though this head had been put on a duel-bladed pike. It was a weird image, but the only one that made sense considering the odd type of tissue damage.

All he knew for sure was that these bodies were several hours old at least. Maybe close to a day.

"There's nobody in the RV," Norman said.

Diego pressed into the woods.

"Hey!" Ross said. "Where are you going?"

"There was one more person in their group," Diego said. "If he's still out here…"

"For all we know, he's the one who killed these people," Norman said.

"Trust me, if you've seen this guy, you'd know he didn't do this," Diego said. "Let's just say, he lacks the muscle mass needed to cleanly take a man's head off."

He pressed into the woods, now gripping his knife firmly. Every tree was vetted thoroughly by his eyes. Each sound was taken into consideration. Diego was not only listening for potential killers, but any stiff motions of anyone hiding in the woods. There was still the possibility that the missing victim may have gotten away and was cowering behind a bush somewhere.

Two hundred feet into his search, his sense of smell rang alarm bells in his brain. Right away, he knew there was another body in the woods. He turned to the left and went another hundred feet, which led to another small clearing.

At the tree line, he found the skinny activist kid who challenged him at the gas station. At least, he was *mostly* certain this was him. There was no head left to identify. Unlike the other victim, whose head was severed, this one was crushed into the dirt. The body was bent backward, the spine clearly broken near the L3 vertebrae.

There was more.

Diego looked into the small clearing and saw a small camp nearby. A small tent was put up near a white Jeep.

"Hello?" He approached the tent, walking around to the other side. "Anyone there? Hello—"

He peeked inside and saw the naked corpses. The female was beheaded, seemingly a trademark of the maniac doing all of these murders.

The male... Diego coughed, then cupped his handkerchief over his mouth again. It was hard for him to estimate what had happened to the man. It was as though his flesh had been broken down at the cellular level. At first, he thought it to be a chemical injury, then realized the tissue damage was consistent with insect bites. Except, this was far more extreme. It was as though an entire colony of ants had helped themselves to his body.

Adding to that train of thought was the sight of motion in the exposed ribcage. Diego didn't want to, but he looked anyway.

"Jesus!" He jumped away from the tent. There was no other way of describing it. Those were *worms*! Then again, he had never seen worms like that before. Not with spiked bodies and huge insectoid jaws.

It didn't matter. Diego had seen enough.

He sprinted through the woods until he rejoined the others. Just looking at him, the three vacationers knew the situation had gone from bad to worse.

"Get in the truck," Diego said. "Right now. I'm gonna call the Sherriff. Hopefully I can get a signal."

"How bad is it?" Kelly said.

Diego looked her in the eyes. "Worse than any murder case I've ever investigated."

CHAPTER 14

Pam opened her eyes. She was on her back, hands bent behind her head, feeling the warm breeze grazing her body. She had nearly dozed off during her bliss-filled cuddling session with Ted. He was lying in bed beside her, eyes shut. Pam looked over and kissed him on the lips. She got a snore in return. He was out cold.

She smiled and took a moment to appreciate his form. As far as she was concerned, Ted had earned his nap. Maybe it had something to do with the fact that she was one-hundred percent submissive, giving him an added sense of power. Regardless, he performed particularly well today. Well enough for her to crave more.

Good things would have to wait. Her attempts to nudge him produced louder snores. She got a laugh out of the ordeal. Ted would probably need time to recharge his batteries anyway.

Pam stretched, then climbed over her boyfriend. As much as she enjoyed watching him, the snoring was getting to be a little much. Also, lying in bed was starting to get a little boring. The time would be better spent outside enjoying the lake before the weather rolled in. First, she would do Ted a small favor and shut the window. The last thing he needed was for that big bird to come back and potentially fly into the room. Though, that thought was a funny one.

She put her bikini back on and stepped out of the room, gently latching the door in order to not wake the love of her life. Happy and invigorated, she skipped down the stairs, grabbed a beer, and went outside.

"Hello, nature." She stretched her arms and strutted to the lounge chairs. To her surprise, there was no crude remark from Jamie. In fact, there was no Jamie at all. Pam glanced around, seeing nothing but quiet lakefront property. "Jamie? Where'd you go?"

She immediately felt stupid for asking. It was Jamie, the guy who was passed out drunk after falling out of the kitchen window. In all likelihood, he was in a similar state nearby. Judging by the empty bottle on the ground near the trees, it was easy to assume he was in the woods.

"A drunk Jamie wandering alone in the woods," she said to herself. "He probably tripped over a branch two steps in." Suddenly, she remembered his vomiting session which led to his temporary exile from the cabin. "Oh, damn it. I guess I better check and make sure he's all right."

A glance at the water triggered resentment. She would rather be swimming right now. Part of her wanted to say 'the hell with it' and just assume Jamie was fine. He probably was, but she had already committed to being a decent human being.

She entered the woods. "Jamie? You over here? I swear, dude, when we get home, we're throwing an intervention. You're going a little too heavy on the sauce, even for vacation."

There was no response. However, there were footprints and crushed grass. She was no tracking expert, but those looked pretty fresh. She followed the trail a little further.

"Jamie? You okay? You out here, dude?" She gave thought to quitting the search. There were a hundred things she would rather be doing. The temptation grew more powerful until it overwhelmed her. "You know what, to hell with it. If you're out here, you're on your own. Drunk idiot."

She turned around and took a step back toward camp.

Right away, she felt the sting of a small pebble striking her back. Pam whipped around, hearing the sound of running footsteps somewhere in front of her.

"Jamie, you dumb prankster! I'm gonna kill you!"

She took off running, grunting as her bare feet came down on dead bark and twigs. It was worth smacking the loser across the face, and maybe kneeing him in the groin.

Yeah, definitely doing that. Might spill all of his beer stash too. Force him to drink lemonade for the rest of the—

A massive pain filled her ankle. It was as though she had stepped into the mouth of a shark. Pam fell face-down, screaming again as her leg twisted in the grasp of… whatever it was she stepped on.

Propped on her hands, she looked at her foot. A small metal clamp with pointed teeth had snapped shut over her ankle. It was a snare, like those used to trap coyotes. It had a death grip, its razor teeth digging right into her bone.

Gasping for breath and holding back tears, Pam sat herself upright. She grabbed the thing and stuck her fingers into the gaps, trying frantically to pry it open.

The effort produced an agonizing grunt. Frustration and anxiety followed. The damn thing wouldn't open, no matter how hard she tried.

"Jamie! Ted! Help me!"

She cursed herself for shutting the bedroom window. It was bad enough that Ted was practically in a coma.

"Jamie?! Help, please!"

A twig snapped somewhere behind her. Pam turned around, expecting to see the drunken friend emerge. Her heart raced. Warm blood oozed from her ankle, worsening her sense of fright.

Pam shook madly in another attempt to pry the snare open.

"Where are you, dude? Come on, help me! I'm hurt. I'm caught on this thing, and…"

She turned her eyes back toward the sound. Paralyzing tension stiffened her body. For a second, she wondered if she was hallucinating. This *person* that emerged from behind the trees could not possibly be a person. Its height, its claws, the technology on its wrist, the strange, metallic attire, the gadgets… none of it was human.

That sentiment was reinforced when she saw its hands and the flesh exposed through the gaps in its outfit. The thing's natural color was a charcoal color, almost green in places, as though it was some species of bipedal insect or shellfish. Its humanoid figure was the only common physical trait it shared with her species.

Pam's mind was caught between shock, confusion, and terror. It was hard to comprehend what she was looking at.

It stared back at her, tilting its head curiously. Though she couldn't see through that mask, she recognized the type of intense stare. It signaled desire and intent without regard for her well-being. Matched with the unnervingly intense breathing, she realized what was on this thing's mind.

She had been to shady clubs in the past and had walked alone in the streets of Manhattan at night, where she had seen that same evil gaze. She learned to recognize when someone was eyeing her with, at best, impure thoughts.

Some things were universal. Though this being was not human, it possessed some of the same *inhuman* traits that plagued civilization.

"No…"

It stepped forward, its gaze firm on her nearly naked form.

"No!"

She got on her hands and knees and tried crawling away, only to be immediately stopped by the snare. It stood over her now. A huge hand pushed her face-down against the earth, pinning her.

"NOOOO!!!"

CHAPTER 15

"Oh, you cheating bastard."

Eddie Wingard watched the digital rook take down his queen, cornering his king in the process. The words *YOU LOSE* flashed on the screen, as though the computer was rubbing it in. He refreshed the game, eager to try again.

It was what a typical Saturday afternoon looked like for the Sheriff. The early morning hours consisted of drinking coffee and doing some paperwork. Depending on the weather, he would follow that up with some vehicle patrol. Often, the fieldwork was left to the deputies, but Eddie didn't care to be couped up. Neither in an office nor at home.

Eddie's wife frequently complained about his tendency to work the weekends. His response was "why would I *not*?" The other option would be to work on the never-ending honey-do list and listen to her news programs. Eddie would rather deal with a block full of crackheads. Fortunately, out here, the worst he usually had to deal with were drunks, underage teenagers, and the occasional meth user. Such events were few and far between.

His patrol resulted in the consumption of two donuts and a hundred extra miles on his SUV. Back in the office, he committed to his sworn duty… to beat this damn computer at chess.

"Still here, Sheriff?"

He looked at his door at Deputy Ford.

"Not leaving until I beat this sucker."

"That's what you said last Saturday."

"And I didn't leave until ten that night."

Ford snickered. "And you still didn't win."

"Yeah, yeah, yeah." Eddie leaned back and put his feet up on the desk. "So, I rage-quit like some basement-dwelling man-baby. Won't happen this time. I've brought my A-game."

"Evidenced by your colorful use of the words 'cheating bastard'," Ford said.

"Ah, shut up." Eddie pointed at the white cup in Ford's hand. "And bring me one of those."

Before Ford could step away, the dispatcher's voice streamed through their radios. *"Sheriff. You still in?"*

Eddie stood up and leaned out the door to shout down the hall. "Mandy, you could've just walked back here and seen the open door."

"Can't!" she shouted back. "Got someone on the line. Stating there's an emergency over by Lake Fairview."

Eddie's grin disappeared. He and Ford raced down the hall before arriving at the dispatch office.

Mandy was on the phone, jotting down notes on a spiral pad. "Uh-huh... uh-huh... Hello?... I can't hear—oh, there you are. Start from the beginning, please. Five people in an RV... Where on the lake is this?... I didn't quite catch that... Hmm... You there? Hello? Hello?" She looked at the phone, shrugged, then redialed. "Hmm. Weird. No signal."

"The hell's going on?" Eddie said. "Who was that on the line?"

The dispatcher turned in her seat to look at him. She did not have the look of a concerned dispatcher sending people to a potentially violent situation. Instead, she looked skeptical. Borderline amused, even.

"That was Diego Tritton," she said. "The damn line kept breaking up. Could only get a few words at a time, so I'm not fully sure what he was trying to explain. Something about people in an RV. Need police right away, apparently. Every time he tried to elaborate, the freaking signal cut out."

"Did he say something about an RV?" Eddie asked.

"Yeah," Mandy said.

"Oh, hell." Eddie dug his hands into his pockets and rocked back and forth on his heels. "I bet it's those people he ran into at the gas station yesterday. They got all up in his business over the whole Willie Stader thing, and he was getting pretty agitated. Didn't seem too pleased that I was there to keep tabs on him."

"You think he's playing a joke?" Ford asked.

"It's one hell of a prank if he is. The guy ought to know he could be arrested for this..." After a few additional moments of consideration, Eddie dug out his keys. "Yeah, I guess we'll go check it out. God help Tritton if this is some kind of scheme to get back at me. I saw the case of beer he was loading into his truck. Wouldn't be surprised if he's sitting alone, in his cabin, all depressed and irritable. All pissed at the world for holding him to account for the incident."

"You think he's the type to hold a grudge?" Ford asked.

Eddie shrugged. "All I can say is that hardly anything happens around these parts. Then he shows up, and all of a sudden all hell's breaking loose? I'm not buying into it." He looked to the dispatcher. "Did he say where the RV was at?"

"Not specifically. I lost him before he could say," she said. "Maybe if he calls back, I can find out. All I know is that it's somewhere by the lake."

An audible groan filled the room. Eddie tucked his thumbs under his belt and lifted his chin, squeezing his eyes shut to blind himself from the current misery.

"Great. That's a hell of a lot of ground to cover," he said. "We'll be out there all afternoon, and probably for nothing."

"If you want, I can run out and take a look," Ford said. "It'll give me something to do." He glanced at the clock. "As long as you don't mind paying overtime."

Eddie snorted. The knucklehead was always looking for some excuse for overtime, especially when the budget didn't call for it. Still, Eddie didn't care to go all the way out to the lake. There hadn't been a murder in this area for over twenty years, let alone anything as brutal and violent as what Mandy described. Maybe it was the fact he was nearing retirement, or the fact that he had his doubts about Diego Tritton, but he did not want to drive all the way out to Lake Fairview.

"Yeah, alright. Go check by the cabins first. They're on the south end of the lake. That much I know for certain."

"Sounds good!" Ford yanked his keys from his pocket and pranced down the hall.

Eddie followed him out with a grin on his face. "You know, I'm gonna download that and show it to the entire department." He pointed at the security camera in the ceiling corner.

"You just wish you could move as gracefully as I can. Without breaking a hip, at least."

"Oh! You wise ass! I hope there's a maniac in a hockey mask out there waiting for you," Eddie said. Happy with his verbal retort, Ford went to the door. Eddie followed him out. "Check-in. Let us know you're still alive. Don't spend countless hours out there. I'm not paying you *that much* overtime."

"I'll see what I can do, boss."

"Yeah, sure."

"Go back to losing at chess."

"Alright. I will!"

Eddie shut the door and marched to his office. With his feet back on the desk, he tapped the spacebar to wake the computer up.

Once again, the words *YOU LOSE* flashed on the screen.

"Wait a second! You can't time out the game, you cheating bastard!"

CHAPTER 16

"Shit, shit…" Diego walked up and down the road, holding his phone high in a vain attempt to get a signal. He dialed the number for the umpteenth time, only to get the same frustrating result. "Damn it!"

Kelly stepped out of his truck. "Nothing?"

"I had them on the line for a minute, but I lost them. Now, I can't get through to them again."

"Did you say where this spot was?"

"I didn't get a chance." Diego raised his phone and walked around some more. After another minute of futility, he marched back to the truck. "It's no use. We need to go."

"Thank God," Ross said. "We need to get the hell out of here."

"Wait," Kelly said.

"Wait, what?!" Ross exclaimed. "Kelly, that killer could still be around here somewhere."

"Exactly." She looked to Diego. "We're not too far from Patrick Gawdy's cabin. I'm wondering if we should go check on him."

"Oh, lovely," Ross muttered.

"He might have a landline," Kelly continued.

Norman perked up. "She's got a point. I can't get a signal on my phone either. And there's no landline at our cabin."

"Mine neither," Diego said. He clipped his phone to his belt and stepped into the cab. "Good idea, Kelly. Best to check on Mr. Gawdy anyway. Hopefully he's alright."

He started the engine back up and drove north.

Everyone watched the trees, half-expecting to see some insane lunatic creeping under a tree or behind a bush. Every sway of a branch made their hearts leap.

In the backseat, Norman dug out his own pocketknives. While Ross was breathing nervously and looking out each window, Norman was rigid, watching out the passenger side window for anything unusual. That military training, ingrained from day one, was dying to be put to good use. He never had the satisfaction of combat. All that training was spent idly guarding posts or policing his own brothers-in-arms. Now, he may finally get to put it to use against a mass murderer. It was clear the killer liked getting up close and personal. Norman was more than eager to give the piece of shit exactly what he craved…

He flipped his knife open.

…and a little something extra.

Ross looked at him. "You're not gonna go all *Rambo*, are ya?"

"Not unless I have to," Norman said.

"Right…" Ross took a breath and looked straight ahead at the driver's seat.

Diego glanced at the rearview mirror, noticing the journalist's uneasiness.

"You alright, Ross?" he said. Ross didn't answer. Diego wasn't sure if his anxiety was from finding those bodies or being stuck in the truck with who he saw as a 'murderous criminal'. "This should only take a minute. Once we get to Mr. Gawdy's place, we can use his landline to call the cops. Then we'll haul ass back to the cabins and get your friends."

"And we'll get far away from here," Kelly added.

"I'm down with that," Norman said. "Definitely don't want to be here when it's dark. God only knows what hours of the day that creep likes to operate. Hell, I've heard some of these guys operate on hardly any sleep. They're so buzzed by their crazy activities, they—Whoa."

Diego slowed the truck and looked back. "Something the matter?"

Norman put his face to the window. Interestingly, he was looking *up*, rather than straight into the woods.

He shook his head. "I don't know. Thought I saw something that looked like…" He chuckled nervously, unsure of how to describe it. "Lightning, I guess."

Ross peeked at the sky. "Looks fairly clear to me."

"I'm telling ya. I saw a flash up that way." Norman pointed northeast. The others looked in that general direction but saw nothing. Norman shrugged it off. "Sorry. Probably just my imagination."

"Yeah. Probably thought you saw aliens landing," Ross muttered.

"Relax," Diego said. He pointed up ahead at a jeep trail that led east. "Look, we're almost there. This goes straight to Patrick Gawdy's place."

He made the turn and drove the truck through the narrow trail. Tall trees cast dark shadows over the truck and its passengers, adding to the feeling of claustrophobia and bewilderment.

Even Diego felt the hairs on the back of his neck stand on end. His grip on the steering wheel tightened. His sense of awareness tripled. Every movement from the tallest branch to the tiniest blade of grass was noticed.

The sense of vulnerability was never worse than this moment. Never again would Diego leave home without his gun. It was the old saying "Better to have one and not need it than need it and not have one."

The sight of Patrick Gawdy's cabin brought a feeling of levity. It was a charming little place. A single-story place with two bedrooms and a large, open living room, it was no surprise why Mr. Gawdy enjoyed coming here. The view of the lake was beautiful, the space around it open and green. There was a nice big firepit in front of the cabin. Several fishing poles leaned against the side of the building.

In the driveway was his old pickup truck. The blue paint was starting to fade, but Diego had no doubt the mechanics were well maintained. He was well aware how handy Mr. Gawdy was. Had circumstances been normal, Diego would have considered hiring him for repair work on his cabin.

He parked behind the truck and stepped out. "Hello? Mr. Gawdy?"

The others stepped out and began to branch throughout the property. Diego and Kelly walked around the corner to the front door.

Kelly knocked on the door.

"Hello? Sir? It's me, Kelly Dawson." She knocked again. "You home?"

Ross appeared in the yard to the right of the building. He glanced every which way, then looked at Diego and Kelly.

"He's gotta be around here. Truck's here."

"Door's unlocked," Kelly said. She slowly turned the handle and opened the door. "Mr. Gawdy? Hello?"

Ross shuddered. "I don't like this."

"Relax," Norman said.

"Will people stop telling me to relax?! We found a bunch of dead bodies, for chrissake! To top things off, there's no sign of Mr. Gawdy."

"Like you said, he's gotta be here somewhere," Norman said. He pointed at the dock. "Hell, he's got an open tacklebox over there. Does he have more than one boat? Maybe he just went fishing." Norman took a few steps toward the dock to investigate, only to stop in his tracks at the shoreline. "Oh…"

He lifted his knives from his pocket.

Diego and Kelly joined him, then sucked in a deep breath when they saw the rotted corpse. The water had pushed it under the dock, where the limbs had bunched up. The clothes were ratty and torn, as was his flesh. Bones protruded from greyish skin. The jaw was hyperextended with no muscle tissue to hold it together. The eyes were gone, revealing empty sockets.

"Diego…" Kelly grabbed his arm.

Ross ran inside, cupping his mouth.

Norman opened both of his knives and looked back and forth.

Diego put his arm around Kelly and backed away from the dock. "It'll be alright."

"No… I mean, that's an acid burn."

He looked at her. "Huh?"

"I'm a chemist. I know what chemical burns look like," she said.

"Whatever it is, it's definitely related to what happened at the RV," Norman said.

Diego nodded. "You're right. This is no coincidence."

They turned around to the sound of footsteps stumbling onto the front porch. Ross, pale and sweaty, clung to one of the awning pillars as he caught his breath.

"Phone's dead," he said, pointing behind him with his thumb. "I tried calling 9-1-1. Nothing."

"You've got to be freaking kidding me," Diego muttered.

Norman marched into the cabin and found the landline. He raised it to his ear and tapped on the keys. Shaking his head, he put the phone down.

"Son of a bitch. No dial tone. Nothing. The lines must be down somewhere." He stepped outside and joined the others. "Diego, you think they might send some deputies? They know we're at the lake, right?"

"They do," Diego said. "Hopefully they'll be smart enough to drive to our cabins."

"Good." Norman marched to the driveway. "Then I vote we get the hell out of here and…" He stopped in his tracks and went dead silent, staring to the north. "Whoa. I thought I imagined that."

Kelly clasped her hands and nervously held them to her chest. She saw it too.

Ross and Diego happened to be looking in the other direction at the time. Diego stepped beside Kelly and followed her gaze. All he saw was a partly cloudy horizon over a forest of green trees.

"What is it?"

"I don't know," she muttered. "It kinda looked like… lightning."

Norman pointed to the sky. "There!"

This time, Diego saw it.

It was a violet flash of twisted energy. It did not extend from the heavens, but instead the earth itself. A second flash followed, disappearing as quickly as the first.

"I don't know what that is, but it's not lightning," Diego said.

"We should go check it out," Norman said.

"I…" Kelly inched toward the truck. "I'm not sure I feel safe doing that."

Diego nodded. "She's got a point. It may not be lightning, but it definitely looks electrical. I'm not sure going near it is a good idea."

Norman tightened his grip on his knives. He reversed his grip on one, holding it in a ready position.

"Then don't come. I'm gonna check it out."

"Dude!" Ross said. "Macho man, you're not a superhero! I'm with the detective. You might get zapped."

"*Or*, this thing could start a forest fire," Norman said. "Stay here if you want to. I'll be back in just a minute."

"Norman, don't..." Diego's words went unheard. Norman darted off in the direction of the flash, disappearing in the maze of thick woods. He dropped his hands to his sides, frustrated. He liked Norman, but he had to agree with Ross that the guy was a little brash. There were plenty of people like that in Denver, always rushing headfirst to take matters into their own hands. Once, he was in the middle of pursuing a human trafficking suspect. A foot chase led to a brief shootout near a hardware store. A good Samaritan, crouched behind a pickup, attempted to tackle the suspect. Putting himself in the line of fire had obvious consequences. He was struck, both by police bullets, and by the suspect. In spite of immense blood loss, he survived, though only because Diego drove him to the hospital, saving time.

"That dumbass," Ross said.

"What should we do?" Kelly said.

"I don't know," Ross said. "If something happens to him, we'll never know. Yet, if we leave without him, we'll be looked at as the assholes."

Again, Diego agreed with Ross. Perturbed, he looked over at Patrick Gawdy's rotten corpse. He was still in his waders. He couldn't be sure how that acid chemical got on him, but it was clear Gawdy was in the water when it did.

The detective in him went to work. This killer, assuming there was only one, was capable of beheading someone with a single swipe. Somehow or another, he was able to crush one person's skull as though it were a grape. Then there was the man in the tent, who was eaten alive by bizarre carnivorous worms. As evidenced by Gawdy's death, the killer had access to some kind of chemical weapon. Now, there was some sort of electrical activity occurring in the woods.

And Norman was running right towards it.

He thought about the fool at the home improvement store. The guy was an idiot, but a well-meaning idiot. Same with Norman in this case. Regardless, the call to duty pulled at Diego's conscience.

You're not a cop anymore. Don't feel like you have to go after him.

Despite what he tried to tell himself, his conscience prevailed.

Diego looked through the cabin's open doorway. Memories flashed from one of his visits during hunting season. While out fishing on his boat, he went to the north end of the lake and saw Patrick Gawdy with a six-point buck on the hood of his truck. Leaning on the front porch was his .30-.30 Winchester rifle.

He hustled into the cabin, glanced around, then went into the bedroom. The weapon was in the closet, hidden in the corner behind some clothes. Patrick never bothered locking it up, since he never left the cabin during his visits.

On the shelf above it was a full box of ammo. Diego loaded the rifle to its six-shot capacity, then stuffed some more bullets in his shirt pocket. He cranked the lever and stepped outside.

Ross' throat tightened at the sight of the former detective with a gun. "Uh…"

"I'm going after him. Stay here." Without waiting for a reply, Diego went into the woods.

Kelly was right behind him. "Yeah, sorry. I'm not on board for splitting up."

"Great! Just great!" Ross said, trailing behind her.

The woods were eerily dark, despite the bright sunshine. They even got darker as a cloud passed overhead, coating the area with an enormous shadow. The trio slowed after a couple hundred yards of travel. Sticking close together, they continued north.

A breeze passed over them, wiggling long thin branches. Pine needles fell from wavering branches… right onto Ross' neck. He yelped and spun around.

"Shit! Fuck! Damn! Shit!"

Diego spun on his heel, rifle shouldered.

Ross flapped his arms then dug the needles out of his shirt collar. He calmed down, only to get riled up at the sight of the rifle muzzle pointing in his general direction. Diego kept it angled down, but that wasn't enough for the journalist.

"Don't you even think about it!"

"I told you to wait by the truck," Diego said.

"Starting to think I should've," Ross said. "Frankly, I'm not sure if you're the one who should be handling that thing. Considering…"

Diego turned his back. Even under these circumstances, he knew it was a matter of time before the Willie Stader case got brought up.

"Just go back," he muttered.

"I'll keep it in mind." Ross looked over his shoulder at the seemingly infinite stretch of woods between him and the truck. The cabin was already out of sight. Visibility ended at thirty feet. The feeling of safety-in-numbers took hold. He cleared his throat and continued following Diego's lead. "Right now, I'm committed, unfortunately."

They went a few dozen yards further, with no sign of Norman.

"Norman?" Kelly called out. "Norman? Answer me!"

"Over here!" he called back.

They glanced about, unsure of the exact location he was calling from.

"Where's 'over here'?!" Ross said.

"This way!" Norman replied.

This time, Diego was able to determine the direction he was shouting from. He led the others through a group of pine trees. Past them was a relatively large clearing. Broken branches were sprinkled throughout the ground. Many of them were covered in leaves. The wood was still bright in color, as were the leaves. They were still partially hydrated and maintaining their natural green color. It had not been long since they were broken off the trees.

Kelly looked up, seeing the damage to the surrounding trees. The damage extended all the way to the top, especially to the group huddled on the east side of the clearing.

On the left side was Norman, standing still with a perplexed look on his face. He was staring into the middle of the clearing as though he had seen a ghost.

"You alright, man?" Diego said.

"Yeah." Norman's eyes did not move.

"What's wrong?" Ross said. "What do you see?"

Norman pointed straight ahead. "There's something there."

Everyone looked into the clearing, then at each other. *You see it? No? Me neither.*

Frustrated and out of patience, Ross stepped forward. "Dude, there's nothing out here."

"Dude, you're about to walk right into it," Norman said.

"Into what? There's nothing here—"

THUD!

"FUCK!" Ross staggered back, pressing his hand to his brow. "What the…" He stared at the space in front of him, seeing nothing. Yet, he walked into something as rigid as the side of a building. Slowly, he extended his hand. The sensation of cold metal embraced his palm.

Something was in fact there.

"Holy…"

A purple flash of light engulfed the area.

"…SHIT!"

Ross jumped back to the safety of the group and watched as the 'lightning' flickered. Each flash revealed a monstrous, mechanical insectoid image. Its sides resembled the hull of a battleship. It stood on six stilts, its center mass at least forty-feet wide and disc-shaped. For a split-second, the group thought they were looking at a gargantuan spider. After another flash, it was clear this thing was mechanical in nature.

There were ports that functioned as thrusters. On the top were instruments that served as antennae. There were structures on the underside of the disc with exhaust ports. Engines. The feet of its legs were long and flat. Landing struts.

"Nuh-uh," Ross muttered.

"No fucking way," Kelly said.

"Glad you saw it too," Norman said. "I thought I was crazy for a moment."

"Oh, you are," Ross said. "Just not in this case."

"Is this what I think it is?" Kelly said.

"Unless the military is conducting top-secret technological research out here," Ross said, "I'd say we're looking at an honest-to-God spaceship."

"This isn't military tech," Diego said. "There are many better places for them to test this sort of thing out."

Another flash revealed its shape.

"It looks like it's malfunctioning," Norman said. He waited for it to reappear, then shuffled around the back. Pointing his knife, he exclaimed, "There's an opening back here!"

The others ran over to join him. Sure enough, there was an open hatch with an old-fashioned stairway leading into the interior of the ship. From the other side, it looked like another one of the landing struts. Whoever, or whatever, piloted this thing, probably assumed its cloaking system was perfectly functional.

Norman approached it.

"What are you doing?!" Ross said.

"If it's in there, we might be able to get a jump on it," Norman said.

"Get a jump on it?!" Ross pressed his hands against his head. He felt as though he was going mad. He was still processing the existence of an extraterrestrial lifeform on Earth, as well as the obvious fact that it had gone on a killing spree. Meanwhile, the overzealous Army Ranger wannabe was attempting to fight the thing with knives. "Do you even hear yourself, Norman?!"

"Norman, wait," Diego said, his voice barely above a whisper. If there were aliens inside, the last thing they needed was to draw them out. Judging by the size of this vessel, there was space for at least a few crewmembers—assuming they were human-sized, of course.

"You'll be killed," Kelly said. "If not by whatever's in there, then by the air particles. There could be bacteria you're not used to. Some strain of disease, or... oh, you dumb shit!"

Norman went up the ramp and into the ship.

That protect-and-serve vow kicked in. Groaning, Diego ran after the veteran, disappearing into the spaceship behind him.

All of a sudden, he was no longer surrounded by woods. He entered a world of technology he could not even comprehend. He stood beside Norman in what he guessed was the bridge of this ship. It was a fairly wide room with an instrument panel on the front.

Smeared on the floor was a crusty green substance. Like a slug's slime trail, it stretched from one hallway on the back of the bridge, pooled in the center, before continuing into a second corridor on the right. Both corridors appeared to lead to different compartments within the ship.

Norman studied the instrument panel. It was flat, with strange symbols marking the surface. He lowered his hand to touch it but changed his mind at the last second.

He backed away from it, turning his attention to the passageway on the left side which headed aft.

"Where do you think this goes?"

Diego didn't answer. His attention was on the crusty substance on the floor. The way it was smeared resembled the blood trail from a murder victim whose body had been dragged through a house. It ran through both corridors, the smears appearing to originate from the one on the left. Looking down its length, it appeared to be a short distance to whatever was on the other end.

"Well, we're already committed to exploring this vessel. Might as well find out," he finally said.

The two men slowly walked the length of the corridor. Diego kept the weapon level, ready to blast anything that even resembled a threat. He arrived at the compartment and turned the corner.

He swallowed. Despite the vast difference in technology, he immediately recognized this compartment. It was a brig, similar to those on a Navy ship. There were three different holding cells, two of which were sealed off with some kind of energy grid.

"Diego?" Norman muttered, looking at the body lying on the floor.

Diego nodded. There was no denying what they were looking at. Though humanoid in its basic shape, there was nothing *human* about this thing. Considering the fact they were standing inside a real-life spaceship made the answer obvious. This thing was an alien.

A dead alien.

Together, they observed the thing's red-silver clothing. Both men, from their backgrounds in tactical training, recognized the attire as some kind of uniform. There was even an emblem on the left shoulder. The thing was nearly seven feet in height. A metallic mask covered its face. Its hands had opposable thumbs and three elongated fingers tipped with pointed nails.

"Whoa…" Diego muttered.

"This is beyond nuts," Norman said.

"That's putting it mildly," Diego said. He looked at the injuries the alien had suffered in its final moments, then looked to the center cell. Another member of its species had been tossed through the laser grid barrier, reducing it to cubes of flesh.

"Looks like they had some sort of disagreement," Norman said.

Diego turned to the third cell. From what he could surmise, its grid had been disabled. He inched closer, then after hesitating, took a look inside. Looking on the floor left of the entryway, he saw a small steel panel which had been flipped open, revealing circuits. The mechanics had been painted with scorch marks, as though someone had poured gunpowder onto the components and ignited it.

He had seen enough. Something had killed these aliens, and it didn't take a strong IQ to know it was connected to the murders in the woods.

Both men returned to the bridge. Diego continued for the exit, while Norman walked toward the other corridor.

"Dude, come on," Diego said. "Let's get out of here before the pilot comes back."

"I think there's something down here," Norman said.

"Oh, gee," Diego groaned. "That's all the more reason for us to vacate… what the hell are you doing?... oh, fuck!"

There was nothing Diego could say or do, short of knocking him out, that could stop Norman from wandering down that second corridor. The foolish idiot. Diego didn't think he was a bad guy, but he clearly had a macho complex which led to a desire to look for fights. Maybe the guy thought he was going to fight a killer alien hand-to-hand and kill it with his knife. Whatever the case, he was exploring the rest of the ship whether Diego liked it or not.

Looking at the smeared green substance on the floor—blood—it was evident that another of those aliens had crawled through the ship.

What was it doing? Trying to get help? Trying to send out a signal? Reach an infirmary?

Those questions would have to wait for another time. At the moment, all Diego could do was go after the overly-macho Norman.

Diego proceeded with caution, constantly looking over his shoulder in fear that one of the ship's occupants would suddenly show up. He caught up with Norman, who had stopped at the doorway at the end. Something inside had caught his attention.

He made room for the former detective, who quickly laid eyes on a third alien corpse.

"Another one," Norman whispered.

Diego nodded. "Yeah."

Its uniform matched those worn by the others. This particular alien had really gone through the wringer. After staring at it for just a few seconds, it was obvious this one had gone toe-to-toe with an enemy with a bad attitude.

Its right arm was misshapen in a way that the left one wasn't. Both men knew what broken limbs looked like, especially if untreated. In addition, they both knew what a stab wound looked like. No doubt, some kind of blade had punctured its chest. Green blood oozed from the incision, coating its uniform. In its abdomen was another, larger wound. That one was mostly cauterized, though it still oozed blood.

Norman looked at the room. There were several items on racks, laid out in specific order. He did not recognize any of the tech, but he did know the method in which they were set up.

"It's an armory." he said.

At this point, Diego was also studying the room. Though he couldn't know for sure, he suspected this compartment served two purposes, one being an armory. The right end of the room was void of weapons, instead holding steel container units. Some of them resembled refrigerators, others cabinet drawers, just more high-tech. He would have assumed it to be the galley, had it not been for the operating table. Some designs were truly universal.

"An armory and infirmary."

"These guys doctors?" Norman said.

Diego looked at the details on the uniform, then at the weapons.

"No. I don't think so."

"Whoa…" Norman knelt by a mechanical object lying on the floor. It was the length of his forearm, with a small tunnel running through its length. "I think it's a gauntlet."

Diego glanced between the object on the floor and one of the racks on the left wall. Definitely a weapon.

"Don't touch it," Diego said.

Norman froze, arm extended. It wasn't Diego's words that stopped him, but a shift in the 'dead' body.

A tense silence filled the room.

This time, Norman regretted his foolhardiness. He felt that he had knelt near a sleeping giant, and that any movement would awaken it. For several moments, he was motionless, even holding his breath.

Slowly, he retracted his arm.

The alien shuddered. It raised its head and arm, lashing at the gauntlet. Norman jumped back out of reach.

"Sweet Christ!"

Both men retreated to the bridge where they filed out through the exit. Kelly and Ross immediately noticed their frantic body language.

"What happened? Did you see one?" Ross said.

"Yeah, there's one in there," Norman said.

Ross jumped back. "Then let's get the hell out of here before it comes after us."

"I don't think we have to worry about that," Norman said, catching his breath. "It's pretty messed up. Something went down on this ship."

"Went down?" Ross said. "What went down? What do you mean?"

"We'll tell you on the way back," Diego said. "Right now, let's get to the truck and get the others."

Together, they raced through the woods toward Patrick Gawdy's cabin.

"'Bout damn time," Ross said between breaths.

CHAPTER 17

"He plays guitar... ... ... For out of... ... businessmen..."

"Oh, for the love of God." Deputy Ford twisted the volume knob, as though that would somehow improve the crummy radio signal. The Joe Diffie song hit its chorus, of which Ford heard every fifth or sixth word between static. He gave up and turned the radio off, opting to switch to his cell phone instead.

He glanced at the road as he got on his music app. The fact that he had pulled people over for doing similar things was of no consequence. A never-ending loading screen opened up. Ford cursed the phone under his breath.

"Oh, come on, you piece of shit."

He closed it and opened it again. The app never got past the loading phase. Ford gave up and decided to drive in silence. Before he put his phone away, he remembered he had not texted his wife that he would probably be getting home late. He brought up the text screen, typed his message, and sent it.

A moment later, a red exclamation point appeared near his text, followed by the message: *your text failed to send.*

Ford groaned. He had no cell service out here. He found it odd, since he had driven out here before and never had an issue. The cell tower was on the other side of the lake. He gave thought to checking it out while he searched the area. It would give him an excuse to milk this assignment and get some overtime hours. If it turned out he had to call a maintenance person to take a look at it, he could justify staying longer to oversee its completion.

A blur of motion in the sky made him look up.

"Jesus."

For the third time, he saw that weird bird darting between the trees. It moved real quick, was brown in color, and almost resembled a dragonfly in form. He assumed his mind was playing tricks on him regarding its shape. Though he was no expert on birds, he knew there were no species that looked like that. Each time he saw it, he was certain it was the same bird. It maintained an altitude of twenty-five feet, and every time it appeared, it was twenty meters or so ahead of the patrol car. It almost seemed as though it was keeping pace with him.

Ford shrugged it off. Was it weird? Yes. Was it significant? No. If nothing else, it would make for a funny story. When he got back to the station, he could tell the other deputies how he was tailed by a big-ass, weird-looking bird.

His eyes went to the road.

"What the hell?"

He hit the brakes and stared at the downed powerlines on the right side of the road. After putting the vehicle in park, he stepped outside and observed the scene. The ends of the cables were scorched, as though someone had climbed to the top of the pole and taken a blowtorch to the thing.

Ford raised his mic. "Hey, Sheriff?" He waited for a response. "Sheriff? Eddie? Turn off the chess and pick up the radio, please. I just discovered something weird." No response came through. Ford groaned. The Sheriff was probably in the john. "Hey, Dispatch? We're gonna have to call someone from DTE to take a look at this. We've got a downed power line, roughly a half-mile east of the lake."

No response came through.

"Dispatch? Hello? Unit Four, do you copy? Unit Five? Anyone?" He switched channels to try reaching the State Police. "Bixby Station, this is Deputy Ford from the Poncho County Sheriff's Department. Please respond." As he feared, he was met with dead silence.

Ford tried the car radio. "Dispatch? Sheriff? Hello?" Nothing. It was as though everyone on the planet had disappeared. He was out here with no cell service, no radio signal, and no backup.

"What the hell is going on?"

He debated on what to do. At this point, he wasn't comfortable with being out here all by himself. At the same time, he wasn't far from the lake. At the very least, he should go the rest of the way and check on those cabins.

Cursing under his breath, he buckled himself in and floored the accelerator. The idea of working overtime was no longer appealing. He wanted to be in and out as quickly as possible. With that thought in mind, he wondered what the nature of Diego's call really was. All the dispatcher said was 'incident' and 'emergency'. At the time, it was easy to write it off as either an exaggeration or a prank.

But now?

He was zooming along at seventy miles an hour. About a thousand feet ahead was the three-way intersection. A right turn would take him straight to the cabins on the south side.

A blur of motion lifted his eyes to the trees.

There it was again! That weird-looking dragonfly-bird-thing, still making pace despite the fact that he increased his speed by thirty miles per hour. It vanished behind the trees on the right.

Ford tried to force it from his mind. *Just a bird.*

As he came within five hundred feet of the intersection, he began to ease on the brakes.

Out from the trees came that bird. This time, it was not twenty-five feet above him, but instead, level with his vehicle.

"Whoa!"

It truly was shaped like a dragonfly. Its wings buzzed as such. It had an abdomen like a scorpion's tail and numerous appendages that resembled insect legs. The 'foot' of one of those legs spun like a drill bit. Next, the impossible happened. Hot blue fire spat from its end, like the flame from a blowtorch.

The thing landed on the hood and pressed the flame to the windshield. It cut through the glass as though it was paper. Screaming, Ford swerved to the left, cutting across the road directly into the woods. Miraculously, he managed to miss the first several trees before plowing directly into one.

The engine crumpled and the front tires burst. Ford's head came down on the wheel, resulting in a gash across his brow. The bird-thing took off to the sky, its wings giving off a mechanical whirring sound.

Ford fumbled with the door handle with his left hand, eventually finding it. To his relief, the door wasn't jammed, though it needed a good push to get it open all the way. He stepped out, then leaned against the wreckage. He shut his eyes and put his hands to his temple. His whole skull was throbbing.

Partially disoriented, he patted his shirt for his speaker mic. "Dispatch? Sheriff? Anybody?" The lack of response triggered full-blown panic. "Come on! Pick up, damn it! Why the hell is nobody answering?!"

Zip!

His eyes went to the next tree over. High on its trunk was that *thing* which caused him to crash.

Ford stared, frozen by awe, fear, and confusion. As he had previously observed, the thing did in fact have an insectoid shape. Oddly enough, that wasn't the weirdest thing about it. The sun's rays stretched through the canopy and bounced off its brown body.

It was made of metal.

Ford didn't ponder over what it was and why it attacked him. Those questions would come later. For now, he was solely interested in preventing future attacks.

He drew his sidearm and pointed it at the bug-thing. "Sayonara."

Slash!

Ford saw the glint of metal moving vertically, then the splattering of his blood. His severed arm hit the ground in two pieces, the hand still gripping his pistol.

He staggered backward, watching the blood fountain from the stub at his elbow. Slowly, he turned his head to the right. Had he not been disoriented and fixated on the bug-thing, he might have noticed the giant humanoid emerging from the woods.

The creature looked at the wreck through a high-tech, yet ancient-looking helmet, then cocked its head back as though hit with inspiration. It grabbed Ford by the shirt and forced him to the tree. With amazing strength, it pushed against his Interceptor with its other hand. The vehicle scooted back a couple of feet, which was all the thing apparently needed. It forced the Deputy's head between the engine and the tree trunk, then slipped its fingers through a gap in the hood and pulled the Interceptor back down.

Smash!

Ford's legs spasmed as his skull and shoulders were sandwiched by his own patrol car.

Satiated by a day of sadistic events, the Convict watched the twitching lawman gradually slow to stillness. Though from a distant galaxy, it recognized authority when it saw one. This human wore a uniform and was equipped with a department-issued vehicle, communication equipment, and weapons. Fortunately, it was all primitive compared to the technology of its drone.

Over the course of monitoring the human's approach, the drone was able to home in on its radio signal and create interference. The lawman was never able to call for help.

Eventually, more lawmen would come in search of their man. When that time came, the Convict's fun would reach new levels. Picking off a whole squad of armed humans would not only be satisfying, but exhilarating. Hunting dumb, unsuspecting victims would never get old—especially not this species—but battling armed opponents was something else entirely. Sometimes, the Convict enjoyed a challenge. Victory fed its ever-growing superiority complex. All it had to do was wait and let its drone monitor the road.

In the meantime, it moved south to return to the lakefront habitats. Those other humans would be arriving shortly.

CHAPTER 18

"How many of those things were in there?" Kelly said.

"At least three," Norman replied.

"I don't get it," Ross said. "What do you think happened in there? Did they get cabin fever or something? Did one go berserk?"

Diego kept the pedal floored. The truck juddered as it sped over the uneven dirt road, giving its occupants the feeling that it would break apart.

"You're asking about the psychology of something we didn't even know existed until a few minutes ago," he said. "Something that isn't even from Earth."

"That doesn't mean there aren't a few constants across the galaxy," Kelly said. "Just because something's technologically superior doesn't mean it does not succumb to mental illness. Or evil."

"I don't know," Diego said. "We don't know what happened, why they landed here, if they're all dangerous or if there's a bad apple in the group."

"You saw what those things were wearing," Norman said. "I don't know much about aliens, but I know about uniforms. There was something 'formal' about that one."

"What? You think they were ambassadors?" Ross said. "Secret service agents, maybe? What are you getting at, Norman?"

Diego sped past the main road, putting them roughly a minute away from the cabins. He looked to the darkening sky to the south. He had hoped the incoming weather would blow east, but sure enough, it was heading right toward them instead. In an hour or so, the heavens would have this whole area drenched.

The trees were already shaking in the breeze. Like swells from an incoming storm, the wind was gradually picking up strength.

"Everybody, keep it together. Let's get the others and get the hell out of here. Then we can speculate all we want."

The cabins came into view. Ted's van was still there. Everything outside appeared normal. Mostly normal. Nobody was out.

"They must be inside," Diego said.

Kelly made a face. "Well, in Ted and Pam's case... Let's just say there's a good reason why they're probably inside."

"Oh..." Had the occasion been different, Diego would have laughed. He steered into the driveway to park alongside the van. "I'll leave it to you guys to handle that situation. I'll run over to my place and grab—"

POP!

"Whoa!"

Everyone shifted in their seats as the front tires erupted in a display of black rubber shreds. As the truck scooted to a stop, the back tires burst as well.

Diego stepped out and looked at the damage. All four tires were not only flattened but completely ravaged.

The others exited the vehicle, equally dumbfounded.

"How... just... how?" Kelly said.

"There's no sharp gravel or glass in the driveway," Norman said.

"Unless Jamie did something stupid," Ross said. "Like dropping beer bottles in the driveway. I wouldn't put anything past him."

"Glass wouldn't make the tires rupture like this," Diego said. He looked at Ted's van, then inhaled deeply to control the fresh wave of anxiety that coursed through his body. "This wasn't an accident."

The others joined him beside the van, each having their own unique reaction to the sight of flat tires. Unlike the ones on Diego's truck, they had not burst but instead were slashed.

Diego checked the front passenger tire. There were two lacerations, spaced out at six inches. It was the same for the other three tires as well. Either the perpetrator was meticulous about the way he slashed tires, or a dual blade was used.

Diego knelt beside the left rear tire of his truck. With his knife, he moved some of the gravel and rubber shreds.

"What are you looking for?" Norman asked.

"Anything out of the ordinary..." He lifted a large flake of tire rubber which lay behind the wheel. Beneath it was something that appeared to be tiny pieces of glass.

Kelly stood over his shoulder, intrigued by the find. Having worked in a lab, she had seen small vials dropped, shattered, and crushed. This was a similar thing, only the glass had that greenish tint.

Ross knelt by the rear passenger tire. "Got some over here, too."

"Over here," Norman said. He was standing a few feet behind Ross, looking at the gravel. At his feet were little items that resembled green marbles.

Diego approached, waving his hands in warning at the others. "Don't touch them. Definitely don't step on them." He knelt for a closer look. The green texture inside the glass appeared to shift as if it was a tiny

Rorschach image. Like clouds in the atmosphere, the stuff moved constantly.

Diego looked at Kelly. "You're the chemist. You recognize this stuff?"

"No, but I suspect it has an explosive capability," she said. "Considering you ran over a few of them, the fact that we know there's an extraterrestrial presence in this area..." She could not believe she was saying that in a serious sense, "...the slashed tires on Ted's van..."

Everyone connected the dots.

"It's here," Diego said. *And it doesn't want us to leave.* He grabbed Patrick Gawdy's rifle out of his truck and passed it to Norman. "I trust you know how to use one of these."

Norman accepted the weapon and pointed the muzzle down. "What's the plan? We've got no ride."

"I'm gonna run to my cabin and get my gun. Then we'll hole up inside your cabin until help gets here." Diego looked at Ross. "Hey, that computer of yours. You upload articles on it?"

"Yeah..." Ross replied.

"You need the cell tower, or do you upload via satellite?"

Ross smiled with relief. "Satellite."

"Good. Get a message to the Sheriff. Hurry." Diego turned on his heel and sprinted for his cabin.

Kelly watched him until he disappeared behind the trees. Afterward, she walked with Norman into the cabin. Ross was at the picnic table collecting his laptop. Its battery was low and needed to be charged. He followed them inside and took it to the living room couch where the charger was plugged in.

To everyone's surprise, the inside of the cabin was dead silent.

"Jamie?!" Norman shouted. "Ted? Pam?"

Kelly went up the stairs. "Guys?!" She was relieved to hear one of the bedroom doors open. A hazy-eyed Ted poked his head out. He was shirtless and wore a towel over his waist.

There was no need to ask whether he saw or heard anything strange while they were gone. After his fun, he had obviously fallen asleep, making him oblivious to the damage to his van.

"Everything alright?" Ted asked.

"No. It's not," Kelly said.

"You and Pam need to get dressed," Norman said. "I'm not kidding. This is an emergency."

Ted was wide awake now. At that moment, he realized Norman was holding a rifle. "Where'd you get that?"

"It's Patrick Gawdy's," Norman said. "He's dead. So are many others. There's a killer in the woods."

"Yeah," Ross shouted from the couch. "Get Pam and join us down here. And where the hell is Jamie?"

"He… I don't know. Pam and I made him go outside." He glanced into his room and back at them. "She's not in here either. Her bathing suit is gone. She must've gone for a swim."

Kelly, Ross, and Norman shared the same alarmed look. The journalist went to the window. "I don't see her out there."

"Oh, shit…" Norman shouldered the rifle and went out the door. He was greeted by a gust of wind and the sound of distant thunder. That storm was an hour out at most. "Fucking weather."

Kelly ran to the middle of the yard, cupping her hands over her mouth. "Pam?! Jamie?! Where are you?!"

Ted and Ross followed them out, the former now dressed in a t-shirt, shorts, and sandals.

"Pam?!" Ted shouted.

For several minutes, they continued calling for their two missing members. The only one to respond was Diego, who jogged back onto their property. He had his pistol strapped to his thigh. A pouch on the belt contained two spare magazines.

"Someone missing?" he asked.

"Jamie and Pam," Kelly said.

"Maybe they went for a walk," Ted said. "I'll get in my van and take a drive."

"You can't," Ross said. "Your tires are slashed. Can't use the detective's truck either. Something came by and boobytrapped the driveway."

Ted's brow furrowed. "Some*thing*?!" He looked at everyone's faces, hoping somebody would announce that this was all some stupid joke. "Will someone please explain what the hell is going on?" Ted frantically said. "You guys said something about finding bodies in the woods? Patrick Gawdy's dead? Now my girlfriend's missing."

Diego watched the darkening skies to the south.

"Pretty soon, we won't have much visibility. We need to find them now."

"Over here," Norman said. He picked up an empty bottle that was lying near the trees. "Some of the grass is bent over here. Looks like Jamie went in this direction."

"What about Pam?" Ted asked.

Kelly put a hand on his shoulder. "We'll find her. Just keep calm."

With his hand resting over his holster, Diego pressed into the woods. Kelly was right behind him, and Ted behind her. They veered to the left, taking one section of the woods while Norman and Ross took the right.

Both groups yelled for Jamie and Pam, with no response.

The wind coursed through the trees like an angry flood, producing a whistling sound. Over the course of the next few minutes, that whistle began to resemble a demented howl. Kelly did not consider herself superstitious, but she felt a strange spiritual presence, and not a good one.

The sunlight had faded under grey clouds. Distant thunder rumbled a few miles behind her, its echoes adding to the haunted atmosphere. All of a sudden, Kelly wished for the mundaneness of her normal life. The thought of that chemistry lab which she found painfully boring now seemed warm and welcoming. Her mild depression, her resentment over her recent breakup, the lack of excitement in her life—she would never take what she had for granted ever again. If there was any positive to take from this nightmare, it was that.

First, she needed the nightmare to end.

"Guys?!" It was Norman's voice. "Over here."

They hustled through the woods and found Norman and Ross standing by a tree. They were looking down, alarmed and disturbed. At their feet was a puddle of dried blood. Bugs and worms had helped themselves to it. Mosquitoes buzzed around their heads, drawn by the odor.

Diego knelt by the puddle. It had mostly absorbed into the soil. The little bit that splattered onto the nearby tree was still a bit wet.

"This happened while we were out."

"Whose blood is it?" Ted said. He didn't want to know the answer. He turned around, face beet red, and shouted Pam's name.

Ross went to comfort him. "Ted, bud, we don't know if anything's happened to her—" He jumped after his foot came down on something soft and squishy. Looking down, he felt the blood drain from his face. "Th—th—th… that… that's a…"

The others gathered, each having their own sickened reaction to the sight of Jamie's severed manhood being picked at by bugs.

Ross leaned against a tree, his head spinning. He was barely keeping himself together. The urge to vomit and pass out was strong. Only his resilience kept him from succumbing.

"I think… I think I'm gonna go back to the cabin."

"Good idea," Diego said. "Get online. Get a message to the police. Hell, send one to the Governor's office at this point."

"Okay." Coughing and dry-heaving, Ross turned south and hurried to his cabin, clumsily stumbling over roots and branches in the process.

Norman stayed close with the others. Splitting up no longer seemed like a good idea.

"Which way?" he asked.

Diego looked at the trail of blood and bent grass. The body had been dragged in that direction. He unholstered his pistol and gripped it with both hands, keeping the muzzle low.

"Let's keep going." He looked at the others. "If anyone wants to turn back…"

"No," Ted said.

"I'll stay with you," Kelly said.

Diego nodded. "Okay."

Together, they pressed on.

***

Watery eyes clouded Ross' vision as he trudged through thick underbrush. He arrived in the yard, taking a quick look around before continuing for the cabin. It did not appear that anyone, or thing, was here waiting for him.

He sprinted for the front door, latching it shut behind him. He went to the couch, where he found his laptop in sleep mode. Again and again, he tapped the spacebar to wake it up. As though deliberately trying to irritate him, the stupid computer was slow to activate.

Ross dug his fingernails into his scalp, quickly succumbing to hysteria and anger.

Eventually, the bass code bar came up. Ross tapped his four-digit code and watched the home screen come into view. He tapped the internet icon. The window popped up, showing nothing but a white screen as it struggled to load. As usual, the stupid internet was always slow around here, even with the satellite connection.

Ross rapidly tapped his foot on the floor. "Today please…"

The wind outside kicked up. Feeling moist air striking the back of his neck, Ross spun toward the kitchen. With a pounding heartbeat, he braced himself to see something horrible staring back at him. Instead, all he saw was an open window, the same one Jamie had drunkenly fallen out of yesterday.

He put a hand on his chest and calmed himself. "Whew." He stood up and walked into the kitchen area, keeping his fists closed, as though that would somehow be useful in defending himself. There was nothing in the kitchen and utility area. Nothing but cool summer air warning him that an ugly storm was approaching.

Ross shut the window and returned to the living room couch. By the time he sat down, the Microsoft Firefox home page was up. Ross typed Google in the search bar so he could look up the sheriff's department email.

Sure enough, the internet was slow enough to drive him to madness. The search results appeared, showing the email in the first link. Ross clicked on it, groaning as another slow loading process unfolded.

***

Ted relentlessly called Pam's name, begging the Lord for her to emerge from behind one of those trees. They crossed over two hundred feet of distance, after which the blood trail vanished.

"Maybe we should head back in," Kelly said.

"No!" Ted said. "Pam is still out here somewhere."

"Maybe she went somewhere else," Norman said. "There's no evidence that she wandered out here."

"If you guys want to hide in the cabin, that's on you," Ted said. "I'm not going to write her off."

"I'm not saying that, dude," Norman said. "I'm just exploring all possibilities. We don't even know where Jamie's body has been taken. I don't know…" All four of them went quiet. Beyond the whistling wind was the sound of droplets trickling onto the ground. "Is it raining already?"

Everyone looked at the sky and held their palms out to test the weather. Not a single drop came down.

Diego listened carefully to determine which direction the trickling was coming from. He looked to his left.

"It's coming from over there."

With his gun pointed, he led the group northwest. The sound of buzzing insects created a discomforting ambience. A vile but familiar smell pierced Diego's nostrils. Even without seeing the blood and body parts, he would have known he was walking into the scene of a murder.

They weaved around a grove of underbrush, finding a pool of blood soaking the grass. Everyone looked about, not seeing a body…

…until they looked up.

There he was, slung over a branch. His face was barely recognizable, for his head had been cleaved into three rigid slabs.

The four companions stared open-mouthed. Even the hard-boiled detective was momentarily paralyzed with shock. Once he regained his wits, his attention to detail kicked into gear. There were two incisions in Jamie's skull, spaced four inches apart. It was the same weapon that slashed the tires on Ted's van and beheaded that poor girl in the tent.

Kelly's legs shook underneath her. She backed away, nearly collapsing with each step. Her hands shook over her mouth, her throat compressing. Her frantic mind fired numerous contradictory signals. She wanted to scream, but her tight throat made it difficult to do so. She wanted to run, but her legs were turning to jelly.

On the contrary, Ted easily succumbed to the terror his eyes beheld. He pivoted on his heels and ran.

"Oh, God! Oh, Jesus! Oh, Gah—" He came to a sudden stop. "OH GOD!!!"

The others ran in his direction, finding him standing over Pam's naked corpse. She was lying face-down in the dirt, her eyes wide and pointed upward, her arms stretched high over her head. Her fingers were coiled, the ground around them scuffed, and her fingernails blackened with dirt. There was mild bruising between her shoulders, but no lacerations and no blood. By the looks of it, she had died of fright.

Diego checked for a pulse, confirming the obvious.

"What did it do to her?" Kelly said.

Diego stood up, noting the position of her legs and the nauseating redness in-between. The answer was something he did not want to ponder heavily on. All he knew was that this killer had a mindset that was fucked up beyond all recognition.

"Pam!" Ted cried over and over.

"Let's get back to the cabin," Diego said.

"We can't leave her here!" Ted said.

"We have to," Diego said. "I'm sorry, but she's gone. There's nothing we can do for her now. We need to get indoors and hope to God that Ross managed to get a message to the Sheriff."

Ted gave one last look at his dead girlfriend, then conceded to the detective's point. Numb with grief and shock, he followed the others south to Ross' property.

***

Poncho County Police Department

Please send help. My name is Ross Harker. We are located in a cabin on the south end of Lake Fairview. There is someone or something in the woods. We found one of our group members dead. Our vehicles have been damaged. We can't escape. We need help immediately.

We have already found several other bodies in campsites near here. Patrick Gawdy is dead. The phones aren't working, nor is the landline. Bring all of the firepower you can. Alert the government. We have a confirmed sighting of an extraterrestrial spacecraft a quarter mile or so northeast of the lake.

Ross shook his head and put his finger on the backspace. "No, they'll read that and think it's a prank. Better to leave out any mention of a killer alien. We'll cross that bridge when they get here."

He began typing a new second paragraph, emphasizing the finding of bodies and their lack of transportation. He kept it short and concise, limiting it to three sentences.

"Much better... Oh, wait... No, no, no!" The computer tab went white after losing connection once again. It was at this point where Ross nearly violated his own sacred rule of computers: don't punch the screen. Violence and technology were not good bedfellows.

He twirled his hand, trying to will the computer to reconnect. As soon as the signal came back, he clicked send. Another loading symbol...

Message sent.

Ross fell against the back of the sofa. "Thank God." It didn't bring much comfort. Not much did after catching the sight of Jamie's 'remains' in the woods. Nature's commotion aggravated his nerves further. The whistling of the wind outside, the chirping of birds escaping the nearby storm, and the rumbling ambiance was making his knees shake and his bowels enflame. He felt as though an evil spirit hovered over Poncho County.

A brisk chill struck his shoulder, making him shiver. Next came the realization that the wind was actually entering the cabin through the back window. He got up and looked.

To his dismay, the window was open again.

Didn't I shut that?

He stepped into the kitchen, this time holding the fireplace poker. Holding it high, he approached the window. Nothing was there. He even went as far as to poke his head outside. Nothing was standing behind the cabin or in the driveway. Despite this, his nerves were nearing the breaking point. He distinctly remembered closing that window. There was no way it would open again by itself.

Ross noticed the sprinkling of dirt on the sink and on the floor pad. The nozzle was bent forward slightly, as though something heavy had leaned on it. Ross did not hear anything. Then again, he had spent the last few minutes cursing nonstop at his computer.

Now, he was cursing nonstop at his current predicament. It had come in through the window.

"Oh God… Oh shit!"

He looked in every direction, unable to locate it.

It's in here. It's toying with me. It's sick! It's demented! It's completely fucked up!

Ross had no intention of standing around, waiting for the thing to ambush him. He spun on his heels and ran for the front door. He twisted the knob, yanked it open… and beheld the sight of the seven-foot giant standing on the other side. It stared at him through that bizarre mask, eyes flashing red.

Dual blades protruded from its wrist gauntlet.

Ross backed into the living room area, the invader promptly following him. It raised its gauntlet, the blades shining from the ceiling light.

"No… NOOOOO!"

SLASH!

He felt a swift, cold sensation in his belly, then the warm wet drizzling of blood and intestines. They fell onto the floor like spilled pasta, coiling into a small red and brown mound.

Foggy curtains clouded his vision. By the time those curtains closed, Ross had fallen backward, reduced to a stiff corpse who stared blankly at the ceiling.

The Convict watched with great amusement as the life left the stupid human. Part of it wished it had toyed with him a little more. Like a moth to the flame, he had gone to the open window which the Convict had opened from the outside. The dummy fell for the trap, and in an attempt to flee, essentially let his killer into his home.

It was a good kill, one that the Convict was glad it managed to pull off. Its travel time from the large road to the habitats worked to its advantage. The group had split up, allowing it to isolate one of its members.

On the furniture was an electronic device. The Convict took a look at the screen, seeing a human message on the computer having been sent. Somehow, despite using its drone to destroy the power lines and disable the communication tower, the dead human was able to get a signal out. Possibly through a wireless connection to orbiting satellites. It was common sense to believe that the human, in the last minutes of his life, was alerting the authorities of their predicament. If the message successfully made it to its destination, then reinforcements would be arriving sooner rather than later.

No matter. The Convict was up for a challenge. First, it would have its fun with the remaining group members.

With a swipe of its blades, it carved the device into three pieces, completely cutting the group off from the outside world. Not that it made a difference. Their lives only had a few minutes remaining.

The drone completed a new scan of the surrounding area and sent the data to the Convict's helmet. It was delighted to see that they were returning to the habitat. As it turned out, their lives only had a few *seconds* remaining instead.

It shut the door and waited.

***

They emerged from the woods, exhausted, flabbergasted, and flustered. Even Norman and Diego, both highly trained in professions that included great stress, had to work to keep their wits intact. As they retreated to their fortress, they exchanged information on defensive positions and how to barricade the doors and windows. There was no debate, no clash of egos. Just unified men with a goal to survive.

"Ross better have sent that email," Norman said.

"He did. I'm sure he did," Kelly said.

"I don't understand. What's happening?!" Ted cried. "Will someone tell me what's out there? None of this is making sense!"

Norman went for the door. "I'll give you the short version. There's a killer out there and it's not from this world. Yes, literally an alien. We'll tell you more after we're inside." He grabbed the doorknob and began to twist.

"Norman!" Diego shouted.

Norman looked at the former detective, who was pointing at the door's bottom edge. Red fluid had pooled under the door. Norman touched it with his fingertips. Blood.

He nodded at Diego, then gently shushed at Kelly and Ted.

Diego made them back up, mouthing *it's behind the door.* He stepped in front of him, finger on the trigger of his pistol. With his other hand, he counted down from three.

At zero, Norman shoved the door open and jumped back.

The alien lunged, its blades missing him by inches. It stepped outside to pursue. Sunlight burning through the grey sky cast its gloomy radiance on its monstrous figure.

As Diego and Norman suspected, it was exactly like the ones in the ship, except its attire was different. There was no uniform, no sign of allegiance to anything but itself. Its mask was marked by years of combat, its boots dirtied by a life off the grid. Its attire and technology indicated intelligence. Thus, its actions were driven purely by bloodlust and not some kind of horrible instinct.

It stopped, recognizing the weapons that were now pointed in its direction.

"Welcome to Earth," Diego said.

BANG! BANG! BANG! BANG! BANG!

He and Norman unloaded their weapons into the creature. It shifted with the many impacts, jolting to the left, then the right, backing up into the cabin.

Diego shot mercilessly, emptying thirteen rounds within seven seconds. The last two rounds were reserved for the creature's head.

BANG! BANG!

The alien threw its head back, then fell. It landed with a thunderous *boom*, cracking the floorboards underneath the carpet.

Kelly and Ted uncapped their ears and looked at the extraterrestrial. It lay on its back, motionless, its arms out to the side like a holy figure. The armor plate was scarred and dented from bullet impact.

"Is it dead?" Kelly asked.

"Hope so," Norman said. He cranked the lever of his .30-.30. "Because I'm out."

Diego ejected his magazine and loaded a fresh one. Slowly, he approached the alien.

Just for good measure, he put a few more bullets into it. The body twitched as the bullets made contact. This time, he saw a little bit of green blood pooling on the floor.

One thing was certain: he'd done some damage.

Laying a few feet farther in the living room was Ross with a torn-open midsection.

"Is he…?" Kelly already knew the answer.

Diego shook his head.

Ted stood straight, his grief shifting into anger. "That's what killed Pam?! That's the thing that…" He couldn't bring himself to speak of what it did to her. Uncontrollable rage birthed from the thought.

Fuming, he marched up to the thing.

"Wait," Diego said, raising a hand to stop him. Ted smacked his arm away and went up to the alien. With great pleasure, he stepped in the blood that leaked from its wounds.

"You still alive?! I hope so; that way you'd feel this!" He kicked it in the head, then in the side. The fact that this thing was an extraterrestrial had no bearing on his emotion. To Ted, it was no different than an escaped felon from a state prison. It was evil and deserved to feel all the pain in the universe before dying.

Each hit felt good. So good, that he wanted more. It wasn't fair that he was not able to join in on shooting the thing. All he had was the hope that it had enough life left to experience his revenge. He kicked it again. "That's for Pam, you twisted, stupid… MONSTER!"

Ted stomped twice more on its head before moving to its pelvic area. He raised his foot over its groin.

"I hope you're still alive, so you can feel *this*." With all of his might, he drove his foot onto its crotch.

His hopes were realized.

The thing sprang up with a high-pitched shriek. One of its hands found Ted's neck and squeezed. He gagged and grabbed at the creature's wrist. Suddenly, his feet were dangling beneath him.

It stood, holding the human with one hand. Ted's eyes bulged as the grip on his neck intensified. He floundered, his feet thrashing several inches over the floor.

Diego took aim but could not get a clean shot. With no choice but to get close, he ran through the doorway for a point-blank shot at the alien's head. That metallic head turned like that of a praying mantis. Still holding Ted high, it swung its left arm, backhanding Diego across the chin.

A moment later, he was on his back, dazed, the pistol bouncing from his grasp.

He leaned up, propping himself on his elbows. When his vision cleared, he saw the thing driving Ted to his knees. The alien stood behind him, holding him by the back of the neck. It pulled its bladed arm back, lining the tips up with the back of Ted's skull.

No amount of struggling could free him of its grasp. He shook, he clawed, he squealed, after which he spasmed.

The alien drove the blades home. The tips reappeared out of Ted's face, one of them through his eye socket. On its tip was the eyeball, gooey as a crushed grape.

It ripped the blades out of the side of his head and set its gaze on the man who shot it.

"Diego! Get out!" Kelly shouted.

He was on his feet but could not go anywhere. The creature stood between him and the door. There was no back entrance to this cabin. The only alternative was through the window.

Norman had realized the same thing.

"Heads up, Diego!"

A moment later, he was on the other side of the window with the .30-.30 raised like a baseball bat. A powerful swing reduced the window to small shards. He swung a second time, removing the shards that protruded from the bottom frame, allowing Diego safe passage.

The thing took a step forward with intent to kill.

Diego dove through the window, somersaulting to his feet on the other side. The alien slashed, the tips of its blades nicking the back of his shirt on the way out. Without hesitation, it followed him out the window. Despite its size, it moved with the grace of a ballet dancer or a seasoned martial artist. It was a being of superior strength, one that Diego did not want to go toe-to-toe with, even if it didn't have the blades.

Norman, however, did not share the same mindset. He threw the rifle at the creature, the butt striking it in the helmet. The blow was enough to make it take a couple of steps back, but otherwise, the alien was unfazed. Norman was not intimidated. He saw the blood leaking from its sides. Some of their bullets had made their way through its Kevlar-like gear. It was not immortal. It *could* be killed. With it injured, there was probably no better opportunity for him to fight it.

"Let's go," Diego said. "Back to my cabin."

He clasped hands with Kelly and ran for his hideout. For a moment, it seemed Norman was following them. When they looked back, they saw that he had instead gone for the log pile. Norman yanked the sharp ax from the top log, then turned to face the alien.

"Norman!" Kelly shouted. "What are you doing?!"

"Don't do it," Diego shouted. "Come on, man. Run!"

Norman shook his head. "You guys go." He held the ax in one hand and one of his knives in the other. "This motherfucker is unwelcome here." He pointed the ax at the fiend. "You hear me? You *understand* me?! You killed my friends. Now you're going to wish you invaded some other rock."

The alien seemed to acknowledge his challenge. It took what appeared to be a fighting stance, slowly advancing on the human. It held its arms out, the bladed arm tucked back like a boxer ready to throw a hook.

Kelly screamed. "Norman, DON'T!"

The veteran charged, bringing the ax down with all of his might. The alien quickly deflected it with its gauntlet blades, parrying the ax and throwing Norman off balance. He swung again, this time in a horizontal motion. The alien simply caught the ax by the stem, keeping the blade at bay.

Norman tugged, unable to outmuscle his foe. Not ready to concede, he lunged with his knife.

SLASH!

The knife—and his hand—fell to the ground.

Norman stared at the raw stub at the end of his forearm, which was now gushing blood. As shock and lightheadedness set in, so did the realization of his failure. All of his life, he had trained hard with the anticipation of having an epic battle. Fate had brought him to that moment, with the worst of mankind's foes. Not only did he fail, but he failed miserably and in a matter of seconds.

The alien yanked the ax from his other hand, tossed it up in the air, and caught it by the handle as it came back down. It gave the manmade weapon a brief glance of admiration, then brought the blade down on Norman's head. His skull opened like the mouth of a Venus flytrap.

With Norman dead, Kelly and Diego resumed their retreat. The alien let the corpse fall and sprinted to pursue.

"Go! Get inside!" Diego said. They raced through the sunroom and into the cabin's living room entrance. When he turned to slam the door shut, the alien was already on the other side of the screen window. He latched the door, then stepped back.

He heard the sunroom door get ripped off its hinges. A moment later, it effortlessly passed through the living room door, exploding it into a dozen pieces which flew into the cabin.

It was not wasting time with its last two victims. There was no sense in trying to lure them out, or toy with them. All it wanted was to end their miserable lives for its own entertainment.

For Diego, it was obvious that this was the case. He knew how killers operated. Some had motivations ranging from revenge to jealousy. Every so often, there came a demented bastard who simply enjoyed it. It didn't matter that this thing was from some other galaxy. The trademarks were all there. It killed indiscriminately. Not even its own species was off limits.

It had probably killed a thousand species on a thousand planets. Now, he was next.

"Get back," he said to Kelly. "Get out the back door."

"What about you?"

"Just go."

"But…"

"GO!"

Kelly retreated out the back door, leaving Diego alone to face the intruder.

Diego waited for the blades to rise, then dove to the left, dodging the creature's attempt to behead him. He scampered on all fours, with nowhere to go but the bathroom.

The alien came after him, encouraged by the fact that the stupid human had boxed himself into a compartment with no escape.

Diego was back on his feet. He turned around and faced his doom.

"You wanna rip my guts out? Go ahead!" He put his arms out, daring the thing to follow through. "Whatcha waiting for?"

The alien advanced, gauntlet raised. With a mighty thrust, it committed to impaling the former detective, only to be foiled by the simplest of hazards.

Its foot snagged on the buzzsaw cord, catching the creature off guard. Diego hopped onto the toilet seat right as his attacker plummeted onto the floor. Three hundred pounds of extraterrestrial mass splintered the tile with a thunderous thud.

Diego seized the opportunity, hopping over the alien and landing behind it. He found the buzzsaw cable, which had been yanked from the outlet by the alien's foot. He plugged it back in and activated the saw.

The creature propped itself up on its hands and looked over its shoulder, just in time to see the spinning blade cut into the soft, exposed meat on its calf.

It reared its head back and let out an enraged trumpeting sound. Diego drove the blade through the muscle and into the bone, triggering another cry. He withdrew the blade and jumped back as the alien clumsily slashed at him. The blades missed him, but did manage to catch the cord, deactivating the power tool.

Diego threw the buzzsaw, bouncing it off the alien's helmet.

It stood up, screeching again after putting weight on its injured leg. Now, it advanced on Diego with the same intent, but with added motivation. It was angry now and desired revenge. Diego's death would be slow and excruciating.

Knowing this, he bolted out the back door.

Kelly was standing near the shed with a shovel in hand, ready to take a swing at the alien. She was relieved to see it was Diego coming out the door instead.

"Oh, Diego. Thank God."

"Keep back. It's coming."

As soon as those words escaped his throat did the thing emerge on the back porch. Limping on its bad leg, it left a trail of green blood as it pursued its victim.

"We should run," Kelly said.

"No," Diego said. "Stay off the driveway. It might've left more of those boobytraps."

"What do we do?!" she said. Her voice grew frantic as the thing advanced. "Diego?! What do we do?!"

"Give me the shovel!"

"You're gonna fight it?!"

He looked at the alien, now a mere ten feet away from him. "Yes."

Kelly cursed under her breath, then tossed him the shovel. She backed away, keeping to the side of the driveway to avoid being injured by those marble-things. She shut her eyes, not able to bear another horrible death.

Diego moved at the thing, shovel held high. It raised its arm, ready to block a swing directed at its head. Anticipating this, Diego swung low, hitting the injured leg with the blade.

The alien screeched and moved back. Now even more enraged, it moved with a bloodlust unmatched by anything in the universe.

Diego backed toward the shed, holding the shovel like an ancient spear. "Aw. Did I piss you off?"

The thing growled, ignoring the pain in its leg in favor of the satisfaction of slaying this earthling.

Diego passed by the front-right corner of the shed, slowing to let the alien close in. He brought the shovel over his shoulder for another swing. The alien did not slow. It closed within reach, ready to yank the tool from his hand and break all four of his limbs with it.

Instead, he swung straight up.

The blade struck the hornets' nest, splitting it down the middle. A swarm of angry black insects took to the air, forming a black cloud. Diego dropped the shovel and ran as fast as he could, leaving the dumbfounded alien in the midst of the attack.

It spun on its feet, completely perplexed. Its armor could only defend against so many stings. Like ants overcoming a huge beetle, these wasps easily found chinks in the armor, repeatedly stinging and biting.

It slashed and spun, baffled by the abrupt attack by these tiny earthbound creatures. They operated as one unit with a single hive mind. Their objective was simple; eliminate the threat to their hive.

Pain flooded the creature's senses. No amount of slashing would deter the swarm. They were dead set on injecting its veins with venom until it dropped dead. Their small size worked to their advantage. It was as though the alien was battling an angry mist.

A rare moment occurred in the creature's life. It turned north and fled, shrieking as the swarm continued to sting it. It disappeared behind the grove of trees, its screeching echoing as it crossed Ross' property and into the woods.

Kelly and Diego regrouped at the back door and slammed it shut, keeping the angry swarm outside.

Diego hurried to the front of the cabin and found the screen door. The hinges had been ripped off entirely, forcing him to use electrical tape in a creative way to prop the door up. With them being stuck in this cabin, the last thing they needed was for any hornets to make their way inside.

When he reentered the living room, he was greeted with a hug from an emotionally overwhelmed Kelly.

"You okay?" she said.

"Yeah, I'm in one piece," he said. "How 'bout you?"

She shook her head. "It killed them. It killed them all."

"I know." He hugged her again. "It's gone now."

"But will it be back?"

Diego chose not to answer that directly, for neither of them would like the answer.

"Let's hope the calvary gets here first."

CHAPTER 19

For over two hours, they hunkered down. The storm had arrived, pounding the roof with large raindrops. Kelly had started a fire in the fireplace. She knelt close to it, stirring it with the poke. Despite the summer heat, Diego didn't object. It was human nature to need to control something during uncontrollable times. Besides, there was something soothing about a fire that somewhat quelled his own anxiety.

Diego went from window to window, monitoring the area around the cabin. Every time he looked in the direction of Kelly's cabin, he felt a surge of frustration. His gun was still over there. In normal everyday life, he hated being unarmed. There was a sense of vulnerability he felt when he didn't carry. Today, that vulnerability was multiplied by a hundred.

Of all the times to be unarmed, it had to be while a homicidal alien was stalking his cabin.

He checked the rear window and tested the backdoor lock. Not that it would make a difference. The alien would bust through that door as though it were made of toothpicks. All he could do was keep checking the windows and hope he wouldn't see the large humanoid figure in the yard.

"Damn that rain. As though it wasn't hard enough to see out there," he said. Watching Kelly stir the fire, he realized she needed to hear something a little more optimistic. "Doesn't appear to be anything out there, though."

"Maybe it had a violent allergic reaction to the wasp venom," she said.

"That's actually very possible," Diego said. "It's not from here. If it's new to this planet, its immune system may not be able to handle the diseases and bacteria this world has to offer. Kinda like *War of the Worlds*."

"You think that's why it hasn't returned? You think it's dead?"

"If it isn't, it's thinking twice about coming back," Diego said. He wished he went with the comforting lie that it was dead. Kelly hung her head low. She was barely holding herself together. After losing five friends in gruesome fashion, who could blame her? Her life was forever changed. This lake, which always signified peace and serenity, was now the setting of ungodly horror.

"Sorry," Diego said. "I'm sorry about your friends. I didn't know them well, but it's clear they were all good people."

"They were. Obnoxious, but good," Kelly said.

"Aren't we all when we're in our twenties?" he said. Kelly gave a weak chuckle. Diego sat on the floor next to her. "Sooner or later, the cops will arrive."

"Will they even believe us when we tell them what happened?" Kelly asked.

"We'll take them to the ship," Diego said. "Or, at the very least, tell them where it's located. Even so, they'll see the aftermath of what happened here. As soon as they arrive, I'll tell them to get you into town."

"*If* they arrive," she said. "It's been a few hours since you called."

"Come on, Kel. Don't give up," Diego said. He squeezed her shoulder reassuringly. "We will get out of this. I promise."

He leaned up to glance out through the front door and back windows. Still nothing. Hopefully, Kelly's hypothesis was correct and the creature was dying from the wasp stings. There was no way to know for sure. For now, all he could do was keep her spirits up the best he could. The best way to do that was to keep her mind off their situation.

"So, what was it you did back home? Something to do with chemistry, was it?"

Kelly prodded the fire once more.

"I'm a chemist for a water treatment plant," she said.

"That sounds interesting."

She snorted. "No. It really isn't. It's a bunch of routine work. We check water samples brought in by businesses and residential areas and do checks on the river in our city. It's mundane. *Boring.* As is my life. Everything in my world was boring and uneventful." A long sigh followed the statement. "And I've never appreciated it until now. I swear, if I get out of this, I'll never bitch and moan about my daily grind ever again."

"I guess once you've experienced a seven-foot killer alien coming after you, your priorities kind of change," Diego said.

Kelly chuckled. "Yeah, I suppose you're right." After stirring the fire some more, she felt comfortable enough to move to the sofa. "It's weird how things play out."

"What do you mean?" Diego asked.

"This lake was always my safe haven from misery," Kelly said. "The misery that is… was my life. I don't consider myself an entitled person. We make our own happiness. It's just that I allowed myself to fall into a rut. College and credit card debt, bills, groceries, a boring job I don't care for that pays for all of it. I guess I could make a better effort to improve my situation instead of scrolling through my phone every evening, but I convince myself that I'm trapped. Even my relationships suck. The last guy I dated left me for an eighteen-year-old Instagram-obsessed chick.

"Every time I came to this lake, it was with the intent to forget about everything. Instead, I end up fixating on it even more. This year is different, though. That thing you said about priorities is true. I feel a whole new appreciation for the things waiting for me back home. I have a nice apartment, a decent-paying job with a pension and good benefits. I've known people who'd love to have what I've got. And that ex-boyfriend of mine?" She chuckled again. "Why am I so beaten up over him? I dodged a bullet!"

"Took the words right out my mouth," Diego said.

The two of them shared a laugh. His mission of alleviating Kelly's anxiety, even if only a little bit, was successful.

"What about you?" she said.

"What about me?"

Kelly looked around at the interior of this cabin. "You come here—all alone, considering the vacant state of the guest room. This was the first place you came to following being cleared of criminal charges following the Stader situation. If I were to play 'armchair psychologist' I'd say you were coming here to forget about the woes of your life as well."

Diego kept silent for a moment. He wasn't sure if he was avowing the question because it was too personal, or because she was right.

He took a seat next to her and watched the flames dance.

"I was a detective," he said. "I've put away all kinds of people and seen all kinds of heinous acts. I don't have any sad backstory. I became a cop because I wanted to kick the shit out of criminals. Pure and simple. I'm not talking about traffic violators. I mean murderers, traffickers, rapists, drug smugglers… Simply put, I don't like criminals. I get a thrill seeing the looks on their faces when I bust their asses. If they resist arrest, it's even better. It's gotten me in trouble with the department, but believe me, I've received more 'thanks' than you can count from victims and their family members."

It was his turn to sigh.

"Unfortunately, no matter how hardened you pretend to be, you can't shake some of the stuff you encounter. Sometimes, you feel like you need to get away from it all." He gestured at the porch and lake. "Then, you make a mistake and shoot someone who didn't need to be shot. The department quickly throws your name under the bus to ease their own backlash. You find out they would happily have indicted you had it not been for irrefutable video evidence. You say to hell with it all."

He looked over at her, seeing a young woman who felt safe in his presence against the evildoer that lurked somewhere outside.

"You were right. We come here to forget, but instead we remember. I remember why I became a cop in the first place."

"Because you want to protect people?"

"That…" He stood up and grabbed a beer from the fridge, "…and I fucking hate criminals. *Especially* ones from space."

He drained the can and crushed it in his grip.

CHAPTER 20

"Of all the idiots that had to be stuck with this car on this godforsaken day, it had to be me."

It was the fourth time in ten minutes Deputy Jimmy Baile mouthed that same phrase. Car Six was the bane of the department's existence. Though referred to as Car Six, it actually wasn't a car, but an old Ford Ranger. Once it was going over forty miles per hour, Jimmy felt its engine would explode at any moment. The muffler always had a hole in it, the air conditioning didn't work, and to top things off, the front right headlight wasn't working.

He could barely see the three vehicles in front of him. After Deputy Ford failed to check in via radio or phone, Sheriff Eddie Wingard started growing concerned. Next came a deeply concerning email from someone named Ross Harker, stating that he and his party had discovered dead bodies near the lake. Following Ford's odd radio silence and Diego Tritton's bizarre phone call hours earlier, the Sheriff went from nonchalant to borderline frantic. Every attempt to contact both Ford and Tritton went unanswered.

The string of oddities was lengthened by the sudden lack of cell service in this part of the county. Once the team of deputies left the station, Eddie radioed to Jimmy Baile, *"Car Six, when we near the cell tower, make a turn on the trail and check it out. We might have to have someone come out and take a look at it."*

Jimmy watched the rain pelt his windshield as he followed the line of cars down the main road. He could barely see Car Four, an Interceptor roughly a hundred feet in front of him.

On each side of them, the trees were dancing in the wind, pelting the puny vehicles with leaves and pinecones. It was hard to see anything at this point. If there was a crime scene in the woods, it would be easy to miss.

Easier to miss was the trail which led to the cell tower. Had it not been for the yellow sign, Jimmy would have passed it altogether.

"Shit!"

He hit the brakes, nearly putting the Ford Ranger in a tailspin. As he backed up, he quickly lost sight of his fellow deputies in the fog and rain. It came as a surprise that none of them chastised him over the radio for his clumsy driving, or that Eddie didn't offer a reminder about checking out the cell tower.

Not that Jimmy was complaining.

He carefully drove the truck through the narrow trail. The world around him grew increasingly dark and ominous as he pierced the woods.

Of course, the stupid county couldn't have placed this tower in a less inconvenient spot. There were plenty of areas farther back where the tower would have done its job while being more accessible. But no, it had to be here of all places.

Wiper blades brushed away green leaves and blotches of water, barely granting him adequate visual of the trail. Twice already he flinched, hearing the crunch of a broken branch under his tires.

"This is just great. I'm gonna get a flat! Or crash. Whatever the case, this stupid so-called truck is gonna meet its end, and I'm gonna get the heat for it."

Crunch!

Another stupid branch.

None of the sensors lit up—assuming they were even working to begin with. Jimmy didn't think about that. He assumed they were working and pressed on.

After what felt like an eternity of dirt trail, he reached the cell tower. It was surrounded by a metal fence which was locked shut. Opening the gate was not the issue—each deputy had the key on their keyset. Figuring out which key it was, in this rain, was the issue.

"Oh, hell."

He put the truck in park and opened the door. Braving the weather, he ran to the gate. Sure enough, the first key didn't work. Nor did the second. Or the third.

"Oh, come on! Why do we need so many damn keys to begin with?! We don't even use most of them. It's not like we're operating in a big city block for chrissake!"

Rain stung his forehead as he fumbled for the next key. Much to his relief, this one worked. He pushed the gate open and ran to the cell tower. Already, he was at his wits end. All he planned to do at this point was take a quick glance at all the boxes, assume everything was fine, and get the hell out of here. He was no electronics expert anyway. Unless there was obvious damage, he wouldn't know if anything was wrong to begin with.

Jimmy reached the foot of the tower.

"Oh…"

He stared through the mist and rain, perplexed at the sight of a smoking distribution box. The base band unit looked as though someone had taken a blowtorch to it. Fibers were exposed and split. He couldn't see the remote radio unit up near the top of the tower, but he could see plenty of scorched markings lining the steel. The transceiver section was completely in disarray, with parts peeled out and heavily burned.

The damage was, in fact, obvious.

Jimmy retreated to the Ford Ranger and got on his radio. "Hey, Sheriff? This is Baile. Someone did a number on this cell tower. It's a mess. Completely busted up." He waited for a response. "Hello? Sheriff? Dispatch, did you copy?" He waited again, only receiving silence. "Hello?! Anybody?!"

Numerous radio attempts followed, with similar results.

Meanwhile, he watched the haunting view of the cell tower, its box panels split open and blackened with burned marks. Indecision plagued his mind.

Nobody's responding. Should I go find Eddie, or should I try and head back to the station?

After careful consideration, he decided Eddie was closer.

Jimmy turned the truck around and started the long, tedious trek back to the main road. Right away, he hit a bump.

"Fuck." He held his breath and leaned toward the windshield. *If I focus, I can get out of here without hitting another…*

CRUNCH!

"FUCK!"

The question of whether the sensors were working was answered.

Jimmy stopped the truck, glaring at the yellow tire pressure symbol behind the steering wheel. Groaning, he stepped out. As his luck would have it, the front passenger tire was flat.

"Lovely. Just lovely," he said. To make his day even more miserable, there was no spare tire or donut. Now, he had to drive with one headlight and one flat tire in pouring rain. "This stupid truck. I hate this stupid truck. Gosh, I swear this truck will be the death of me! The only way it could make my life worse is if it ran me over then backed over me. Damn piece of junk."

With clenched teeth, he eventually made it to the main road. He took a right turn and eased his way toward the lake. Hopefully, he could join up with the others and ride with them. He could just leave the truck on the side of the road to be repaired tomorrow.

Slowly but truly, Jimmy made his way toward Lake Fairview. The rain continued to bombard the vehicle and obstruct his view. The grinding sound of the rim against the pavement made his stomach churn. He gave thought to pulling over and waiting for the others.

After crawling for a while, he decided to turn on his brights to determine how much farther he had to go. The extra light shone against the pavement, exposing the black skid mark a few yards ahead.

Jimmy followed the semi-circular trail with his eyes, spotting what appeared to be tire marks in the grass that led up to the trees. At first, he thought it possibly may have been some idiot on an ATV going crazy. Except, whoever did this went with enough force to expose the dirt.

"Hold on a sec…"

He parked the truck and briefly entered an internal debate on whether or not he should investigate. Obviously, Eddie and the other deputies weren't here. Either they didn't think it was worth looking into, or they missed it entirely. Jimmy assumed the latter. Had he been driving at normal speed, he would have missed it altogether in this weather.

"Oh, hell!"

With his flashlight in hand, he stepped out. Punished by the weather, he sprinted for the trees where the tire marks ended. Wind assaulted his face as he entered the dark and angry woods. With his flashlight pointed, he passed by a few trees, only to stop suddenly when he saw the crashed Interceptor.

Sticking out from between the smashed engine and a tree trunk were Deputy Ford's stiff legs. Birds, bugs, and other critters had assembled at the soft gooey flesh, helping themselves to an easy snack.

Dry-heaving, Jimmy stumbled back to his vehicle.

"Sheriff? Dispatch?" His words came out as coughs. It did not matter, for his transmissions went unheard. All he could think to do was catch up to the Sheriff and tell him face-to-face.

He boarded the truck and gunned the engine, no longer concerned about the flat tire.

CHAPTER 21

"You hear that?" Kelly sat up and looked out the back window. "I think someone's coming."

Diego put his face to the window, squinting to see through the rain. Three vehicles were approaching. All of them police SUVs.

"I gotta get out there," he said, grabbing his jacket. "They don't know the driveways are sprinkled with booby traps."

He sprinted out the door and waved his arms at the lead car. The Sheriff flashed his lights and approached his driveway.

Diego put his hands forward, gesturing *stop*. The driver's side window rolled down, giving him a view of Eddie Wingard's face.

"Mr. Tritton? What on Earth is going on out here?"

"Sheriff, first of all, *do not* bring your vehicles into the driveway," Diego said. "Trust me, I'll explain, but there's something in the gravel that'll burst your tires on contact."

"Burst tires? What the hell are you on, Tritton?" Eddie said. The look on his face said it all. Already, he thought Diego was a crackpot.

"Listen, just stay off the driveways," Diego said. "Don't walk on them either. God knows what'll happen if you step on one of those things."

"Step on what?" Eddie said. He put his vehicle in park and stepped into the rain. "Mr. Tritton, I'm not going to ask again. What the hell is going on out here? Where's Ross Harker? Do you know him? We received an email alert about possible homicides in the woods. Is that what you were calling my department about earlier?"

"Have you seen Deputy Ford?" one of the deputies said.

"I... no," Diego said. "Has he come out here?"

"I sent him out after you called," Eddie said.

"Just one deputy?"

"Yeah. The signal cut out... either that, or you hung up, and you never called back. All we heard was something about an RV. Then we received an email from Ross Harker. Please, Diego, tell me you didn't get into another spat with those people at the gas station."

"No, no, no... you gotta listen to me," Diego said. "Ross is correct; there are several bodies in the woods. There's an RV, a tent, a deceased person at the cabin on the north end of the lake."

"Alright," Eddie said. "We'll set up a perimeter."

"Before you do, you need to listen very carefully," Diego said. Eddie and the deputies stared at him, sensing that what they were about to hear would be very unusual. "There's some*thing* out here. It killed most of the people in the cabin next door."

Eddie looked at his six deputies, all of whom shared the same 'what the fuck' expression on their faces. Each of them had the same question, but nobody was sure how to voice it.

Something and not someone? Was this guy talking about an animal? Or was he simply going crazy?

"Hooooly shit!" one exclaimed. He was at the back of the line of vehicles, pointing at the neighboring cabin. "Sheriff! We've got a body over here! At the end of the driveway!"

"A body?" Eddie said. The Deputy was out of sight thanks to the tree barrier. "Talk to me, Gonzales."

"Sir… it's bad," the deputy named Gonzales said. He sounded as though he was trying hard to keep his lunch as he spoke.

Other deputies hurried in his direction.

"Be careful," Diego said. "The killer may still be around here somewhere."

"Quit with the riddles," Eddie said. "You've given plenty of buzzwords. 'Killer'. 'It'. What exactly happened?"

Diego knew he had to tell the truth, and he dreaded the results of it. His internal struggle was momentary, for Kelly stepped out of the cabin.

"I'll tell you what happened. We were attacked by a fucking alien!" she said.

Eddie's only response was a stare of puzzlement and mild anxiety.

"It's true," Diego said.

"Oh, for godsake," Eddie muttered.

"It killed her whole group. It's been slaughtering people all across the lakeside," Diego continued. "There's a ship, not too far north of Patrick Gawdy's cabin. There are bodies inside of it. *Alien* bodies. They're in some kind of uniform. I suspect they were like the equivalent of U.S. marshals. I think the one that attacked us was being transported and managed to overtake the ship. It's an escaped prisoner—a *convict*."

"Oooookay, I've heard enough," Eddie said.

"Sheriff," Diego said. "You've got to listen—"

Eddie raised a finger. "No, I don't think I will. Wait inside. I'll speak to you in a moment." He turned around to approach Ross' cabin, stopping near one of his deputies. "You got your breathalyzer?"

"Yeah."

"Go inside and have them blow on it."

"Dude, we haven't been drinking!" Diego said.

Eddie continued walking toward the neighbor's property. Frustrated, Diego and Kelly jogged after him. From the road, they could see the deputies converging on Ross' driveway, nearing Norman's soggy corpse.

"Wait, wait, WAIT!" Diego said. "I said stay off the driveway."

"We're not on your driveway," Eddie said.

Diego ran after him. "*Both* driveways! You dumb idiot!"

Eddie turned around, his hand defensively going for his sidearm. "Ah-ah! Hold it right there."

Two of the deputies stepped in Diego's way. He caught a glimpse of their nameplates as they grabbed him.

"Chill, man," one named MacLean said.

"If you fight, we'll cuff ya," the other, Deputy Fowler, said. He had a hint of a smile on his face. "Don't worry, we won't let any aliens abduct you."

"You pricks," Kelly said.

"Knock off the jokes," MacLean said to Fowler.

Eddie, confident that his men had Diego under control, resumed walking to Ross' cabin.

"Guys, you gotta listen to me," Diego said.

"I've got a missing deputy, a dead body over here, and here you are spouting off nonsense about aliens—all of this *after* you shot an unarmed man in Denver," Eddie said. "I don't know if you've lost your mind, Tritton, but I'm gonna find out."

"No... Sheriff!" Diego said. He pushed against the deputies, who refused to loosen their grip.

"Get the cuffs on him," Eddie said without looking back.

Fowler and MacLean grabbed Diego's wrists.

"Come on, fella. Don't fight us," MacLean said.

Diego twisted, doing everything in his power to resist arrest without resorting to striking the deputies.

"Stop it!" Kelly yelled. "He's telling the truth. There's something out here. We saw it. It killed my friends."

Eddie, now at the driveway entrance, turned back to look at them. Even through the rain and mist, the look of contempt on his face was plain as day.

"Put them in the car." He turned to walk up the driveway.

"Sheriff..." Diego put all of his power into his lungs. "DON'T!"

One step. Two steps. Three steps.

Four...

Splat!

Eddie wobbled in place, waving his arms around. He was standing on one foot—and not voluntarily. Next thing he knew, he was on the ground. It wasn't his shoulders or back that was hurting, but oddly his shin.

"I… it's… I… it's gone…" It was all he could muster in the perplexity and shock. He was not even aware his left foot had exploded until he sat up and saw the stub where his ankle had been.

All of a sudden, he was a believer.

"Holy…" MacLean and Fowler released Diego and ran to their boss' aid. Diego and Kelly were right behind them, keeping a sharp eye on their surroundings. At this point, the safest place was around the men with the guns, even if those men didn't believe them.

The other deputies abandoned Norman's corpse and ran over to Eddie's aid.

"Watch out," Diego said. "If you see any little green marble things on the ground, avoid it at all costs." He cut through the crowd and knelt by Eddie's side. He brushed away the greenish shards that lay near the stump. He turned to Fowler just in time to point at the little round glass boobytrap near his foot. "Left foot! Watch out."

Fowler looked at the little marble thing. Thirty seconds ago, he would've assumed it was a normal, man-made marble. Now, after seeing what just happened to Eddie, he was willing to take Diego's explanation a little more seriously.

"Lay him back," Diego said. "Get something under his head and get his legs up. We need to tie something around his leg. Come on! Come on! Hurry it up."

Deputy MacLean unclipped his duty belt and removed his pants belt for the tourniquet.

"What the hell are those things?" he said. By the sound of his voice, it was evident he was willing to entertain the 'alien nonsense' explanation.

"I'll tell you on the way back," Diego said. "First, we need to get the hell out of here."

"I'll call an ambulance," Fowler said.

"I've already tried," another deputy said. "Nobody's responding."

"I didn't hear your call," MacLean said. "Sure your radio's working?"

Fowler tested his. "Check." Nobody heard it on their receivers. "You think something's blocking the signal?"

"We'll figure that out later," Diego said, tightening the belt around Eddie's thigh. The Sheriff winced in pain, watching his bloody stump with a sense of disbelief. "Hang on, Sheriff. We're getting out of here."

"Can't leave the crime scene," Fowler said.

"If we stay here, we'll be added to it," Diego said. "Only way you'll get your investigation is if we get a superior force out here. State troopers, the national guard."

MacLean nodded. "Let's go, gentlemen. Help us get Eddie into the back of my vehicle. The rest of you, depart."

"Wait," Kelly said, looking to the front of the property. "There's only five of you. Where's the other deputy?"

Everyone glanced around. Gonzales, the one who pointed out the location of Norman's body, was nowhere to be seen.

"Gonzales?" MacLean said. Holding his duty belt, he walked to the front of the house. "Gonzales? Where the hell are you? Get out here, man. We're getting out of—"

He looked down at something on the ground. Diego recognized the look—it was the same kind he had whenever he discovered a body. He recognized the next look on MacLean's face as he looked *up*—showing the same astonishment and shock Diego had when he first saw the seven-foot-tall alien figure.

MacLean turned to the group, ready to run.

"Everyone get to your—" *Splat!*

The flash of energy and splatter of brains and skull were almost simultaneous.

MacLean's headless corpse shivered in place, the right hand still pointing at the other deputies while blood spouted from the neck and still-intact lower jaw. The tongue, still in place, flapped as though he was still trying to speak.

The Deputy collapsed.

To his fellow officers, the only thing more shocking than his death was the arrival of his killer.

The Convict emerged from around the corner, proudly standing over MacLean's body. Its gauntlet blades were extended, their tips still red with Deputy Gonzales' blood.

It gazed at the humans, arms down, shoulders hunched. It was challenging them to a duel.

"Holy sweet savior!" Fowler shouted.

The extraterrestrial dipped back around the front corner.

All remaining deputies drew their sidearms.

"No, don't!" Diego said. "Return to the vehicles. Get out of here!"

"No fucking way," Fowler said. "It killed Gonzales and MacLean, and maimed Eddie. We've got an opportunity to stop it right now." He turned his attention to his other deputies. "It's moving around to the other side. I want two of you to go around back. Stephan and I will circle around the front. Let's go!"

Two of the deputies hurried to the back of the cabin.

As they neared the rear-left corner, their flank came to a dead stop. Three narrow streams of light extended skyward. One of the deputies shrieked as he ran through the lasers. He fell to the ground… in pieces.

His partner stopped, looking in shock at the remains. Stunned by shock, he was oblivious to the alien's presence until it was right in front of him.

Fowler wasn't wrong. The creature was, indeed, moving around the building. And it had anticipated the Deputy's attempt to intercept it.

The Convict grabbed partner by the neck and lifted him off his feet. Holding him close to its body, it swiveled on its feet to face the front yard.

Fowler and the other deputy emerged from around the corner and pointed their guns. Multiple gunshots shook the air.

The Convict stood in place, letting the human shield take all of the bullets.

Fowler took his finger off the trigger, realizing he had just killed one of his co-workers.

The Convict extended its gauntlet. A small device protruded from between the blades, glowing red hot. Fowler turned on his heel and ran, leaving his last remaining partner to suffer the wrath of what was coming.

From that extension came a bolt of hot blue energy. It struck the Deputy square in the chest, blowing his charred lungs and a segment of spinal cord out his back.

"Diego! Let's get out of here!" Kelly screamed.

She knelt by Eddie and helped Diego drag him toward the vehicles. As they retreated, they saw Deputy Fowler emerge in the front yard. Several energy bolts strobed past him. A few of them struck the ground near his feet, resulting in small explosions which knocked him off balance.

He yelped, falling face-first against the dirt.

There was nothing they could do to help him. All they could do was focus on escaping.

"Here," Eddie said, pulling his Beretta from its holster. "Take this." He shoved it into Diego's hands. He grabbed his two spare magazines and offered them to the former detective.

"Don't give up on me, Sheriff," Diego said.

"Go…" Eddie's head dropped, his eyes half-shut.

Diego checked for a pulse, finding none. Shock and blood loss had gotten the better of Eddie Wingard.

"Damn it." Diego grabbed the gun and mags, tucking them into his waist as he and Kelly ran for one of the SUVs. Diego got in the driver's seat. For once, something went in their favor.

The keys were still in it, the engine still running.

Diego waited as Kelly got in her seat. As she buckled herself in, he took a look in Deputy Fowler's direction in hopes that he could be saved.

It didn't look good.

Fowler was struggling to get to his feet. He was still in the front yard, whimpering incoherently as the Convict strutted in his direction. It was no longer shooting the deadly energy projectiles. Of course not—it preferred to kill up close and personal.

Fowler leaned back on his heels, extending his pistol in its direction. A few bullets deflected off its rigid mask. He aimed lower for a neck shot. A swipe of the gauntlet blades knocked the weapon out of his hands.

Unarmed and helpless, Fowler stumbled backward.

The creature swiped at his midsection.

Fowler kept retreating, initially thinking it had missed. Then he felt the warmth of his own blood running down his pants. He looked down at his abdomen. It was split open, ready to drop its contents on to the grass.

His mouth agape, Fowler slowed to a stop, trying to hold his guts in.

The Convict approached. To the surprise of everyone watching, it retracted the blades.

With a powerful thrust, it plunged its hand into the wound. Fowler hollered as guts freely fell out. There was a *crack*, followed by another scream.

The Convict retracted its hand. In its grip was one of Fowler's lower ribs, pointed down like the tip of a dagger. With that rib, it silenced the Deputy's screams by putting it through his eye socket.

Fowler hit the ground, his rib sticking out of his face.

The creature relished its kills, delighted in having successfully defeated this planet's version of law enforcers.

Its celebration was cut short by the sound of an engine. It turned toward the road just in time to spot Diego and Kelly turning around in one of the SUVs.

Diego turned the vehicle around and pointed it north.

"It's coming," Kelly said.

Sure enough, it was. Fast.

Diego gunned the accelerator, raising a middle finger to the alien. "So long, fucker."

They sped north past Ross's cabin. Looking in the mirrors, they saw the alien on the road behind them. It appeared to be tapping something on the side of its gauntlet with its finger, as though pressing keys.

"The hell's it doing?" Kelly said.

"I don't know, but I don't like it," Diego said. "All I know is I don't plan on being here to find out. As long as…" A flicker of movement in the trees caught his attention. He kept his eyes at an upward angle. His gut instinct warned him that whatever it was that he saw, it wasn't good.

That instinct proved to be correct.

The flying thing reappeared, keeping pace with the SUV. In appearance, it resembled a giant dragonfly, complete with legs, antennae, and a wingspan of two feet. A flash of lightning glinted off its exoskeleton.

If it were any other day, I'd think I was going crazy…

It swooped down onto the hood of the SUV. Instead of spattering on the windshield, it secured a grip on the hood and wipers.

Up close, they could see that this thing was mechanical, comprised of some kind of technology. A drone with God knows how many purposes and functions. Surveillance, sabotage, assassinations, maybe even first-responder purposes. Whatever its original purpose, the Convict had corrupted it for its own sick purpose.

It raised one of its legs to eye level, the foot rotating with incredible speed. A blue speck of hot light appeared. A moment later, it extended into a three-inch blade of fire.

The windshield cracked under the intense heat. The leg punched through the incision and extended its flame within an inch of Diego's chest.

"Whoa!"

The former detective slammed on the brakes, bringing the vehicle to a halt. Momentum robbed the insect-thing of its footing. It slid several inches down the hood before gaining a new foothold.

"Kill it! Kill it!" Kelly shouted. "*Shoot* it!"

Diego yanked the pistol from his waist and pointed it at the drone. He fired off several more rounds, striking the thorax. Metal legs and wings thrashed as though the machine felt pain. Sparks flew, the abdomen bending like a scorpion's tail. A final shot knocked the thing clean off the hood.

Rainwater splashed through the slit in the windshield, sprinkling onto Diego's lap. Still pointing the gun, he caught his breath. He could see the thing in the glow of the headlights. It was on its back, twitching in the exact same manner as a dying insect. The torch on its front leg was still burning, now resembling a tiny volcanic eruption.

Kelly looked out the rear windshield. "Diego?!"

He glanced at the rearview mirror, witnessing the Convict spring toward them. "Shit!" He gunned the accelerator, shooting the SUV forward.

He felt two violent vibrations. The first was from the front left tire rupturing, having accidentally passed over the drone's torch. The second came from the impact of the Convict leaping itself onto the bumper.

Clinging tight, it peered through the glass at its next victims. A thrust of its fist shattered the rear windshield. Holding on tight, it slipped its upper body into the trunk. It was a narrow fit for its head and shoulders, and an impossible one for its midsection.

Keeping an eye on the mirror, Diego kept speeding. The vehicle shook with every inch of uneven ground, juddering its passengers and intruder.

Unable to fit itself through under such turbulence, the Convict settled for a blaster kill. It extended its fist and took aim with the projectile weapon on its gauntlet.

"WHOA!"

Diego swerved to the left. The force of the motion shifted the creature's aim. A blue, scalding ball of energy zipped to the left of Diego's head, shattering the window.

The Convict readjusted its aim, the firing mechanism glowing.

He weaved to the right, foiling the creature's second attempt to blow his head off. The second blast punched through the windshield, blowing a mix of fire and glass onto the hood.

A rush of wind and rain invaded the SUV.

"Take the pistol," he said to Kelly. "Just point and shoot."

She snatched the gun from his lap and extended it toward the alien. Several rounds struck its helmet, throwing off its concentration. The gauntlet prepped for firing again.

Fearing that its third shot would hit its mark, Kelly shifted her aim toward the device and fired off every remaining round in the magazine.

"Die! Die! Die!"

Clank! Clank! BEZEEERRRRKKK!!!

A fountain of hot energy spat in all directions, heating the inside of the SUV. Kelly had successfully landed a lucky shot, her bullet igniting the energy projectile before it was even fired. The inside of the gauntlet erupted in sparks, severely scalding the Convict's arm.

It reared its head and growled, using its other hand to free itself of the now-torturous device.

"The trees!" Kelly said. "Pancake the fucker."

Diego hit the brakes again, then picked a tree to line the vehicle up with. To his left was one with a nice smooth trunk and little undergrowth in the way. He put the SUV in reverse, cut the wheel, and floored the gas pedal.

Realizing what he was doing, the Convict slid its upper body out of the trunk. Had there been one more millisecond, it would have been able to throw itself clear. Alas, it found itself smashed between nature and machine.

Its arms flew to the side, its center mass threatening to implode. Ribs compressed, on the verge of snapping.

Diego kept the pedal floored, the three full tires kicking up dirt as the vehicle continued driving against the tree. He cursed himself for running over the drone's torch. If not for the flat, the vehicle may have gained enough force to actually kill this thing.

The Convict let out a roar. Like a sound from the Mesozoic, it struck fear into the adrenaline-crazed humans.

That fear fueled Diego's desire to kill this thing once and for all.

He put the SUV in forward gear and drove off several feet, only to fly back in reverse. For the second time, the Convict was sandwiched with crushing force. This time, it let out a low-pitched squeal. Green blood dribbled from under its mask.

This time, a few ribs cracked.

Pain fueled the creature's resolve. It reached into a pocket on its vest.

"The hell's it doing?" Kelly said.

Diego looked back, noticing a glass vial in the thing's hand. In that vial were small, wormy things.

In that moment, his mind flashed to the tent near the RV. That corpse, which had been grossly mutilated by such organisms, only larger ones. Now he knew where they came from. They fed on flesh and had grown.

"Holy—"

He put the vehicle back in forward and sped off.

The Convict fell forward, securing a hold on the window frame with its left hand. For several yards, it was dragged behind the vehicle, holding the vial in its right hand.

Diego swerved left and right again, trying to shake the thing off.

"Look, we're approaching the main road," Kelly said.

Diego put pressure on the accelerator. Maybe a sharp left turn would shake the alien loose.

Three hundred feet… two hundred… one hundred…

Sparks flew from the front left hubcap as it scraped against the pavement. They were now on the main road… directly in the path of a crappy looking Ford Ranger with one headlight. It too had a flat tire, yet it was traveling in a hurry.

"Shit!"

Diego performed a sharp U-turn, putting the SUV back on the dirt road.

He heard a thump on the pavement behind him.

Kelly looked back. "It fell off."

Diego glanced in the mirror, seeing the Convict face-down on the intersection. It pounded the pavement with its fists, then stood up. The Ford Ranger closed in. There was the screech of brakes as the driver realized there was someone in his path. The realization came too late.

The Ford Ranger—a police vehicle, to Diego's surprise—struck the alien in the back, knocking it forward for several feet.

After putting the vehicle in park, the Deputy stepped out. They could hear him exclaiming "oh my God!" as he approached the body.

"Oh, no, no, no…" Diego muttered.

"He thinks he hit a person," Kelly said.

"Yeah." Diego backed the vehicle up, then poked his head out his window. "Hey! Deputy! Don't go near it!"

Deputy Jimmy Baile was rife with shock. He didn't even see the person until he was right up on him. That stupid vehicle.

His mind, in its defensive state, went to work assigning blame. Whoever was in the SUV had distracted him, pulling onto the road in his lane, only to turn around and drive off. Had they not done that, his eyes would've been focused on what was ahead.

Then there was that stupid Ford Ranger, which should have been in a junkyard somewhere. Had it not been for Eddie Wingard's instruction, he wouldn't have even been driving that stupid thing. Especially not in this weather.

What was Eddie thinking, having me drive that thing?! Hell, why is that truck even in service?! WHY, DAMN IT, WHY?!

None of these excuses stuck. He just hit a person with his truck. He would be lucky if this only cost him his job and not a charge for vehicular manslaughter.

Jimmy approached the person. It was a large fellow, lying face-down, unmoving.

"Hey!" shouted the guy in the SUV. It was one of the cop cars, yet, Jimmy did not recognize the person inside. Whoever he was, his voice was intense. "Stay away from it!"

"Are you crazy? This man needs medical attention," Jimmy shouted back. He knelt by the guy he'd hit and went to check for a pulse. It was then he noticed the strange attire and scaly skin. In the blink of an eye, everything the SUV driver was shouting made complete sense. Even the next part.

"THAT'S NO MAN!"

It was too late.

The thing rose. Lightning reflected off its metal mask, giving Jimmy a quick glimpse of its horrible eye slits before it grabbed him by the neck.

He coughed and gagged, his feet dangling twelve inches off the ground. There was no outmuscling its grip. Whatever this thing was, it had the strength of Greek titans. All he could hope to do was draw his sidearm and put a round in its head.

Hope was the key word there.

That hope quickly died. The creature was already a step ahead of him. With its free hand, it removed the pistol from Jimmy's holster. It admired the weapon design, then gripped the weapon properly. Its hand was a little big, but it was still able to get its finger through the trigger guard.

Jimmy shook frantically, feeling the muzzle prod his gut. Then came intense heat and pressure as several rounds punched through him. Spitting blood, he looked down at his ruptured midsection.

The thing threw him on his back. Fascinated with its first use of the weapon, it took aim at the SUV.

Unable to help the Deputy, the driver floored the pedal, speeding north on the dirt road. Several bullets struck the vehicle, shattering a taillight and one of the rear windows. The driver, however, was unharmed, resuming his retreat into the distance.

Jimmy spat blood as he gasped for breath. The wounds in his gut burned. His insides felt as though they were aflame. He cursed the fact that he was still alive. He did not know what this monster was, nor did he care at this point. The suffering was excruciating, far beyond his tolerance. All he wanted was for one of those bullets to enter his brain and put him out of his misery.

Alas, the pistol was empty. The creature tossed it away, no longer interested in the firearm. It stood over him and gazed, weirdly captivated by his suffering.

"K—" Jimmy spat more blood. His gut now felt as though a fiery tornado was twisting about in there. All three bullets were lodged in his stomach or intestines. Either way, it was obvious he had severe internal bleeding. "Kill me."

The thing looked to the vehicle. After a moment of thought, it stepped over him and moved to the driver's side door. It got inside and studied the controls. The first attempt resulted in the thing driving in reverse. After more experimentation, it got the general idea of how trucks worked. It shifted into forward drive and gunned the accelerator.

Jimmy squealed as the truck passed over him. Bones and ribs cracked. His body rolled with the motion, his gut now split wide open. The truck stopped, the driver now looking back at the roadkill.

Except it technically wasn't roadkill yet, for Jimmy was still clinging to life, even if involuntarily. His body was twisted out of proportion, his palms and toes skyward even though he was face-down. His neck was cracked, his jaw slack, tongue tasting wet gravel as he watched the thing put the truck in reverse.

Tires screeched.

Spatter!

It backed over him, mangling his body all the more. The thing turned to an angle, striking a tree and breaking the rear axle.

The thing stepped out and stood over Jimmy Baile, just in time to witness the life finally fade from his body.

CHAPTER 22

For the past ten minutes, Diego had watched his rear-view mirror more than the road. The rain continued to pelt the windshield, partially obscuring his view. The lack of sunlight didn't help matters, nor did the wind blowing through the hole in the glass. It was as though the weather was deliberately helping the alien remain invisible.

Finally, after minutes of feeling the vibrations of the wheels grinding against the ground, Diego finally took a chance. He parked and stepped outside to get a look at the vehicle.

As he suspected, there was no rubber left on the front left wheel. The torch from that damn dragonfly-shaped drone had shredded the thing to bits.

"Well, great," he said.

"What can we do?" Kelly asked.

"I'm thinking," he said.

"There should be a road on the east side of the lake. Maybe we could take that and find a way to circle back to town."

Diego shook his head. "Don't think that'll work, I'm afraid. There's no way this hunk of junk is gonna make it." He took a breath and looked into the darkness in the direction of the main road. Somewhere behind that darkness was a blood-thirsty alien murderer. "Then again, we can't stay here either."

"Maybe… maybe we hurt it enough when we rammed it against the tree," Kelly said. "Maybe it's dying."

Diego so badly wanted to believe that. It was tempting to grab on to the optimism that they were now safe. The fact was, they were not safe. At best, the Convict was slowed down by its injuries. But dead? He would have to be standing over its cold corpse before he believed that.

"No. It's alive. We saw it go after that deputy as we drove off." He climbed back into the driver's seat and shut the door. He looked at the police radio. *Why the hell haven't I tried this yet?* He lifted the speaker mic to his lips. "Hello? This is Detective Diego Tritton. If anyone is picking up on this transmission, please respond."

Silence.

He repeated the call twice more, then tossed the mic against the dashboard.

"So much for that."

"You mean to tell me that thing can block police frequencies?" Kelly said.

"Looks like it," Diego said. He groaned, on the verge of losing his temper. It seemed everything was working against them. They couldn't drive much farther. They couldn't call for help. The ridiculous weather was only adding to his anxieties. "Our help is already dead. Can't run. Nobody's coming. We're on our own."

Kelly put her head against the back of her seat, absorbing her reality. For a few moments, she appeared as defeated as he was.

A change in attitude caused a shift in her posture. She looked to Diego again, her hand grabbing his shoulder. A new idea had come to mind—and she was convinced it would work.

"There is one fella that might be able to help us."

Diego squinted, trying to think of who else lived on the lake. At that moment, it dawned on him who she was referring to.

"You're suggesting we go back to that ship?" he said.

"Yes."

"You want us to deliberately encounter another alien?"

She shrugged. "Yes!"

"Assuming it's even still alive," he said. "Last I saw, it was in pretty bad shape."

"Listen," Kelly said. "You said it wore some kind of uniform... that it appeared to be some kind of intergalactic marshal. If that's the truth, then it's safe to say that it's not a fan of that... *convict*, since that's what we're calling it, apparently."

"Even if it's not a marshal, I think it's safe to assume those two didn't get along," Diego said. "I highly doubt it got busted up and stabbed over a friendly chat."

He glanced at his rear-view mirror once more. A decision had to be made. Eventually, he would look into that mirror and see that monstrosity emerging from the darkness.

Groaning, he eased on the accelerator. The SUV scraped the dirt road as it moved forward. Before long, he would be seeing sparks.

Still, it was better than driving on foot.

"Thank God I'm not in Denver," he said. "Imagine all the people who'd be honking at me."

Kelly snickered. "I'd kill to be in Denver."

"Yeah?"

"Uh, yeah!" she said. "Because then I wouldn't be in the woods getting chased by a killer alien."

Diego nodded. "Good point."

CHAPTER 23

There was a sense of buyer's remorse when they arrived at the spacecraft. It was still there, the entryway still open. The energy flickering had ceased, the cloaking mechanism having died completely, putting the vessel in plain sight.

At this point, they had no other choice. The SUV barely made it this far. If they needed to go anywhere else, they would have to steal another vehicle. Their best bet was Patrick Gawdy's truck, assuming they would be able to find his keys.

"You sure about this?" Kelly asked.

"It was your idea," Diego said.

"Yeah, I know." She brushed a few strands of hair off her face. "Kind of a lots happened since then… I mean, I'm realizing I'll actually have to walk in there this time."

Diego opened his door. "Come on."

He stepped outside and gave a quick glance at the sky. The storm was finally starting to die down. The wind was now a gentle but constant breeze. The grass here was thick and soaked with rainwater, squelching under his boots, which left small craters in the tiny jungle as he walked to the spacecraft.

As he walked, he kept a sharp eye on the ground. Though he couldn't see any in the thick grass, he suspected that the Convict had left some of those explosive marble traps around its ship.

Kelly, thinking the same thing, stepped in his footprints as she followed him. They arrived at the entrance.

Slowly, Diego stepped in, holding the pistol in a tactical grip. The alien marshal, if it was still alive, would either be hostile or accommodating. There was only one way to find out.

They arrived at the bridge. Kelly winced at the sight of the crusted green blood on the deck. That shock quickly shifted into astonishment. Even after everything she had endured that day, she was still lost in wonder. She was inside a real-life alien spacecraft.

"Everyone at work will never believe this," she muttered.

"Yeah," Diego said. He proceeded for the second corridor. "This way. Let's take it slow. It's hurt and, if it's still alive, probably pissed."

"Great," Kelly said. "Now I'm *really* glad I suggested coming here."

Down the corridor they went, stopping about halfway from the armory entrance.

"Best to announce ourselves," Diego said. He cleared his throat, thought up a few phrases, ultimately settling with "H-hello?! Mr… Alien, sir. Do not be alarmed, we come in peace." They made their way to the entrance. "We're coming in…"

He took a breath and stepped inside, the gun pointed at the floor.

The alien was slumped against the wall, its head tilted down. There was no improvement to its physical condition. Worse, it did not appear to be conscious, or even breathing.

Do they breathe like we do?

Kelly stepped inside and shuddered at the sight of the creature. "It's badly injured."

"Yep."

"Its arm is broken. It has at least one puncture wound."

"Yes, thank you for pointing out the obvious," Diego said.

"It's just that I'm amazed. Its basic physiology looks to be similar to ours," she said. "Bone structure, organs, even waste deposit."

"Waste deposit?" Diego said with a smirk. "You mean…?"

"Yes, yes… *that*," Kelly said. "Not that it matters. The thing doesn't appear to be alive."

Diego looked at its stiff posture and nodded. "No, it does not." He inched closer, then knelt beside it. "I guess it won't hurt to confirm. If it does have a similar biology as ours, then it stands to reason that it has a pulse." He searched for a place to check, ultimately choosing the creature's neck. He pressed in with two fingers, directly under the edge of the mask.

He shook his head. "No, I…" He perked up. "Wait… I feel it. There's a pulse. I think it's alive… Oh, shit…"

The helmet shifted, those eye sockets pointed directly at him.

"Uh… hi."

The alien's left arm lunged, clutching the human by the throat. For a creature that was so close to death, it still had remarkable strength.

Diego gagged, feeling as though his eyes would shoot out of his skull. "D-don't!"

"Stop!" Kelly yelled. She ran to one of the weapons racks. She had no idea what these items were, aside from the gauntlets. With no knowledge on how to operate them, she decided to grab something more familiar. There was a container full of the marble booby traps.

She grabbed a fistful and spun toward the alien, hand raised back to pitch them at the fiend.

The alien, seeing this, threw Diego toward the infirmary section of the room.

Kelly threw the marbles. The alien batted its good arm, smacking them across the room. Like explosive raindrops flying horizontally, they smashed and exploded in various objects.

One of them struck a steel container attached to the far wall. The door split open, the items inside visible through the crack.

In the blink of an eye, the marshal had practically forgotten about the two human intruders, its attention now entirely on that busted cabinet. It rolled to its right and began dragging itself toward it.

Diego stood up and stepped aside. The thing had zero interest in him all of a sudden.

It reached the container, then pushed itself up on its knees. Reaching high, it tried to open the small metal door. Though cracked, it was still latched. Growling in frustration, it rattled the door, unable to muster the strength to get it open.

Frustrated and demoralized, it gave up and fell backward.

Diego stood still, watching it. Not only was their biology somewhat similar, but their attitudes. He knew the body language of someone who had given up on everything and was waiting for death.

He stepped to the container, pointing at the blue objects behind the crack.

"You need this?" he said to the alien. It did not offer a reply. "Don't play dumb. I know you probably don't speak my language, but I'm pretty sure you know what I'm talking about." He looked to Kelly. "Bring me one of those."

She grabbed another one of those marble things and approached.

Diego accepted the small explosive, then looked to the alien.

"Listen, I think we have a common problem," he said. "You see, there's a member of your race that's killed many people. If I had to venture a guess, I'd say it's the same one that made you so pretty. Now, I came here thinking we could help each other. Getting choked out wasn't part of the plan. So, either you're just as fucked up as that Convict, OR you're as eager as I am to get some payback." He looked at the explosive, then at the container. "I guess there's only one way to find out."

He threw it hard against the door. The marble burst into a greenish explosion, busting the latch and opening the cabinet.

Stored inside were several huge syringes with a blue substance.

Now, he had the alien's attention. It looked up at him, now completely at this human's mercy.

Kelly approached the cabinet and took one of the syringes out.

"You know what you're doing?" Diego asked.

"Yeah. Looks like it's self-injecting. It just needs someone to place the needle." She knelt by the alien, then took its left arm by the wrist. The creature pulled back for a moment, not sure if it was willing to trust her. "Dude, I'm having a shitty day. Can you at least cooperate?!" She yanked its arm, extending it. She observed the texture of its skin, then found an area to inject the stuff. Though she wasn't fully sure what this substance was, she knew it served some kind of medical purpose. The alien was eager to get it and was not objecting to the injection.

The substance entered its bloodstream. The alien rested on the floor, its breathing intensifying for several seconds.

Kelly stood up and waited beside Diego, watching the results of the procedure. Rapid breathing followed, along with some minor convulsions. The creature grunted intensely, its left arm feeling the wounds in its torso.

When it came to an end, the alien sat up. Its movements were not nearly as rigid as before. Already, it had a lot more strength than before. It took a few deep breaths, then stood up. It walked to another medical machine in the wall. A small scanning device protruded from a slot in the textures. The alien set its good arm in the slot, then watched in a plasma monitor as the machine conducted a medical scan.

Diego and Kelly could not read any of the figures on the monitor, but one thing they recognized was a squiggly line that represented its pulse. Its heart rate had dramatically improved from two minutes prior.

"Those syringes must be some kind of stim pack," Kelly said. "Causes rapid healing for penetrating wounds."

"Its arm still looks messed up," Diego said.

"Yeah." Kelly approached the alien. It whipped its head towards her, a stern growl warning her off. "Oh, relax," she said. She pointed at its elbow. "Your arm. You're gonna need to have that set."

She reached for it. The alien retracted, much to her frustration.

"Will you just..." Fed up, she grabbed its wrist and began to pull. "Three, two..." *Yank!*

The alien shrieked and stumbled back, clutching its injury with its good arm.

"Sorry, sorry," Kelly said. "The broken ends of the bones were rubbing together. Had to separate them in order to... never mind. Take another healing syringe. You'll be fine."

The alien's posture relaxed. For several minutes, it stood watching them. Already, its arm was looking better. The healing process had begun. Before long, it would have limited use of its arm again.

Shifting its glance between the two humans, the alien raised its left fist and put it over its heart, nodding with a gentle growl.

Diego and Kelly understood.

Thank you.

"You're welcome," Kelly said.

CHAPTER 24

"Uh-huh… wow. This fella learns fast," Diego said.

In the bridge of the vessel, the marshal had accessed the data correlated by the Convict. Through the smartphone it had taken off one of the victims, the computer was able to breach the language barrier of the two species. Thus, they were finally able to communicate.

As Diego spoke, a translator on the monitor would decipher his voice and relay it to the marshal, and vice versa.

The creature replied in its native language. The instruments on the computer glistened as the words were transformed to English.

"Yes. Indeed. As do you."

"At least he's nice enough to give compliments," Kelly said. She was in the bridge, exploring. The marshal did not seem to mind. After all, they had saved its life.

"So, I was right," Diego said. "You guys were transporting a prisoner? It got loose, killed your friends, took control of the vessel?"

The marshal, after hearing the translation, simply nodded. There was a hint of bitterness in the way it cocked its head. Diego sensed the creature's pride had been damaged. It had failed its task, and many had perished as a result. On top of that, its comrades were dead. Diego had been to police funerals. He knew how an officer felt when his partner was killed in the line of duty.

It replied in its native dialect. The computer did its thing, ultimately reforming the words into something Diego could understand.

"It will be back. Only a matter of time."

"I was thinking the same thing," Diego said. "We need to come up with a gameplan. It thinks you're dead. It thinks Kelly and I are helpless."

"It won't like that you're in here," the marshal replied.

"So what? It's planning on killing us anyway," Diego said.

"No, you don't understand. If it thinks you're setting up an ambush in this ship, it will activate the internal defense systems."

"Oh, I don't like the sound of that," Kelly said. "What systems, exactly? Like, lasers shooting from the ceiling, or gas, or…?"

"Both."

The marshal pointed at the ceiling. Diego looked up, seeing what resembled a hose nozzle in the corner.

"Well, that's just dandy," he muttered.

"We can set up a trap," Kelly said. "We've got plenty of weapons. We have the energy blasters, there's the exploding balls, these chemicals in the tiny glass vials..."

"Careful with those!"

Kelly shook, not expecting the intensity in the marshal's voice. She looked at the two different colors in the vials, then back at the alien.

"Let me guess—don't let these different chemicals touch."

"Correct."

"You're right about setting a trap, though," Diego said. "We can still use the element of surprise. We can distract its attention, giving the marshal enough time to land a killing blow."

"There's no choice. You will have to use yourselves as bait," the marshal said.

"I have a better idea," Kelly said. She walked up the corridor into the bridge. "We saw what that sick bastard did to Pam. There's no question it doesn't just get its kicks from killing."

The marshal looked at her, taking in a breath as though repulsed by the implication.

"What did it do?"

"Pam's a female," Kelly said. "It... took advantage of her before killing her."

The marshal exhaled slowly, its suspicions confirmed.

"It is a criminal, guilty of thousands of offenses. It has visited many different worlds, spreading its evil across the galaxy."

"Jesus," Diego said. It was a lot to comprehend. All at once, he was learning the true extent of the Convict's nature, while also discovering that there were, in fact, many different planets with intelligent life on them. "They're going to put me in a nuthouse."

"I don't understand."

"Mm? Oh, just thinking out loud," Diego said. He thought for a moment, his memory revisiting Kelly's recent statement. "Wait a minute. You mentioned what happened to Pam... are you planning...?"

"I'll use myself as bait," she said. "I'll wait outside. The thing will come for me, thinking I'm helpless. Once it comes for me, the marshal can shoot it."

"What about me?" Diego said. "Surely, it won't think I've just wandered off."

"Not unless it thinks you're already dead." Kelly looked at the chemical vial. "You think it laid some booby-traps near the ship? It's got three-quarters of a tank. Maybe the 'explosion' did more damage than the Convict intended..."

"It could work," the marshal said.

Diego exhaled sharply. He put his hands on his hips and hung his head low, pondering Kelly's suggestion.

"You won't be able to claim your life is boring after this."

CHAPTER 25

After the killing of the lawmen, the Convict took a few moments to rest and assess its situation. Its primary weapons were damaged. Its plasma caster was disabled, its acid pistol no longer functional, having been dented during the repeated vehicular impacts that left several ribs cracked, and it did not possess any stim packs. All it had were its blades, a few booby traps, and its superior strength. All of which were more than enough to finish the job, if only it could get its hands on those annoying humans.

No longer having drone surveillance at its aid, it could only rely on short-range scans with its mask. As far as it could tell, the remaining human pair had once again escaped.

Their vehicle was heavily damaged, possibly to the point of breaking down. With this in mind, it proceeded north on foot. Under normal circumstances, it would be an easy journey. Tonight, it was long and tedious. The Convict was in dire need of a stim pack. The drone, having been damaged during the chase, was unable to administer a stim injection. The drone had saved its life after the insect assault, injecting it with a healing substance that counteracted the poison in its veins. Now, it did not appear to have the luxury of the drone. Its only safety net was in the infirmary of its vessel.

The minor setback did not cause worry. The Convict's body needed time to adapt to this new environment. Given enough time, such things as insect stings would be nothing more than a minor inconvenience.

It traveled north, stopping periodically to try and fix its gauntlet. The human projectile weapon had damaged it severely. The plasma caster was irreparably damaged, though the transmitter still functioned. It proceeded to send signals to the drone in hopes that the device was functional enough to crawl its way to the ship.

As it walked, the pain in its side worsened. The human's attempt to crush it against the tree were almost successful. It limped on its right side, the pain worsening the farther it walked.

Pain, while annoying, was a minor inconvenience. The Convict had suffered worse than this in its long life. If anything, pain motivated it to continue its malevolent pastime. Pain was an inspiration, helping the fiend envision new ways to make future victims suffer. In addition, those who caused it pain tended to suffer the most. The Convict knew it was dishonorable, and it did not care. It still sought vengeance to those who inflicted injuries, even in self-defense. As far as it was concerned, it had every right to rid the universe of these stupid creatures.

Their deaths were no great loss. As far as it was concerned, over ninety-nine percent of lifeforms had nothing of value to offer the universe. Not just the humans, but the many other species it had slaughtered. They wouldn't invent any new technology, medicine, or anything else of value. They simply took up space and used up resources until their time ran out. In the Convict's mind, the universe got along fine without these lifeforms.

Not that it ever felt the need to rationalize its actions. Its motive was simple: it killed because it enjoyed it. Nothing more, nothing less.

As the Convict neared the north end of the lake, it conducted another scan of the area. To its surprise, it picked up a fairly large heat signature. It was near its ship.

At first, it thought this reading may have been a large animal it had not discovered yet. Watching the scan in its mask, the Convict realized this heat signature was from a literal fire. Two questions came to mind. What was burning? And why was it so close to the vessel?

Quickening its pace, the Convict sought out the answer.

Nearing the landing site, it activated its gauntlet blades and approached. It emerged from the woods and saw the towering flame that danced over the local vehicle—the same vehicle the humans operated.

The ship was in plain view, its cloaking system having failed somehow. The Convict chose not to worry about that at the moment, instead focusing on the wreckage and the screaming woman who was on the ground several yards away. Sure enough, it was the woman from the group, her mate nowhere to be seen.

She was in hysterics, hardly noticing the creature, instead fixated on the burning truck.

"No! Diego! No! Oh, God!!!"

The alien looked at the truck. It was hard to see inside due to the flames, but judging by the female's state of mind, the male got cooked alive after the SUV went up in flames. There was a ping of regret, as the Convict would have loved to have been witness to that.

Near the rear tire were several shards from one of its explosive pellets. From what it could surmise, the Convict figured the dumb humans ran over one of the traps and went up in flames. The female had escaped, though her partner was not so lucky.

She was on the ground now, breathing heavily while clutching her ankle. Perhaps she had hurt herself during the escape. Regardless, she would soon wish she had died in the explosion.

It slowly approached, its sick mind going over the many horrible things it could do to her. Helpless, weak, and vulnerable... and well-shaped for a human.

"No." She began to scurry backward. "Get away."

It followed her, picking up pace. Unfortunately, the pain in its ribs kicked in again. As fun as taking advantage of this female sounded, it needed a stim injection first. She would certainly try and escape while it tended to its injuries. Then again, this woman had been a real nuisance over the last couple of hours. Such a prize needed to suffer long and hard before given the satisfaction of death.

With this in mind, the Convict approached.

"No! No! Get away."

Her eyes went to the stair ramp. The Convict stopped. Something didn't seem right. This female appeared perfectly capable of getting up and running away, yet all she did was clumsily scamper on her elbows and feet. And why did she seem concerned with the vessel?

The Convict stopped, looked at the ramp, then back at her. It saw something in her eyes it didn't like: frustration. It was as though she actually wanted its attention on her.

Unable to pierce the ship's hull with its scans, the Convict rapidly backed toward the truck. With a hefty yank, it ripped the door off of its hinges, granting a full view of the driver's seat.

There was no corpse present.

It recognized two words muttered by the female.

"Oh, shit."

Raising its gauntlet, it transmitted an emergency signal to the spacecraft. The male was inside, possibly setting up an ambush. Alas, the Convict would have the pleasure of slaughtering him after all.

Diego was crouched near the ramp, pistol in hand, eager to jump into action. The Convict had arrived and was taking the bait... until it wasn't. The marshal stood beside him, watching a monitor in the corner.

It growled after watching their target activate something on its gauntlet.

"What's it doing?" Diego said. He heard mechanical winding in the ceiling. The little nozzles the marshal had warned him about were now starting to spin. "Oh, that can't be good."

The marshal grabbed him by the back of his shirt and shoved him toward the ramp.

A deadly mist began to spew from the nozzles. Their only choice was to abandon ship or die.

As they retreated, Kelly yelled out in pure terror.

"Diego! Look out!"

In the corner of his eye, he could see the Convict coming at them. Its right hand was high over its shoulder like a baseball pitcher. It chucked a glass vial with a mixed chemical inside.

It landed on the ground between him and the marshal. Both ran for cover, ultimately getting knocked off the ground by the tremendous explosion.

Next thing Diego knew, he was flying head over heels, ultimately landing hard on his back. The world above was a blur. Kelly's screams were muffled, as though they were coming from half-a-mile away.

The marshal way lying face-down a few yards away, equally stunned. Despite its wonky senses, it forced itself to stand on its knees and turn toward the fugitive. It extended its arm and took aim with its gauntlet.

The Convict was also aiming. With its plasma caster damaged, it relied on a secondary projectile—the blades.

They spat from the device like arrows from a crossbow.

A cloud of red erupted from the marshal's chest. It let out a deafening shriek and fell backward, its plasma bolt redirected into the air. The extraterrestrial lawman hit the ground in agony, the blunt end of a blade protruding from its chest plate. The other had grazed its shoulder, landing in the grass several yards behind it.

The Convict approached, its hands balled into fists. It was pleased with itself and frustrated all at once. All this time, it had thought the Marshal was dead, only to realize it had been duped. However, its former captor's attempt to ambush it had been thwarted. The Convict was smarter than the pathetic creatures it victimized, no matter which planet they came from.

Diego knelt by the marshal and pulled on its arm. "Come on, get up."

The marshal sat up and removed its mask, revealing its insectoid face. It leaned to the right and spat blood into the grass. One of its lungs had been perforated, causing a buildup of fluid.

Desperate, it shook Diego off and took another aim at the Convict. The attempt was futile. The Convict closed the distance and knocked the marshal back down with a kick to the chin. It stomped again, pinning the marshal's arm to the ground with its heel, preventing use of the plasma caster. The Convict increased the pressure. With remarkable strength, it cracked the plasma caster, disabling it.

Slowly, tediously, it leaned down and grabbed the blunt end of the blade. The marshal grabbed for its hand but was quickly overpowered. It squirmed and shrieked as the blade was slowly twisted.

Diego stood up and advanced on the Convict, ready to trade blows with it. Without looking up from the marshal, the Convict backhanded him across the jaw, knocking him backward.

For the second time, his senses were warped. Sprawled out in wet grass, he listened to the marshal's cries.

He could not believe it. Their element of surprise meant nothing. The plan was on the verge of failing, the immediate consequence being a slow and agonizing fate.

"Kelly… run!"

"I'm not leaving without you," she said.

He grunted in frustration. Another shriek from the marshal jolted his senses. The Convict was taking great pleasure in inflicting a slow, painful death. Overconfident in its efforts, it paid little attention to the human.

Diego rolled onto his hands and knees. He rolled his jaw, feeling a loose crown. "The dentist is never gonna believe this." He looked to his left and spat blood.

The red droplets landed several feet beyond a black object. The *gun!*

He snatched the weapon out of the grass and pointed it at the Convict. *Bang! Bang! Bang! Bang! Bang! Bang!*

The Convict quickly backtracked, green blood spurting from its shoulder and hip where the armor did not cover.

Diego kept firing until the slide locked back. The magazine was empty, his last line of defense completely spent.

The Convict directed its attention at him. Armed with nothing but its fists, it started walking toward him. It did not complete more than two steps before it saw the marshal standing up.

Though bleeding from the chest and jaws, the law officer was dead set on putting an end to the criminal's reign of terror. It pulled the blade from its chest and tossed it aside before activating its own duel set. Silver blades protruded from its gauntlet, ready to cut into the fugitive's flesh.

The Convict put its hands up. Though unarmed, it was more than ready for a good old-fashioned brawl.

It got its wish.

The two aliens charged each other, colliding with incredible force. The marshal lunged and slashed, determined to land a killing blow before its energy ran out. The stab wound in its chest was wreaking havoc on its respiratory system. Already, fatigue was setting in.

A trained warrior, it was not about to let fatigue be its downfall. It had been bested once by the Convict. It had no intention of a repeat. No matter what, the Convict was going to die tonight. To hell with bringing it back to its home planet for justice.

The Convict evaded the attacks. Taking advantage of its opponent's lack of facial protection, it moved in and landed a strike to the face. The marshal's head snapped back, spitting more blood from its mandibles. It slashed again, its predictable attack parried by the murderer. Again, it was hit with a blow to the face.

A haymaker followed, cracking one of its mandibles. The Convict closed in and grappled with the marshal, locking its right arm. Utilizing its thick helmet, it headbutted the marshal.

The officer did not go down. Taking advantage of the close proximity, it reached up with its free arm. Its fingertips reached under the mask. The Convict grabbed at its wrists, but was too late. The marshal pulled the Convict's mask off, revealing its grotesque face.

Seeing this, Diego found an opportunity to step in. Picking up the discarded gauntlet blade, he charged the duo. With a bounding leap, he slashed at the Convict's exposed face.

The blade sliced at a forty-five-degree angle, narrowly missing its right eye. The Convict snarled and moved back, pressing a hand to its face.

Seizing the opportunity, the marshal pressed another attack. This time, the swing of its blades found its target. Blood spewed from the Convict's shoulder, then from its chin. The marshal went in for a third strike, hoping to thrust the twin daggers through its heart.

A sweep of the Convict's left arm deflected the attack. It leapt at the marshal, digging its thumb into the chest wound. Blood jetted as the incision widened. Nerves flared throughout the marshal's body. It gasped for breath, only to spit out more blood from its deflated lung.

Acting with the advantage of strength and breath, the Convict grabbed ahold of the gauntlet, redirecting the blades downward toward its opponent's knee. It freed its other hand from the chest cavity and activated the triggering mechanism. The blades shot through the marshal's left leg, cutting flesh and bone.

All strength vanished from the limb. Roaring, the marshal collapsed to one knee, then was knocked flat on its back after an uppercut imploded its chin.

Triumphant, the Convict stood over its former captor. This time, it vowed to make sure it was dead, but only after enjoying a little torture in the process. It raised its foot and stomped on the marshal's chest, driving out what little breath remained.

Blood splattered from the mandibles. Bones cracked, then bent inward, their broken edges prodding soft organs.

All strength vanished from the marshal's body. Its attempt to shift the Convict's foot were overpowered by its superior strength. Its gauntlet was damaged, its human comrades could not retrieve new weapons from inside the vessel because of the defense systems.

All hope was lost.

Diego, still holding the blade, moved in for a strike. The Convict, not budging from its position, countered by grabbing him by the throat.

All of a sudden, Diego felt the meat in his neck hugging his vertebrae. He gasped for breath but got nothing. It was as though he was in the vacuum of space. He could not even exhale.

His feet dangled over the grass as the alien lifted him. It pried the dagger from his hand, then held it to his face. Still keeping the marshal pinned, it contemplated the slow death it would inflict on the former detective.

"Hey!" Kelly shouted. It looked in her direction. She was on the ground, shaking with fright. Diego waved his hand, trying to get her to run. Yet, she remained on the ground with a horrified look on her face.

A tilt of its head suggested the Convict was enticed. An idea came to mind. It stomped once more on the marshal for good measure, ensuring all of its strength was gone. Next, it rammed the blade through Diego's leg, then dropped him onto the grass.

He yelled out, clutching his injury.

The Convict plowed its foot against his chest, driving the breath from his lungs. Its actions were specific and deliberate. It did not want him dead, *yet*. It wanted him alive, long enough to watch what it was about to do to the female.

It turned toward Kelly. She gasped, then weakly scampered back. Fear, being so powerful, kept her from running away.

"N-no! Kelly, run!" Diego croaked, his throat still feeling crushed.

"Get away from me!" Kelly shouted. Her pleas only enticed it further.

Diego rolled onto his hands and knees, yelping as the nerves in his leg flared. It was hard to breathe, for it felt as though his chest had imploded from the kick. Even the adrenaline failed to gain him the strength necessary to chase after the creature.

Victorious—dominant—the fiend stood over the human female. It was deliberately slow, the anticipation serving as the first phase of its victim's suffering. It glanced back at Diego, making sure he was watching. Even if he tried to intervene, it knew he would be easily overpowered. These humans were physically weak compared to its species. With its lack of compassion and fear, the Convict was unstoppable.

Kelly looked up at it, hugging her chest. She knew what the creature had in mind, and it appeared to make her clutch up.

"Kelly! Run!" Diego shouted. "What are you doing?"

She didn't move.

The Convict clicked its mandibles, then extended its hands to grab her.

Kelly unwrapped her arms. The grey sunshine struck the glass vial filled with white and red powers. She retracted the divider, mixing the grains.

"Here's a *bang* for ya!"

She tossed the vial down between the Convict's feet, then sprang off the ground. Now, Kelly was running.

The Convict stumbled back, its brain still registering the unexpected sight of the chemical weapon.

BOOM!

A cloud of smoke instantly took form, the ground shaking from the force of a tremendous chemical explosion.

The Convict was launched several feet backwards, its armor covered in its own blood. It hit the ground, stunned. Pain, physical and psychological, wreaked havoc on body and mind. It had fallen for the woman's perceived helplessness, not even considering the fact that she may have taken a weapon from the ship's armory.

For the next several moments, all it could do was stare at the sky. It had been duped. Made a fool of. By a *human* of all things.

Diego smiled. Kelly's supposed helplessness, combined with the creature's overconfidence, had been its undoing.

She was standing near the tree line, her hands on her knees. After calming herself, she looked over at Diego and smiled back at him.

"Nice work," he said.

"Thanks." She inhaled deeply, trying to slow her rapid heart rate. "We did it."

As though in response, the Convict sat up. Blood spat from its mandibles and dripped from its torso. Its bloodshot eyes, full of contempt, hit her with a fiery glare.

It rose, blood running from its wounds in long streams. Its anger served as a temporary anesthetic as it stomped toward the female. Even with its injuries, it would still outlast her in a chase.

Kelly stepped back, this time truly stunned that the alien was still alive.

Diego attempted to stand, his leg injury dropping him back to the grass.

"Christ!" He crawled to the marshal. It had rolled to its side, its skin somewhat discolored from lack of oxygen. It was fumbling with its gauntlet. Diego put his hands on its shoulder and shook it. "Come on, dude. We gotta move."

The marshal tapped a few keys on its gauntlet, triggering a whirring sound. After a brief moment, the sound stopped and the lights died out. The marshal growled in anger, then tried again.

"What the hell are you trying to do... oh, I see," Diego said. It was resetting its gauntlet in an attempt to reactivate the plasma caster. Some internal component was either misaligned or broken entirely. Once again, it shut down before it could charge enough energy for a shot.

Diego grabbed the gauntlet and yanked. "Here. Give it to me!"

The marshal looked at him as though about to argue, then shifted its gaze toward the Convict. There was no time to argue. It slipped the gauntlet off and put it on Diego's forearm.

"On this planet, if something doesn't work..." He smacked the device repeatedly with Eddie Wingard's pistol, "...we do this!" He hit it again and again.

The whirring sound returned, the plasma caster shining blue.

"Ha! Okay... how do I shoot the thing?"

The marshal did not need a translator to know what he was asking. It forced itself to sit up and activated the triggering mechanism.

Diego felt a jolt in his arm which traveled through his body.

"Okay... this is weird."

Once the sensation settled, he felt an odd connection to the device. It was as if it was literally part of him. In that moment, he understood.

He shifted the gauntlet in the Convict's direction. The next action was as simple as breathing.

Fire.

The gauntlet, retrieving the signal from his brain, discharged the plasma bolt. The recoil caught him by surprise, throwing his aim off by a few feet. It zipped by the Convict, who turned toward him. It leaned back, perplexed that it was not the marshal wielding the weapon, but a stupid human.

Diego aimed again. This time, he understood what he was doing.

He fired, striking the Convict square in the chest. A second shot hit its stomach. A third struck its lower left shoulder.

It staggered backward, bleeding from large cavities in its body. It rocked back and forth, the energy quickly slipping from its body. Growling, it took a step toward Diego. No way could it allow itself to be killed by a human of all creatures.

Diego clicked his tongue.

"Should've landed on Mars, motherfucker."

A final shot hit center mass. A cloud of green blood burst from the creature's chest as it fell backward. It landed on the ground, motionless. Defeated. By measly humans.

CHAPTER 26

Kelly ran to Diego and wrapped her arms around his neck. The Convict was dead, its reign of terror finally brought to an end.

"You alright?" Diego said.

"Yeah. You?" she said.

Diego turned his attention to his injured leg. "Might need to tie a tourniquet around this thing."

"We can get something from Patrick Gawdy's place."

They turned to the marshal. It was lying on its back, its breathing shallow. Blood bubbled from its jaws.

"Hey, man," Diego said to it. "Let us help you up. Kelly, can you get another syringe from the infirmary?"

She went to the stair ramp, only to quickly back away.

"Damn it! I can't get in," she said. "The place is full of gas."

Diego knelt on his good leg and took the marshal by the arm. "Come on, fella. You've survived this long. Gotta make it to the end."

The marshal put its hand on his, then gently shook its head. Diego loosened his grip, understanding the unspoken message. There was no saving the marshal this time.

He noticed it reaching for its helmet, which was lying in the grass several yards away.

"Kelly?"

She hustled over to it and brought it to the injured alien. It put the mask on and reactivated the electronic mechanisms. The translator came to life, providing its final message to its human helpers.

"Thanks to you two, I DID make it to the end. My job is done. The criminal is defeated. No longer will my civilization have to fear its evil ways."

Diego nodded. He clasped hands with the marshal, a gesture that appeared to be understood.

"Well then, from one law enforcement officer to another..." With his right hand, he saluted.

The marshal performed its own version of the salute, holdings its hand flat in a similar manner and holding it horizontally across its chest.

That was its final action.

Diego felt its grip stiffen. The saluting hand fell limp over its stomach, the head tilting to the side.

He and Kelly knelt beside the deceased, honoring it with a moment of silence. Diego heard her sniffle.

"You okay?"

"Yeah." She gave a weak chuckle. "Never thought I'd ever find myself broken up over a dead alien whom I've only known for an hour."

"A lot's happened during that time," Diego said. "Don't cry. I don't think it'd want you to." The nerves in his leg flared, causing him to wince. "On the other hand, I just might if I don't get this taken care of."

Kelly put his arm around her shoulder and helped him to his feet.

"Oh, don't be a wuss."

"A wuss!" he replied. "I have an alien knife in my leg."

"It missed your femoral artery. If it didn't, you'd already be dead."

"I appreciate your optimism," Diego said. They gave one final admiring glance at the deceased Marshal, then limped south toward Patrick Gawdy's cabin. There, they would commandeer his vehicle and get the hell out of here.

They entered the woods in silence, cherishing the sense of liberation they both felt. The horror was finally over. Now, they faced the tedious task of explaining the day's events to the authorities. This event would make national news and likely make them world famous, whether they liked it or not.

"I think it's safe to say your life won't be boring after this," Diego said.

"I feel like a fool for ever complaining about that," Kelly said. "Gosh, the press is gonna go nuts when they get wind of this. I'm not looking forward to having my face plastered on the television."

Diego squeezed her hand. "Well, seeing as I'm already used to that, I'll help you get through it."

She smiled. "Yeah?"

He nodded. "Yeah."

They stopped and looked at each other affectionately. The moment was ruined by Diego's throbbing nerves.

"Ah, damn it," he groaned.

"Tell you what," Kelly said. "Let's continue this little moment after we get you to the hospital."

"Sounds good."

Determined to put this miserable day behind them, they continued their hike to Patrick Gawdy's cabin.

The End

CHECK OUT OTHER GREAT SCIENCE FICTION BOOKS

LOST EMPIRE
by Edward P. Cardillo

Building on their victory in the last Intergalactic War, the imperialist United Intergalactic Coalition seeks to expand their influence over the valuable Kronite mines of Golgath. Reeling from their defeat, the warrior Feng are down but not out. The overextended UIC and the vengeful Feng deploy battle groups and scramble fighters as they battle for position in the universe, spinning optics and building coalitions. Captain Reinhardt of the Resilience and the elite Razor's Edge squadron uncover the Feng Emperor Hiron's last ditch attempt to turn the tables with a new and dangerous technology. With resources spread thin, the UIC seeks to exploit Feng's weakened position through a very conditional peace accord. Unwilling to submit, Emperor Hiron must hold them off and quell the growing civil unrest of his starving, warrior people just long enough to execute the mysterious Operation: Catalyst. Commander Massa and his Razor's Edge squadron race against time to stop Hiron's plan, and a new race awakens, led by a powerful prophet set on toppling the established galactic order through violent acts of terrorism.

ABSOLUTE ZERO
by Phillip Tomasso

When a recon becomes a rescue . . . nothing is absolute!

Earth, a desolate wasteland is now run by the Corporations from space stations off planet . . . A colony of thirty-three people are part of a compound set up on Neptune. Their objective is mining the planet surface for natural resources. When a distress signal reaches Euphoric Enterprises on the Nebula Way Station, the Eclipse is immediately dispatched to investigate.

The crew of the Eclipse had no idea what they were getting themselves into. When they reach Neptune, and send out a shuttle party, they hope they can find the root cause behind the alarm. Nothing is ever simple. Something sinister lies in wait for them on Neptune. The mission quickly goes from an investigation into a rescue operation.

The young crew from the Eclipse now finds themselves in the fight of their lives!